Praise for
elle and blair fowler

"Fast, snappy, and filled with great insider knowledge of the beauty industry." —*RT BOOKREVIEWS*

"Fans of Lauren Conrad's *L.A. Candy* are going to sweep up *Beneath the Glitter*, the debut novel from YouTube style sensations Elle and Blair Fowler." —*Justine Magazine*

"An end-of-summer fun read . . . quick, lighthearted [that] makes us feel as if we're actually living a glitzy, glamorous life. Oh, how we wish!" —*Miss Literati*

"A GREAT book and even better beach read. It's fun, lighthearted, and a book that everyone should add to their collection. I can't wait for the next one!" —*loveforlacquer.com*

"This book was delicious and addicting and wonderful. The characters were well-developed, the plot line was delish, and the entire idea was fantastic. It reminded me of *L.A. Candy* in a way, but there was better drama . . . I highly recommend this book. It's absolute awesomeness." —*Willa's Ramblings*

"An enthralling, lighthearted, irresistible, and romantic story . . . fans of contemporary, chick lits, and quick, paced funny reads will certainly find delight in this one." —*Itching for Books*

"An enjoyable read that is perfect for the beach . . . about two sisters who'd do anything for each other but have to realize that life might not be as easy as they want it to be. If you're looking for an easy and fast read, be sure to consider reading this one—especially if you're someone who, like me, is easily pulled in by a world of beauty, glamour, and gossip." —*Fictional Distraction*

"If you are a fan of the Fowler sisters I would definitely suggest picking up this book because it is a great insight into their world!" —*Charming Chelsey's*

"Fun characters combined with the always interesting plot line—which included mingling with movie stars, rescuing animals, forty-six courses of champagne tasting, and even sabotage—made for a quick, fun read that I finished in under a day." —*The Mortal's Library*

"Ava and Sophie seemed really down to earth and were just trying to make it big in a city notorious eating up people and spitting them out. I really enjoyed watching their relationship grow through the tribulation that comes with success." —*Charlotte's Web of Books*

also by elle and blair fowler

Beneath the Glitter

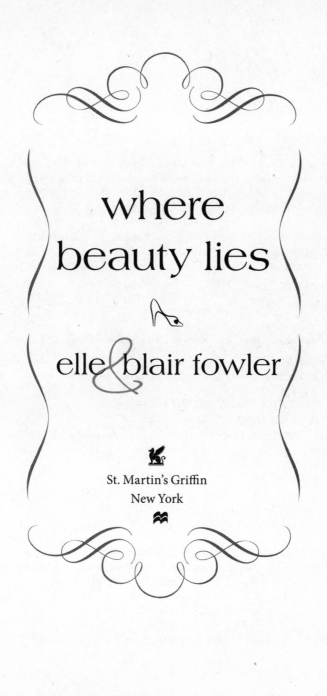

where
beauty lies

elle&blair fowler

St. Martin's Griffin
New York

This is a work of fiction. All of the characters, organizations, and events portrayed in this novel are either products of the authors' imagination or are used fictitiously.

www.stmartins.com

The Library of Congress has cataloged the hardcover edition as follows:

Fowler, Elle, 1988–
    Where beauty lies / Elle and Blair Fowler. —First Edition.
        p. cm.
    ISBN 978-1-250-00619-6 (hardcover)
    ISBN 978-1-250-01713-0 (e-book)
    1. Cosmetics industry—Fiction.   2. Los Angeles (Calif.)—
Fiction.   I. Fowler, Blair, 1993– author.   II. Title.
    PS3606.O8494W54 2013
    813'.6—dc23

                                              2013011190

ISBN 978-1-250-01714-7 (trade paperback)

St. Martin's Griffin books may be purchased for educational, business, or promotional use. For information on bulk purchases, please contact Macmillan Corporate and Premium Sales Department at 1-800-221-7945, extension 5442, or write specialmarkets@macmillan.com.

First St. Martin's Griffin Trade Paperback Edition: June 2014

10 9 8 7 6 5 4 3 2 1

For our YouTube supporters,
who give us more love than
we could have ever dreamed.

And for our parents and youngest
sister, our favorite people in the
entire world.

And for Rose, our editor, for putting
up with our crazy shenanigans.

where
beauty lies

1
contessa your blessings

Mid-November
Soho House, West Hollywood, California
The girl at the door looked up from her computer sleepily and said, "Yes?"

It was 11:03 A.M. on Sunday, so if Sophia hadn't known better she might have thought the girl just wasn't a morning person, but Sophia did know better and knew that Clarabelle would have looked exactly that slow and sleepy at 11:00 P.M. or 2:00 A.M. or anytime. It was part of the mystique about Soho House, the fact that the people who worked the door were so much cooler than the patrons that they literally didn't have time to deal with them.

"Hi, Clarabelle. We're meeting Hunter for lunch upstairs," Sophia said, already moving past her toward the hall with the elevators.

"Reynard?" Clarabelle said, and a large bald man with a tattoo on his face stepped out of nowhere, blocking their path.

Sophia loved Soho House once you were inside, but getting in if you weren't a member—it was, as her sister Ava said, almost enough to make you forget their excellent yogurt-strawberry cheesecake. *Almost.*

"We're meeting Hunter here for lunch," Sophia said patiently. "I'm sure he called it in."

"And your names?"

Her friend Lily couldn't take it anymore. "Clarabelle, don't make me remind you about third-grade PE. You know what I mean."

"It's protocol," Clarabelle hissed at her.

"This is a club, not the White House," Lily hissed back.

"Fine," she said. "Welcome back, Miss London. Miss London. And"—she glared at Lily—"you."

"Thanks, Spot," Lily said, and Sophia couldn't help noticing that Clarabelle's face went from normal to flaming pink in one second. Lily had grown up in LA and seemed to be connected to nearly everyone there by either blood or secrets, which meant she could find a lever to get almost anyone to do almost anything.

"Why did you call her Spot?" Ava asked when they were in the elevator.

Lily gave her a sideways glance. She had cornhusk-blond hair, olive skin, light green eyes, and a face that made people's jaws drop, which would have made her a tedious friend except that she had the sense of humor of a fourteen-year-old boy and was completely nuts. "Trust me when I tell you that you don't want to know." She looked at Sophia. "Don't worry, it's only 11:06."

Sophia tried a smile. "I know." The smile felt tight on her face and she could tell she wasn't fooling anyone.

There wasn't really anything wrong, it was just that she hated to be late. And she especially hated to be late for Hunter because it upset him so much.

"I worry when you're not where you're supposed to be," he told her early on in their dating, with one of his knee-melting smiles. How could she argue with that?

She glanced for the fourth—or maybe fourteenth—time at the Cartier watch he'd given her two weeks earlier on their one-month anniversary. The face was gold with a little blue sapphire on the side, the same color as his eyes. Giving her the watch was so perfectly Hunter, so perfect period.

It was just another example of the way that he never chastised her if she did something he didn't like, just came up with a solution that would charm them both. The watch was his thoughtful, elegant, and effective way of telling her that time mattered to him. He was seriously the ideal boyfriend.

He had been since their first date. That had taken place the day after the nightmare of the Pet Paradise fund-raiser. Just thinking about it sent a little chill up her spine.

After she and Ava had apparently doomed their makeup line with LuxeLife cosmetics by having a knock-down-drag-out sister fight during the big launch, they'd reconciled and poured themselves into organizing a benefit for the animal shelter where Ava had been volunteering. And it had gone spectacularly—until the very end, when they'd been led away by the police, accused of having stolen the money they'd raised. It took less than an hour to get it all sorted out and for the police to arrest Ava's friend Dalton for the theft, but it had still been . . . unsettling.

That wasn't the only unsettling thing about that period, if she was being honest with herself. She'd been surprised not to hear from Giovanni again. She'd seen him for the last time a few days before the benefit, outside the gallery where her photographs were debuting.

"Your work is wonderful, *stella*," he'd said, his face all shadowy planes in the dim light of the parking lot. "It is just that you are more wonderful. What I see is a beginning most impressive. And the more you become comfortable to show of yourself, the more outstanding your pictures they will become. Do you understand?"

She had. "But I'm scared," she'd admitted.

And he'd smiled at her and told her it was natural. "But you won't let it stop you from doing what you want." And then, knowing her too well, he'd added, "And do not say you don't know what you want. You will when the time is right."

That was the last thing he'd said to her, more than six weeks earlier, a compliment and challenge wrapped up together. As though he were saying he believed in her . . . *but*.

Hunter had come out of the gallery to find her then with the news that all of her photos had sold. He'd told her they were wonderful just as they were. That she was wonderful just as she was. There was no "but" with Hunter.

Which was why when Hunter had called the night after she and Ava came home from being arrested and asked her out on a date—"no more playing at just friends," as he'd put it—she'd said yes without hesitating.

And she hadn't looked back since. The next day Hunter had stood in the doorway of their apartment, the sun at his back making a golden halo around his head, and said, "I hope you don't mind, I chose somewhere a little out of the way. I thought you'd like to avoid the press."

Sophia had smiled, and before she could thank him, Hunter had said, "That. Right there."

"What?" Sophia had asked, looking around.

"That smile. It's what I've been waiting to see."

From that moment he'd swept her off her feet so well that she hadn't had time to think about anything except him. She remembered blushing and feeling like she was floating or in a movie, and being so distracted that she hadn't even thought to notice where they were going until the car was turning into the driveway of the Santa Monica Airport.

"A little out of the way" turned out to mean a late dinner at a corner table at the quaint, candlelit garden of a French bistro—in New York City. Afterward, as the car drove them through Central Park toward his parents' place, he got quiet and seemed distracted.

"Did I do something wrong?" Sophia asked.

He shook his head and when he looked at her, he looked like a little boy, his blue-blue eyes wide and vulnerable. "No. You've done everything exactly right. And I'm scared of messing this up."

"You're the perfect one," she said. "This was the most amazing date I've ever been on."

"Really?" he asked, as though he genuinely didn't know.

"Really," she told him honestly.

He'd leaned over and kissed her then and it felt warm and familiar and comfortable. Right. "I could get used to having you by my side," he'd said, squeezing her hand.

"Me too."

They had spent the night at his parents' "little place in the city"—a four-bedroom apartment at the Plaza—and gone sightseeing the next day, before flying back to LA that night. The entire time, everything had just clicked, and by the time they touched down it felt like they'd been a couple for months, not hours.

Hunter was like a good-luck charm. Since they'd been together amazing things had been happening to her, and to London Calling. She couldn't believe she'd ever thought about *not* dating him. In fact, the only thing not perfect about her relationship with Hunter was how little they got to see each other because Sophia was so busy.

Which made being even six minutes late for brunch with him feel even worse.

She knew he would understand, especially when she told him that what had really held them up was Ava waiting to Skype with Liam from the set of his latest movie in Romania. Or was it Slovakia? Sophia couldn't remember, not because she hadn't paid attention but because Ava hadn't seemed sure herself.

She wasn't positive what was going on with Ava and Liam—whenever she asked, Ava said they were just friends, and yet she seemed very eager to talk to him. Much more than "just friends" eager.

Although, looking at Ava now, Sophia thought that her sister didn't seem sad that she hadn't gotten to talk to him, the way she would have when they were going out; she seemed more frustrated.

Trying not to check her watch, Sophia ran her hand through her long blond hair and straightened the French cuffs on her pink minidress. "Is it me or is this elevator set to Sloth?" she said.

"It's you," Lily told her as it dinged a final time.

Sophia practically exploded out of the elevator and into the dining room. Her heart was beating fast as Massie, the hostess, showed them to the corner-view table that Hunter had reserved, but it slowed down when she saw that the table was empty.

Hunter was late, too. She hadn't kept him waiting. Relief flooded through her.

Then she saw that she was wrong. He was there, only his head was on the table and he was dozing.

She rushed to his side and put her hand on his shoulder. "Hi, sweetheart," she said. "I'm so sorry we're—"

His blue eyes opened. "Well, don't you look gorgeous," he

said, standing to take her in his arms. He pulled her close and ducked his head to kiss her in a way that was much more of an after-dinner than before-brunch kiss.

"Wow," she said as they separated and only their noses touched. "You took my breath away."

He smiled at her lazily. "Now you know how I feel every minute I'm with you."

Sophia brushed the dark blond hair off his forehead, struck like she always was by how hot he was. There was a faint line of gold stubble over his square chin that caught the light and made him look like he was glowing. She ran her fingers along his cheek and said, "I wish we could just do this for the rest of the day."

"Me too," he told her. "Only maybe with fewer people around." He yawned. "And I might need a nap."

Sophia remembered that he'd been at a poker tournament the day before. No wonder he was so tired. "How was it? Did you win?"

He shook his head. "Nope, I lost," he said, shrugging it off the way only people with plenty of money can. "But the experience. Some of the biggest names in poker were playing there. It was like getting to play piano with Mozart."

"That's amazing," Sophia said.

"It was an audition, actually. I'm trying to get one of the top coaches to work with me."

"You're really taking this poker thing seriously."

"A prince has to do something while his princess is busy all day beautifying the land," he said. He said it with a grin but Sophia caught the slightest tinge of frustration as well, which made her feel guilty. Luckily, things slowed down from December until February, and she would dedicate herself then to being the best girlfriend in the world.

Sophia smiled up at him and could have spent the rest of the day staring into his handsome face if she hadn't heard Ava say, "No, he just said *every* minute, not *every single* minute."

The two of them were sitting, heads together, on the other side of the table.

"What are you doing?" Sophia asked.

"Collecting dialogue for my new play," Lily told her. "The rule is I can only use things I've heard people say in real life." She grinned at Sophia and Hunter. "Pretty much all the best romance lines come from you two."

Sophia said, "I know Ava's doing a boytox, but you're no shrinking violet. You must have your own romantic dialogue."

"Yeah," Hunter concurred, pulling out Sophia's chair for her. "Get your own."

"Somehow, 'You look hot in that droid costume' doesn't sound as good out of context as," Lily dropped her voice. "'Now you know how I feel every minute I'm with you.'"

Hunter and Sophia grinned at each other. "Be careful," he told Lily, "or we'll start charging royalties."

"Hey hey, did I just hear my favorite word? Royalties?" Rusty Green, president of MeanGreen Productions, had a long red braid and always wore green suits. "How are my favorite future reality stars?" he asked.

"Hello, Mr. Green." Ava said. "We're well."

Rusty Green was one of the first producers to have contacted them about doing a reality show after their charges of theft were dropped by the police, and over the past six weeks he'd also been one of the most persistent.

Sophia hadn't even had time to change her clothes the morning she got back from her NYC date with Hunter before Ava had hauled her out the door to their agent Corinna's office.

Corinna had stood by them through the LuxeLife debacle and their arrest and was always a calm, rational voice.

That morning she'd looked harried.

"Everyone loves a damsel in distress—especially if she's young, beautiful, and nice to animals," she said. "You two have practically attained Disney Princess status now. And boy have people been noticing."

The proposals poured in; reality shows like Mr. Green's, pet-care lines, home-care lines, and many random product-endorsement offers in foreign countries. The one they'd fallen in love with was an offer from HomeSweet to do a line of homewares, starting with a bedding collection that they were launching for Valentine's Day.

Or, as Rusty Green put it now, "How's your little sewing project doing?"

Sophia said in her sweetest voice, "You mean our housewares line?"

He shrugged. "If that's what you want to call it."

"Actually, we're calling it Live Love London," Ava told him, purposely misunderstanding. "And our first collection is called Romp. It's all bedding, sort of country French meets English—"

"Great, great," he said, and Sophia wondered if his reaction would have been any different if Ava had told him they were making couches for baboons. "I've already got someone else on the hook for my project but seeing you two here, if you begged, I would still give it to you. Tell me you've changed your mind."

"I'm afraid we haven't," Sophia said. "We were approached with so many quality reality concepts, but we want to build our brand from the ground up, not just through flash PR."

"I've got to take this," he said, holding up his cell phone and drifting away.

Ava followed him with her eyes to make sure he was really leaving, but said to Sophia, "He didn't have a call, did he?"

Sophia shook her head. "Nope."

"What word do you think it was that scared him off? I want to know so I can use it repeatedly, maybe even have an amulet made."

Lily glanced up from her iPad. "Was he the Martian show?"

Ava laughed. "I'd forgotten about that. No, he was the bachelorette style show set in a rain forest, *Love Is a Jungle.*"

"*House of Mars* was my favorite project you were offered," Lily said. "I can't believe you passed on a show with the pitch line, 'Big Brother set in a biological and gravitationally accurate Martian colony.' What was their slogan?"

"Red. Hot," Sophia told her.

"I might hold you personally responsible if that show doesn't get made," Lily said.

Sophia became aware of people behind her speaking Italian but it wasn't until she heard the phrase *stella mia* that she really began to pay attention.

Giovanni, she breathed, and her heart began to pound.

He'd said it that night at the gallery, *stella.* The last time she'd seen or spoken to him. Said it and then disappeared without another word or text or phone call. He hadn't even bothered to reply to hers.

And now here he was. Presumably talking to a woman, someone else, maybe it wasn't even him, maybe—

"*Stella mia,* for the sake of Pete please do not try to stab yourself with the buttering knife. The tablecloths here are much too nice for such things."

That had to be Giovanni. Unable to stop herself, she turned to look at the table behind them. It was occupied by a model-gorgeous Italian woman in her thirties wrapped in a leopard fur, pointing a butter knife dramatically at her heart, a shorter man with round glasses who gazed at her adoringly, and a boy somewhere around twelve with wide brown eyes and curling golden hair who could have modeled for a Renaissance angel except for the way he winked at every waitress who went by.

No Giovanni.

She wasn't disappointed, Sophia told herself as she turned back to her friends. She leaned back and felt Hunter's arm around her shoulders. Who had time for friends, even funny ones who mangled English and made you see yourself . . . differently.

"I'm going to go take a gallery tour. I need to start working on my Christmas tree," Lily said, picking up her iPad. A gallery tour, for Lily, meant that she was walking around the restaurant taking pictures of everyone's plastic surgery, which at this time of year she would then have printed on Christmas-tree balls. The year before, her tree had been all noses, but she'd been talking about doing all lips and chins this year. Although all of Lily's perfect parts were original, part of her Los Angeles–childhood heritage was a fascination with plastic surgery, both its practitioners and its recipients.

"Am I wrong thinking Lily is wearing one of the sheet sets from the Romp campaign?" Hunter asked as she wandered off.

"You are *not* wrong," Ava said. She tapped the coat draped over Lily's chair. "And this is one of the comforters. There was some extra yardage from the samples they sent over so I repurposed it."

Sophia had always known her sister had a good eye and could put patterns together well, but it seemed Ava's creativity had gone into turbo overdrive since she'd started her boytox.

One day Sophia would get up and there would be an entirely new concept for the throw pillows on the bed. The next, she'd find a dress made from the fabric samples. Ava had made one with leather-fringe trim that they were considering for pillows, which Sophia had been dying to wear for weeks.

"The silk straps were Sophia's idea," Ava was telling Hunter. "She's the trim-and-finishings genius. I just do the grunt work."

"I bet you could sell that stuff," Hunter said. "But I am not suggesting that. I want you to have more free time, not less." He tugged Sophia toward him.

"I'm sorry, Prince Charming. As soon as we finish shooting the Romp campaign, I'll have three, maybe even four days off."

"Four whole days," Hunter marveled.

"Did I say days?" Sophia said. "I meant hours."

"Actually she meant minutes," Ava told him.

"I'll take them!" Hunter went along with the joke. "As long as they're—"

There was a discreet throat clearing, then the same Italian-accented voice Sophia had heard before said, "Please excuse me for the interruption." They turned and saw the man with the round glasses. "The Contessa humbly requests a word with the beautiful ladies, if they are the friends of that one"—he pointed at Lily—"there."

"We are," Sophia said. Her eyes met Ava's and she could tell they were both wondering what Lily could possibly have done now.

"*Prego*," the man answered, holding his arms out to the side, one for each of the London sisters to take. Hunter tagged along, and they made a slow, stately, and as far as Sophia and Ava were concerned incredibly mortifying procession from their table to the Contessa's, three over.

If there was anyone talking or moving or looking anywhere but at them in the dining room, Sophia didn't see them.

When they reached the Contessa, Sophia had a moment of panic about the etiquette when addressing a contessa. Did you curtsey? Kiss her hand? Her ring?

The Contessa herself solved the problem, standing and giving them each two kisses on the cheek. She beamed at them, holding one of each of their hands for a moment, then pointed them into chairs the busboy had brought.

"*Che belle*, how beautiful you are," she said. "We are going to be biff, I know this already."

Sophia and Ava must have looked puzzled, because she said, "Biff? This is an American thing you say, no?" She turned to the boy, snapping her fingers to get his attention, and said something quick in Italian.

"BFF," he explained, with only a slight accent. "You will be the best friends forever with my mother. Good luck to you." He winked at them.

The Contessa leaned toward Ava. "I am told you are the hand that made this." When she said "this," she flourished her right hand toward Lily.

"I made the outfit, yes," Ava said, wanting to be completely clear.

"I am the Contessa Antonia di Bellevista. You have heard of me of course. You know, I do not speak idly. Your outfit is *molto bello*. Or, as you Americans say, the Wow. I must have it. So, it is decided. You will make a fashion collection for me for New York Fashion Week."

Ava said, "Right now we are really focused on—"

The Contessa reached out and placed a perfectly manicured finger over Ava's mouth. "This is not a conversation, blah-blah you blah-blah me. This is me telling you, you will do this."

"All business proposals must go through our agent," Sophia told the Contessa, hoping her voice sounded calming. Since she had just seen the woman pretend to try to kill herself with a butter knife.

The Contessa smiled and nodded, only then remembering that she still held a finger over Ava's mouth. She let go and patted

Ava on the cheek. "*Bene.* You give me the name of your agent. I will go buy him. Very good." She brushed her hands together. "It is done. You are mine now."

"Didn't that sound like that should be followed by an evil laugh?" Ava asked Sophia in the car going home.

"Completely," Sophia told her. "But I don't think we need to worry about hearing from our new *Biff.* She forgot to ask for Corinna's number. Or name."

"What a relief," Ava said.

LonDOs
The truffle-and-cheese pizza at Soho House
Promptness
Serendipity
The Wow
Repurposing
Fast-drying nail pens
New York Fashion Week!!!!!!!!!!!!

LonDON'Ts
Mess with people who had PE with you in third grade
Underestimate the Contessa
Ever say, "But I don't think we need to worry . . ."
Go to sleep without taking off your eye makeup

2
lip lash

Two Months Later

"Three weeks, one day," Ava said as their plane touched down at JFK.

"And two hours," Sophia added without looking up from the magazine she was reading. "Three weeks, one day, two hours, and"—she glanced at her watch—"seven minutes until our very first fashion line goes down the catwalk in one of the most-watched tents at NYC Fashion Week." She flipped a page of the magazine. "Piece of cake."

Ava, seeing that Sophia's hands were shaking, grinned. She was glad to know it wasn't just her.

Although compared to the two months they'd just lived through, it seemed like it almost could be a piece of cake. Ava felt like she hadn't slept that entire time, or maybe she hadn't been awake. Her life had certainly been a lot like a dream since the morning Corinna had called to tell them that some "crazy Italian woman" had forced her out of bed at 5:00 A.M. to say she wanted to buy the London sisters' "bodies and souls" and ask how much that would cost.

Sophia had turned to Ava at that point and said, "I guess the Contessa found the number."

"I thought it was a joke," Corinna went on. "Until I looked her up and saw that her brother just died, leaving her one of the richest women in Europe. What do you say? Are you up for a pact with the devil?"

The Contessa had actually turned out to be much easier to work with than they'd feared. She was generous, enthusiastic, supportive, and seemed to know what she was doing. Not only were her critiques spot-on (once you figured out what she was talking about), but she'd also gotten them a place in Fashion Week's coveted New Young Designers tent and show.

"Must have had to murder someone to do it," Lucille Rexford, the eccentric millionaire who owned LuxeLife and had given them their makeup line, said approvingly, "Just the kind of businesswoman I admire."

In the space of two months they had designed, cut, sourced, and manufactured an entire catwalk line—twelve looks plus two extras. Fabric had been milled, buttons molded, special threads woven, tempers frayed, plans upended, dinners missed, sleep forgotten, and patience tested, but they'd done it.

It was a good thing she'd been doing a boytox, Ava thought, since there was no time for anything like dating. And since technically she was still dating Liam, her movie-star-crush-turned-boyfriend, since he was on location and somehow managed to avoid having a conversation that lasted long enough for her to break up with him. Which she knew she had to do because she'd fallen head over heels for someone else.

Someone else who had been identified by an anonymous call to the police as the person who had actually stolen all the money from the Pet Paradise fund-raiser.

When the police told her and Sophia that Dalton was the thief, Ava had refused to believe it. Cute Dalton, with the sun-streaked brown hair and rich laugh and sculpted surfer shoulders that perfectly filled out his hipster T-shirts; Dalton, whom she'd met at the Pet Paradise shelter, whom her dog Popcorn adored; Dalton, who was in a band with a hit single and made amazing pancakes and who looked adorable in his dark-framed glasses and had eyes the green of the deepest parts of ocean and just as easy to get lost in; Dalton, whose lightest kiss made her feel like her knees had turned to Pop Rocks. He couldn't be a bad guy. He couldn't have forged checks and stolen $110,000 from animals. Wouldn't have.

But she had to remind herself that this was the same Dalton who had told her he was a bad guy, that he'd been in jail for theft before, that she shouldn't get involved with him . . . right before brushing his lips against hers with the gentlest, lightest, most transformative kiss she'd ever—

The evidence against him was impossible to ignore. Not only had he suddenly had money when before he hadn't, but when the police came to arrest him he'd been holding a piece of paper covered with practice attempts at Sophia's signature identical to the forged signature on the check that drained their account. The checks had been stolen during a break-in of their apartment when they were at Sophia's photography opening—an opening from which Dalton had made a hasty exit.

But Ava still hadn't wanted to give up on him. She couldn't believe that he'd just been using her. That everything he'd said and done was a big lie. That he didn't care about the animal shelter or . . . or Popcorn. She'd texted him and called him, but he'd never returned any of them. And the one time she'd run into him—

Her chest got a little tight just thinking about it. She'd been at the park, with Popcorn napping next to her on the blanket, and had just tweeted "at the park with my baby boy. So peaceful, like a little lamb," when his ears stood up and he took off running.

She'd had his leash looped around her ankle in case he tried something like this, and usually he'd stop when it started to tug. But that day he'd been so eager that she ended up being dragged on her butt through the dirt ten feet before she could get him to stop.

She should have known. There was only one person who had that perk-up-your-ears-and-run-to-his-arms effect on Popcorn— on either of them—but she'd been too startled to realize. Until she pushed her long brown hair out of her eyes and saw Popcorn jumping to lick Dalton's face.

For a moment their eyes met and Ava's heart had started to pound so loud that it sounded like it was outside her body. Then his expression hardened and without a word he stood and turned to go.

"Wait," Ava called. "What happened? Why haven't you called? Don't you think you owe me an explanation?"

He wasn't wearing sunglasses, so she was able to see his eyes, how hard and cold they were as he narrowed them. His jaw was so tight that it looked like he had to wrench the words out. "Why? Haven't you and your sister done enough to destroy my life? I don't owe you anything, and I never want to see or speak to you again."

His words, his tone, made Ava's body go cold and her heart slow almost to a stop. She felt frozen in place, unable to reply or move or think.

Popcorn's sad whine brought her out of it. He was looking from her to Dalton's receding back with such a forlorn expression that Ava felt like her heart was breaking.

Only because of Popcorn. Not because of Dalton. She would never let someone who was such bad news break her heart.

"Well, that was unexpected," she'd said to Popcorn as they moped back to her blanket together. Her pants were covered with dust and her face was streaked with dirt.

Popcorn gave a little growl and she looked down to see him gazing reproachfully at her. "What? It's not my fault. I know you like him, but trust me, there's no place for him in our lives." Popcorn's accusing glance said he wasn't convinced. "Sometimes people aren't who you think they are and the only thing you can do is forget about them."

Determined to do just that, she'd thrown herself into her boytox. It had worked fantastically for Sophia, who was really happy with Hunter. Ava would just follow in her sister's footsteps and one day, she hoped, she would feel happy again, too. One day she would look back on the whole Dalton thing and laugh at the thought that she'd ever gone through four boxes of Kleenex (well, three; Popcorn ate one) crying over him.

It had worked. She'd gone from thinking about him a hundred times a day and checking her phone for texts that weren't there, to thinking of him only a handful. Increasingly the feeling of missing him and being sad was replaced almost exclusively with anger and hurt and betrayal. Which, she told herself, was progress. Anything else was foolish hope.

The day before they were leaving for New York she'd been so busy she hadn't even thought about him at all, until she went to take Popcorn for a walk. When they got back she'd found an envelope sticking out of their mailbox. It had her name on it and no stamp, which meant it had been hand delivered.

Inside was a piece of white paper with the words DALTON IS INNOCENT. ASK ABOUT XAVIER laser printed across the center.

She'd dragged Popcorn into the house and woken Sophia. "Look!" She waved the paper in her face. "What do you think this means? We have to take this to the police. It might be important."

Sophia glanced at it and the envelope and handed it back to her. "I don't think the police take anonymous notes too seriously," she said.

"It's not any old anonymous note. It was delivered to our *house.* That means it's from someone who knows we know Dalton."

"Or a crazy person. Or someone trying to stir up even more trouble."

"They could still check the name," Ava said. "Xavier. Maybe there's more to what happened than we know."

"Is this you trying to forget about what Dalton did?"

"No, but this means something and I think we should try to figure it out."

Sophia shrugged, clearly unconvinced. "Call the police then."

Ava had, and although the officer she spoke to was polite, it was pretty clear that Sophia was right. "No, dear, there's no need for you to hold on to the note," the officer told her. "We won't be coming to take fingerprints. That note won't change anything. Go ahead and throw it away."

She hadn't quite been able to throw the note away, but she'd told herself that was absolutely the end of her thinking about Dalton. If the evidence against him was so strong that even the police weren't interested in a new lead, she would be a fool to hold out any hope of being with him. Or rather of his being innocent. He'd made his feelings about her perfectly clear.

The only boy she needed in her life, she decided, was the one in the pet carrier beneath the airplane seat in front of her, where she could now see him curled protectively around Sophia's kitten, Charming, who her sister finally named after joking that no matter who her true love turned out to be, she'd already met her Prince Charming.

A male voice from the row behind her and Sophia broke into her thoughts, saying, "Fashion week ninjas ready to serve." She turned to see MM, Sven, and Lily wrapped in scarves from their necks to their eyeballs. "Hard on cold, soft on skin," he explained. "We don't have time for germs."

"Or chapped lips," Lily added. "They impede the ability to bark orders."

"An unstoppable team," Ava said, feeling very lucky.

Wrapped up like that, the disparity in height between MM, who was five foot five and wiry, and Sven, who was nearly seven feet tall and a solid wall of muscle, was hilarious. Their height was just the beginning of the differences between them—MM was dark, with cinnamon-colored skin and dark hair, while Sven was blond with blue eyes and skin the pink of a peach; MM dressed impeccably with an incredible attention to detail, while Sven's entire wardrobe consisted of jeans and T-shirts.

MM had taken two months off from his clients to join their team as a stylist. His boyfriend Sven had come along to lend moral support, as well as his expertise, having walked the male catwalk once. And Lily had come along as the self-appointed "pet and Contessa wrangler."

In the aisle seat next to her Ava heard Sophia say into her phone, "Yes, all safe and sound. I'll call you when we're settled. You too. Bye." She hung up and smiled at Ava as the line down the exit row started to move. "Ready?"

All that was left to do now was cast the models, put the finishing touches on the collection, and go. Three weeks, one day, two—now one and a half—hours should be plenty.

"No," Ava said. "Terrified. You?"

"Same," Sophia agreed. "But that's always how it starts, right?" They linked pinkies. "Let's go."

Four hours after they landed at JFK they were sitting in the sunken gold-and-black living room of the ten-bedroom, twenty-third-floor condo overlooking the Hudson River that the Contessa had installed them in, drinking tea with a reporter from one of their favorite fashion magazines.

"Your story is really incredible," she said wonderingly. "Two girls with no fashion experience at all launch a runway collection in one of the most desirable tents at New York Fashion Week." She put her teacup down. "I have to say, it sounds almost too good to be true."

"That's what we thought," Sophia told her. "But that's how it happened."

The reporter was young and pretty and chic, wearing a black dress with almost no makeup, black-rimmed glasses, and bright red lipstick. She had handwritten notes on a pad next to her, but there was a recorder on the gold-lacquer coffee table, so it felt more like a conversation than a formal interview. "And you got no outside assistance. There's no designer's guiding hand behind this?"

"None," Ava assured her.

"Every design originated in Ava's brain," Sophia said. "After that, it's sort of—"

"A team effort—" Ava supplied.

"With a lot of trial and error—" Sophia said.

"Until we get something that just—" Ava looked at her sister, who finished the sentence:

"Clicks."

"I guess I just saw that process in action," the reporter said, laughing.

She glanced at the notes in her lap, and her face got serious. "I think the real story is that somehow, in the wake of two PR disasters, either one of which could have sunk you, you continue to find yourselves on top."

"Not on top," Sophia jumped in to say. "Working *toward* that." Ava sensed that something was bothering Sophia but she couldn't tell what. "And although the product launch for our makeup line with LuxeLife did not go well—"

The reporter looked at them sympathetically. "That must have been such a nightmare for you both. Having a fight overheard by hundreds of thousands of people and then running off before the event even started."

Sophia nodded. "We've learned a lot since then. And despite that, demand for our products was so high that they relaunched our line and it is now the biggest seller in LuxeLife's history. So in addition to what you called disasters, we have a track record of success as well."

"Of course." The reporter nodded. "You also have an arrest record," she said, looking a little sheepish. "Can we talk a little about that? You were accused of stealing money from an animal shelter?"

"Right from the mouths of adorable puppies and kittens," Ava answered, referring to some of the less kind news stories. "But we were set up, our arrest lasted less than two hours, and in the end we managed to raise enough money not only to keep the shelter open but to allow them to start work on an annex."

"That's really impressive. You seem to have figured out the magic for turning bad publicity into good."

"We work very hard," Sophia said, and Ava was struck by how serious her voice sounded.

It must have struck the reporter, too, because she said, "I can tell. In fact, let's talk a bit more about your work process. You said every idea originated in Ava's brain. And then what happens?" She looked at Ava.

Ava fluttered her hands. "I just—make it. I've always liked organizing things. In kindergarten the teachers called my parents, worried because I wouldn't build anything with the blocks, I just wanted to organize them. I guess to me this is the same thing, just organizing shapes and colors into something I like."

"That's an interesting take on designing. Organizing shapes and colors. Neither of you have any formal training, is that correct?"

Sophia shook her head. Ava said, "None. When I was little my mother taught me how to sew in the formal dining room but I don't think that counts."

The reporter laughed. "I know the clothes are under wraps, obviously, but do you have some sketches or drawings I could see?"

"I don't really do drawings," Ava said. "I see the designs in my mind and then I just—" She whipped her hands around. "Try to get the basic idea out in fabric. From there, as we said, the pieces just evolve through trial and error."

"A lot of trial," Sophia said.

"And a *lot* of error," Ava added.

"It seems like that strategy has paid off very well for you," the reporter said. "You're calling the line AS. I assume for your initials."

"Yes, but it's also our message," Sophia said, and Ava loved hearing the passion in her sister's voice. "We wanted to build a brand that was fun and exciting, easy to wear but still makes the client feel special, and lets them feel comfortable standing out. It's an invitation. Come AS you are. Because that is our story. We've made mistakes, as you said, some of them publicly. We have flaws. And we've succeeded in spite of—"

"Sometimes because of them," Ava added.

"That's the story of AS," Sophia continued. "That we aren't professional designers, we are normal girls who have a chance to do extraordinary things. Take us AS we are."

The reporter glanced at the pad next to her and said, "I think that's all I have. It was a pleasure meeting you both. Good luck."

"Can you tell us when the story is going to run?" Sophia asked.

The reporter shook her head. "I'm not sure. We'll definitely be doing a profile on you, but this may also become part of a larger piece a colleague of mine is working on. Within the next week I'd say."

After she left, Sophia sat very still on the sofa, toying with the handle of her teacup.

"What's bothering you?" Ava asked.

"She was so *nice*," Sophia said.

"And that's bad?" Ava said. "Do we live in backward world now?"

"I guess I'm afraid this is too good to be true and something will happen to take it all away." Sophia shook her head. "You're right, I'm just feeling disoriented. I mean, where do we live? Look at this place." She spread her arms out, indicating the gold ceiling, black-carpeted floor, black-silk walls, and black-velvet sectional.

"It's what I imagine the inside of a genie's bottle would look like," Ava said, and Sophia nodded.

"Exactly. Only with ten bedrooms. I never really pictured genies having company."

"No, too busy answering their masters' wishes," Ava pointed out.

Sophia's phone rang. "It's Hunter. I have to take it."

Ava said, "Go." As she slid off the black-velvet couch and went in search of her bedroom, she wondered if genies were ever lonely.

LonDOs

Having a genie to grant you wishes

Silver-satin bedroom with mirrored canopy over the bed

Lavender-satin bedroom with pearl-gray canopy over the bed

Footed bathtubs

Heated bathroom floors

Boys who call you just to say they are thinking about you

Hand lotion

Fleece mittens

My sister

Mine too

LonDON'Ts

Boys who are not on Skype when they say they will be on Skype

The phrase I'm sorry, babe, we had to reshoot

The phrase I'm sorry, babe, I was running lines

Boys who growl and accuse you of ruining their lives

Mirrors on the bathroom ceiling

And on the couch

Sleet

Being the genie

3

beauty and the tweet

He was draped across the silver-satin quilt on the bed in her room, apparently wearing nothing but a burgundy robe and dinosaur slippers, when Ava came out of the bathroom, two nights later.

"Hey, *bebe*," Tomasso said. "You feeling lucky?"

Tomasso was the Contessa's twelve-year-old son, and the more Ava saw of him, the less angelic he seemed.

Ava was exhausted. It was only nine but they'd been at the studio at seven that morning, casting models. They'd found fifteen girls they liked and were supposed to convene in the kitchen at nine thirty for Chinese food and to make their final selections. This was the first time she'd had to herself all day and she did not feel like sharing it with a preteen pervert.

Popcorn paced near his feet, growling. "Good boy, Popcorn, protecting Mommy from intruders," Ava said, picking him up.

"Hello, Tomasso. Shouldn't you be in your own apartment? There are what, seven bedrooms there?"

The Contessa, Tomasso, and her husband, Eduardo, lived upstairs, using the apartment the London sisters and their team shared for guests, but Ava was discovering that the boundaries were sometimes a bit loose.

"Ten," Tomasso said. "But this is my apartment too, you know, *bebe*." He patted the bed. "Come and teach me the ways of the world. I like an older woman."

Ava rolled her eyes. "What would your mother say if I called her and told her you were here, Tomasso?"

"She would say, of course he is; it is where he belongs." He grinned and sat up. "She sent me here, you know. To get you. She wants to have a quickie with you."

Ava stared at him. "A what?"

"The short chat. Quickie. You say that, no?"

"No," Ava said. She was wearing black jeans and the over-sized cardigan she'd had on at the studio. She had considered changing but since it was nine at night, and Tomasso was setting a casual tone, she decided to go AS she was.

Adding just a scarf.

And some lip gloss.

As Tomasso escorted her up to the other apartment, which meant to the elevator that opened directly into it, he said, "You should call me Toma. It is more manly, don't you think?"

"No."

"What is a quickie then?"

"Where did you hear about it?" Ava countered.

"From Bobo, the driver. He is always having them with my mother's friend Max. You can learn a lot just from listening."

Yes, you can, Ava thought. She was so tired that it was only when the elevator doors slid open in the Bellevistas' apartment that she wondered what the Contessa might want. This wasn't the first time she or Sophia or any of their team had been summoned, but it was the first time she'd been brought up alone and it occurred to her that maybe she should be worried.

Going from the downstairs apartment to the upstairs was kind of disorienting. While the downstairs apartment was done in Modern Genie style, the upstairs one was like being in a model suburban house, all chintz upholstery and floral curtains and framed prints of geese flying over rivers.

The Contessa was in her office, sitting behind an oak desk. There was a fire in the fireplace, and a comfortable-looking couch in a discreet cream brocade was set against one wall, but Toma showed Ava into an uncomfortable straight-backed chair with an itchy needlepoint cushion across from the desk. He took a much more comfortable upholstered chair next to his mother's desk and settled in as though he planned to be there awhile.

Fantastic, Ava thought.

The floor was wood, with a yellow-and-cream area rug, and the curtains framing the window behind the Contessa were blue-and-yellow paisley. The room was homey, cozy even, and if it hadn't been for the view across the river and the fact that the Contessa was wearing pearl earrings the size of pheasant eggs, it would have been possible to forget you were two dozen floors up in a deluxe apartment on Riverside Drive in New York City.

The Contessa finished writing something, set down her silver fountain pen, and smiled at Ava. Ava was always struck by how perfect she looked, and tranquil, especially knowing that she was prone to rather exciting shows of temper. For example, Ava had come back from walking Popcorn the day before to find the Contessa's husband, Eduardo, pacing in front of their door, waiting for the Thai food delivery guy because he refused to deliver to their apartment, or as he put it "the house of that demon lady with the big knife and crazy eyes" anymore.

But when she didn't have crazy eyes, the Contessa looked beautiful and serene, like someone you could picture singing to birds in a park. Now she smiled at Ava and announced, "I have brought you here to give you the very good news."

"Oh good," Ava said. She'd learned that the best way to avoid seeing the crazy eyes was to keep her replies short.

"I am going to marry you."

Ava leaned forward. "I beg your pardon?"

Toma looked as surprised as she did.

"No not me myself. I will be your half mother." She turned to her son. "How do you say it, Toma?"

"Aunt," Toma answered, frowning.

"Yes, I will be your aunt. You will marry my nephew."

"I don't want to marry anyone," Ava said.

"Yes, it will be perfect." The Contessa leaned forward, tenting her hands over the desk. "Right now you do the boytox, yes? The no men, no dating. It is because your heart has been hurt."

"How do you know?"

"People, they have mouths, yes? *Bene.*" She nodded. "This one who has hurt you, you pretend that you are healing but really you are holding an empty place in your heart for him."

"That's not—" Ava objected.

"Let me tell you about my nephew and why you will do this. You will like him. For one thing, he is rich. Eh. But there is more. He has"—she made a face, like she was searching for words—"a very unusual mind."

"This is true," Toma agreed in a way that made Ava nervous.

The Contessa went on. "He is very, how do you say–*simpatico*—"

Toma offered, "Simple."

The Contessa tapped her forehead, nodding amiably. "And very funny here."

"Are you saying that he is funny in the head?" Ava asked, just to be clear.

The Contessa smiled. "Exactly. Sometimes I am not perfect with the idioms. Funny in the head."

"At least now that he has the right medicine . . ." Toma whispered to Ava.

Ava stared from him to his mother. This wasn't happening. Was this happening?

"And he has much hair," the Contessa went on. "You are young, you do not yet know, but this is very important for men, having the hair. They will not admit it, no, but here"—she patted her chest, presumably pointing to where the hair was—"it means everything."

"Like a beast," Toma said. "My uncle, his father, that was his nickname."

"Is that true?" Ava asked the Contessa.

She got a dreamy expression. "It is. Even in his coffin, people they talked about the hair of my brother. So you will not have to worry, there will always be plenty of hair."

"Oh. Good." Ava felt a little faint.

The Contessa looked delighted. "I see you begin to understand. He is a very good man, my nephew. He has the good eye. He will appreciate you too."

"He has a good *eye*?" Ava repeated.

The Contessa nodded.

"But what about the other—"

"Is best not to mention it," Toma interrupted her.

Naturally, Ava thought. *Probably you didn't even notice the eye because he was so hairy. Or so crazy.* Ava looked at the Contessa. "But why do you want me to marry him?"

"Because you have a broken heart and also he has a broken heart and together you will heal. I realize this today. It is for this one reason that we have been brought together. You two are perfect for one another."

Ava didn't let herself think about what it meant that the Contessa saw her as perfect for her beast-man nephew, and focused instead on the other part of what the woman had said. "I thought we were brought together to put on a fashion show."

"For both of you, it will yield a thing of joy. For him, a pretty wife. For you, a delightful husband *and* a fashion line."

Ava suddenly felt cold. "Do you mean if I don't marry your nephew we can't do our show?"

The Contessa laughed. "But no. I am not the crazy person. You just will go to some parties with him to start. For the Fashion Week. He will be your"—She snapped her fingers and looked at Toma—*"squero."*

"Master," Toma translated.

A master, Ava thought. The apartment was feeling more and more like a genie's bottle with each passing moment.

"And if I say no?" Ava asked, risking the crazy eyes but having to.

The Contessa laughed again. "And why would you do this thing? It would be madness. You must trust me. I am very experienced in the matters of heart, and I know you two will make perfect match. Besides, what will it hurt? It is just one date."

In her head Ava heard, *Funny in the head, hairy, one good eye.*

"And do not forget, he is a count," the Contessa added. "You know this is important, the bloodlines, for breeding. You see my Toma here. Such an angel. And look at his hair. Perhaps one day also he will be the beast."

"Mom," the angel said, batting her hand away from his hair.

"And also there is this," the Contessa said, her expression

earnest. "If you said no, I am afraid I would think you were a not serious girl. Your sister, she is a serious girl I am sure. You, I think you are serious, but what if I am wrong? Eh? Of course I would not back the clothing line of a not-serious girl. A silly girl. A girl who does not know how to say *why not*. I tell you, I do this for your happiness. You and he are made for each other. But you do not yet know how I am always right. So for now is a few parties. Not much. That is all I ask. Then, after, we discuss more." She smiled encouragingly. "*Va bene*? Okay?"

A few parties, Ava thought. That wasn't a big deal. Even with someone who was a little crazy and hairy. And eye patches could be handsome. Very James Bond villain.

Why was she hesitating? She felt like there was something she was missing, a trick the Contessa was playing, that somehow she was agreeing to more than she thought and that this was a bad idea in a way she had yet to understand, but how?

And then she remembered Sophia saying, "I guess I'm just afraid this is too good to be true and something will happen to take it all away," and decided it didn't matter. That something was *not* going to be her. Whatever weird bargain the Contessa was striking, Ava would say yes.

"It would be a pleasure to go to parties with your nephew," Ava said and realized that the Contessa had already gone back to writing.

"Yes, of course," the Contessa said without looking up. She made a gesture with her hand like she was brushing off crumbs and Ava realized she was dismissed.

Ava was five minutes late to the nine-thirty meeting in the kitchen, and still in a daze. When she got there, Lily, MM, Sven, and Sophia were gathered around the large black-granite island in the middle of the room. Open Chinese-food containers were pushed to one side and the pictures of their final model picks were spread in front of them.

"We got you an order of cold sesame noodles, in addition to everything else on the menu," Lily greeted her.

Ava felt sort of odd, like she was floating, there but not there. "Thanks."

Sophia looked up sharply. "Ava? Are you okay?"

Ava laughed. "The Contessa wants me to marry her nephew or else we don't get to have a fashion show."

"That makes no sense," Sophia said. Sven hoisted a stool from one side of the island to the other with a single muscled arm, MM put Ava on it, and Sophia came around to look directly in Ava's eyes. "Are you delirious? Did you take too much cough syrup again?"

"No and no. She says if I won't consider it then that shows I am not a serious person and if I am not a serious person why would she fund our fashion line. Serious like you." Ava smiled at Sophia. "See, perfect sense in Contessa logic."

"Then this is over," Sophia said, shaking her head. "Because I am seriously opposed. There is no way you're getting married. This is not the eighteenth century."

Ava shrugged. "Well, he is a count. That sounds very eighteenth century. But I forgot. He's hairy like a beast and has only one eye."

Lily had pulled out a computer and was already googling the count. "The only thing that came up is an old guy."

"She didn't make him sound old," Ava said, looking at the photo of a man in his seventies. "And the guy in the picture has two eyes. Although he does look hairy." She pointed to the thick mane of hair brushed off his forehead.

"I have a question," Sven said, putting up his hand. He was looking at the computer screen.

"Yes, Sven?" Ava said. "You don't have to raise your hand."

Sven lowered it. "Did she say if he was alive?"

"No." Ava shook her head slowly. "She didn't *specify* that. I just assumed he was alive."

He tapped the computer. "Then is not that man. That man in the picture is dead. It is her brother who died. The last count."

"Rats." Lily pushed the computer to one side. "Think of it as an exciting adventure with a mystery man," she suggested.

Sophia had been frowning the whole time. "Don't be absurd, there's no way Ava is doing this." She made a finish-line gesture with her hands. "The end."

For some reason that made Ava want to cry. "Thank you," she told Sophia. "But for now she says I just have to go to a few parties during Fashion Week. That's not that big a deal. I can do that."

Sophia still looked skeptical.

Sven raised his hand again. "I have another question." They all looked at him and he lowered his hand slowly. "What about Liam? He is your boyfriend, no?"

Ava shrugged. "It's complicated."

Sven pointed to the computer screen. "Here he tweets to you, 'Missing my special lady, thinking of her in NYC.' This sounds like a boyfriend."

"It does," Sophia said, eyeing Ava. "What exactly is going on between you two?"

Ava got very interested in the casting photos. "I really liked this girl. I say we—"

"It doesn't matter," MM said in a strange, soft voice. "Any of it."

"What are you talking about?" Sophia asked.

Before he could answer, the sound of a wild animal roaring in fury shook the walls of the kitchen.

Ava steadied herself on the island. "What was that?"

"I don't know but I think I just understood the phrase *my blood ran cold*," Lily said.

"It was her." MM rolled his eyes to the ceiling. "And I think she must just have seen this." He held his phone out. "It's the magazine piece from your interview."

Ava reached for Sophia's hand.

"How bad is it?" Sophia asked. "Does it say we're amateurs, just lucky, just pretty?" She repeated the things that had been said about them dozens of times before.

"No," MM said, looking like he was in shock. "It's worse. Much worse."

LonDOs
Face wash
Fresh sugar lip balm
Protective pooches
Cold sesame noodles from Szechuan Gourmet

LonDONTs
Trusting reporters
Trusting yourself to not sound like an idiot while talking to reporters
Eighteenth-century marriage practices
Whoever snuck in and finished the cold sesame noodles in the
    middle of the night

4

badison avenue

It started with a tweet:

@reporterwithglasses: "Designing just like kindergarten" and other important things I learned from the London sisters on the eve of Fashion Week. #wisdomefortheages #LondonBridgesFalling #FashionWeek

And by the next morning, it had found a place among the blind items:

We're hearing . . . Christopher Wildwood has an exciting celebrity-guest model, much sought by designers but never—until now—won.

We're hearing . . . *Buongiorno* is the new pickup line, as Manhattan readies for the arrival of a most eligible Italian nobleman (wink wink) and his lady-killing crew for Fashion Week.

We're hearing . . . a spot may be opening up in the New Designers tent at Fashion Week. Rumors are flying that in the wake of an article revealing a certain urban-named duo had no formal fashion training or knowledge of the industry, the Fashion Week Oversight Committee is opening an investigation into their collection. One whiff of impropriety and it's bye-bye show tents, hello Show Over.

"Do you think the Italian nobleman they are talking about is the Contessa's count?" Ava asked as they rode down to the showroom the next morning in a cab.

Sophia didn't look up from her text. "What are you talking about?"

"In the second blind item. I only wonder because it says 'wink wink' and you know, with the one eye—"

Sophia looked up from her text. "I'm sorry, what was that?"

"Nothing," Ava said. "Just trying not to think about what's going to happen with our tents."

"For one thing, this is just a rumor," Sophia said, frowning slightly as her phone chimed again. She glanced at it while she talked, then typed a quick text. "We don't even know if it's true. And it could be some other people with an urban themed name."

"Sure," Ava said. "The Chicago Sisters. Oh no, that isn't a brand."

Sophia squeezed her hand. "Whatever they're investigating, we didn't do it, right?"

"Right."

"So we'll be fine," she concluded. "Innocent until proven guilty."

"Except we do have a way of getting into trouble," Ava pointed out.

"And then getting out of it." Sophia's phone chimed and she sighed. "Excuse me."

"It's only nine thirty. That's so early for Hunter to be up texting," Ava said, partially to herself.

"He's doing some kind of fast he read about in a magazine and it throws off his whole schedule. I'm supposed to text him to give him encouragement."

"What do you say?" Ava asked, leaning over to try to see.

Sophia laughed and twisted away. "It's private."

"I saw the word *bicep*!" Ava told her, grabbing for it.

"Stop." Sophia giggled. "It's all scientific."

"You're sexting!" Ava said as the taxi pulled up to the studio. "I'm telling Mom!"

Sophia jammed her phone into her bag. "Then I'll tell everyone about how the reason you offer to go to Starbucks so many times a day is because there's a cute guy you like to smile at who studies there most mornings and some afternoons from three to seven."

Ava gaped at her as she opened the cab door. "How did you— I mean, that's not—*oh*."

Two dozen microphones bristled at them like a wall.

Sophia reached around to pull the door shut and said to the cabdriver, "Drive around the block." She looked at Ava, who was sitting on the other end of the seat with her eyes huge and glassy and her hands knotted together. "Are you breathing?"

"No."

"Breathe."

"No, thanks."

"Ava, look at me." Slowly Ava's face turned toward her and Sophia saw tears in her eyes. "Sweetheart—"

"Don't be nice," Ava insisted. "This is my fault. It's what I said in the interview that's getting all the bad press." It was true, she knew. Sophia would never have said any of the things she had said.

Sophia shook her head. "You were just being yourself. That's what our whole line is about." Her phone chimed but she ignored it. "If we can't show it at Fashion Week, then they're not ready for us. But that's their problem, not yours."

"Stop it," Ava said. "You're making me cry more."

Sophia hugged her. "I wouldn't want to be doing this with anyone but you, just the way you are."

"I wouldn't want to do this with anyone but you."

"Even if we don't know what we're doing," Sophia said. Her phone chimed another time.

"You do," Ava said. "You always seem like you do."

"Sure."

"How did you know about the guy at Starbucks?" Ava asked.

"I'm your *sister*. I saw you eye flirting with him the other day when we were there together." Her phone chimed again.

Ava glanced at it. "Hunter is really insistent."

"'Hungry' is more like it," Sophia said. "It makes him need so much attention. I would pay someone to go feed him Oreos." She picked up her phone and started reading through the messages.

"Do we go back now?" the cabdriver asked.

Sophia looked at Ava, who nodded. "Yes," she said. "We're ready."

"Just like all those reporters," Ava said. "Hungry and wanting attention."

"I guess that makes us today's Oreos," Sophia answered,

typing into her phone. "Luckily they get stale pretty quickly so they'll have to move on to something else soon."

"Let's hope so," Ava said.

The oversight committee walked into their showroom at exactly one o'clock, right after Daisy, their receptionist, had put her head around the door and whispered, "They're here!" in a scary horror-movie voice.

The AS Collection showroom and studio occupied the entire sixth floor of a building on West Thirty-fifth Street. There was a receptionist's nook just inside the door, and then a large open space with couches, chairs, and a kitchen area stocked with snacks that were used for fittings, meetings, and anything involving the general public.

Beyond that was the work space, with sewing tables, mannequins, their three seamstresses, another sitting area, and their collection hanging on racks. One wall of the work space had windows, which were all covered, and the other was lined with bolts of fabric, fastenings, thread, and trimmings, anything they might need for a fitting or a quick repair. That part was completely closed to the public, since they wouldn't be unveiling their designs until the show. Not even the models they'd had through had seen the clothes they would be wearing yet.

But the oversight committee was different from the general public and the first thing they'd done was ask to see the collection. After they'd looked through it, exchanging annoyingly meaningful looks, they'd taken seats on one couch, with Ava, Sophia, and the Contessa seated opposite them. Lily, MM, Sven, and Toma were perched on stools at a worktable behind them, like a pit crew waiting to jump in.

There was one woman on the committee with shocking pink

hair, wearing a yellow body suit, yellow boots, and a yellow fur shawl. She was a well-known fashion critic, MM told the sisters in a quick whisper as she walked in, and a fixture at Fashion Week for years. Now she glanced at a paper in her lap and looked up at Ava with a puzzled, hurt expression. "'Designing is just like kindergarten'—did you say this, Miss London?"

"No, I said that in kindergarten I enjoyed organizing things and to me designing is like that, organizing shapes and colors," Ava said, and Sophia could have sworn she heard her whisper, *breathe* to herself under her breath.

"Sounds the same as saying designing is like kindergarten," the man sitting next to her said. He had silver hair and an impeccably cut three-piece suit and was, MM told them, the dean of a fashion school.

The third man had dark hair woven into a long braid, dark-framed square glasses, and wore all black. He was a professor of fashion design, MM said, famous for his braid and his avant guard parties. "What else did you learn in kindergarten? Handwriting?"

Ava's expression was confused, as though she wasn't sure if they were serious. "I guess."

"Tracing?" he went on.

Ava nodded. "Maybe."

The Contessa made a face. "Why do you ask about child school?"

"Because it would appear that your 'designers' were actually using other kindergarten skills in their work," the man with the braid said smugly. "Like tracing, copying, and playing pretend."

Sophia's stomach started to twist. "What are you talking about?"

"I'll show you." The woman took a sheath of papers from a folder and walked toward the AS mannequins wearing the collection. Picking up pins from the worktable, she walked from one look to the next, pinning a paper on each of them.

She stepped away and said, "See for yourself."

Ava, Sophia, and the Contessa swarmed around them, with Lily, MM, and Sven following behind. The photocopies all showed a drawing of a dress with the produced dress next to it. In every case they looked almost identical to the AS designs they were pinned on, only in a different fabric.

Sophia felt hot anger flare inside her. "Someone has stolen our designs."

"But how?" Ava said. "Who?

"*Ma no,*" the Contessa said. "These are just knock-ups. Look, you can see the fabrication, it is hasty."

"Knockoffs," Sophia corrected.

"Up, off, around, is all good," the Contessa said, giving Sophia's arm an encouraging squeeze. "Imitation is the empire state of flattery, yes? It means they see your designs and feel"— she searched for a word—"the Wow." She turned to the committee, smiling. "Who is it that knocks these up?"

The man with the silver hair clapped. "Bravo. Nicely done. Sounded authentic."

Everyone turned to look at him. "No, really," he said, playing with his ear. "That was a perfect way to handle it."

"This is not a handle, I am serious," the Contessa said. "Who is it that flatters us this way?"

"Best part," the guy with the silver hair said, pointing at the Contessa. "She's your star."

Sven raised his hand halfway and whispered to MM, "I do not understand what goes on."

MM shook his head. "No one does, sweetheart. Just get tense and stay that way."

The woman in yellow made a face. "Enough grandstanding.

The charges against you are very serious and, as you can see, the evidence is compelling."

"Evidence of what?" Ava asked.

"That you stole your designs from Christopher Wildwood."

The Contessa laughed, and Sophia thought she saw the crazy eyes peeking out. "That is absurd. This Christopher Wildman, he is a hacky sack."

"It's just 'hack,'" the man with the braid told her condescendingly.

Her crazy eyes looked at him. "Oh? The thing you kick with your foot until is dust and cries for mercy like the small piece of garbage it is?"

"No, okay," the man with the braid said, backing off. "That's a hacky sack."

The Contessa started muttering darkly in Italian, then turned to Toma and snapped her fingers for the translation.

"My mother says that even if Christopher Wildthing took male pills and grew a second head he would not be able to design such clothes."

"And I thought all it took was kindergarten," the silver-haired man mused, apparently to himself.

"These are ours," Ava said, and her voice sounded lost and forlorn to Sophia. "We designed them. My sister and I. We have movies of us working on them. Give them your phone," she said to Sophia. "Show them."

Sophia put a hand on her sister's arm to steady her. "That's right. We document our process as we go along. I film it either on my phone or our iPad, which automatically register the date."

"Easily faked," the woman in yellow said. "Not conclusive."

"Can't you level the same accusation against Christopher Wildwood?" Sophia demanded.

Ava bounced to her feet then. "What if I could show you something new?" she asked, excited. "We've got a new piece we just started. That way you could see it's ours." Circling behind one of the workbenches, she pulled out another mannequin. "This is an extra look. I just got an idea a few days ago and decided to—" she whirled her hands around, "so it's not far along but I can tell you how it came about."

She tugged the mannequin closer to the couches. "I took the fabric and draped it, like this, first, then over here, and thought of a back that did this." She gestured with her fingers, then turned the mannequin to show the finished project. "Originally, we had the crystal trim here"—she pointed to the waistband—"but then yesterday Sophia suggested moving it along here"—she showed it edging the bottom hem—"and it just popped."

"It's beautiful," the woman in yellow said. "When did you say you started it?"

Ava looked at Sophia. "I remember it was almost sunny."

"It was the day I went with you to Starbucks," Sophia said, with a wink.

MM nodded. "And you were wearing the black leather shorts and over-the-knee boots with that silk top."

"And we had tacos," Lily said

"I had a fried muffin," Sven announced.

"That was Tuesday," Ava told them. "Two days ago."

"*Bene,* you see," the Contessa said.

"I do," the woman in yellow said. "Because the designer bringing the charges did this sketch the day before." She held out her tablet to show a drawing of a nearly identical dress, in a different fabric and with the trim around the waist in the first place Ava had shown them, dated Monday.

"That's—that's not possible," Ava said.

"But our version, it is far superior," the Contessa told them.

"It's the same dress, with the trim moved," the man with the silver hair said, staring up at the ceiling.

"How do you know he didn't steal it from us?" Ava asked, and Sophia saw that she was shaking. "He could have written a false date on the drawing."

The man with the ponytail said, "He could have. But why would Christopher Wildwood need to? He's a pro. Whereas you—"

"Are brilliant newcomers," Lily announced.

The man with the braid gave her a patently fake smile. "Exactly."

The committee pulled off to the side to consult, and when they came back the woman announced, "We've decided to recommend that your credentials be pulled, and your place in the tents suspended."

Sophia felt like she was in a dream, like all the voices were coming from far away. She and Ava had worked harder on this than on anything else in their lives. They had dreamed up every inch of every garment. The fact that someone was stealing them and was going to get away with it—it was mind-bending.

"This isn't a game," she said suddenly. "You are all acting so casual but do you have any idea of how much work we've put into this? My sister and I?"

"I'm sure you think you have," the man with the braid said.

Ava stepped in front of Sophia. Her voice was calmly curious as she asked, "Why do you believe him over us?"

"He has a track record, he has drawings, he's been to design school," the woman in yellow said primly. "And he never compared our profession to kindergarten."

The man with the braid nodded smugly. "You need to learn

not to bite the hand that feeds you. It has a tendency to bite back."

"You wish to see the biting," the Contessa said, crazy eyes blazing. "You want biting?" She picked up a pair of sheers and began snapping them toward the committee. "I bite you, all of you, into tiny pieces and then make gypsy stew." She went up to the man with the braid and grabbed it. "And this," she said, snapping the scissors. "This I cut right now. I make perhaps bracelets for my biffs."

"Help!" he said, pulling away from her and rushing to the door. "She's crazy. Get her away from me."

The Contessa stood smiling at the two other committee members, opening and closing the scissors. The woman in yellow said, "Consider your certification revoked and your place in the tents gone," and stomped out the door.

The man with the silver hair laughed, pointed at the Contessa, and said, "An absolute gem."

LonDOs

Oreos

Our designs

Tear-proof mascara

Boyfriends who pay attention to you

The Contessa with the scissors

Friends who remember what you wore. And ate.

Cute guy at Starbucks with the sleepy eyes

Kitties that fit in your slippers

Puppies that lick you awake

LonDON'Ts

Wearing hot pink and yellow together if either of those is hair

Discussing kindergarten with reporters

Reporters with stupid Twitter names

Thinking anything will be easy

Whoever is stealing our designs

"Just being yourself" when it means that it ruins things for everyone else

Kitties who ate through the cord of the bedside-table lamp

5

did you hair?

"Run, braidy, run!" the Contessa called after the committee. She snapped the scissors twice more, then dropped them onto the table. "That was fun, yes? You see him fearing?" She laughed and looked around the table at Ava, Sophia, Lily, MM, Sven, and Toma.

Sven managed a tepid smile but everyone else just stared at her. "But what is this?" she demanded. "Why is everyone so frowning? We do not eat this picnic basket of lies. We fight. So they say you cannot play in our big box of sand blah blah blah. *Beh*, we will find our own box of sand to play in. This is all—" She snapped her fingers. "Warm breath. It means nothing."

Lily nodded slowly. "That's true. All you need is another venue."

"It might be hard to get press coverage," MM warned. "Writing about designers without credentials can get a publication in trouble."

"The press is no problem," the Contessa said, running her finger along the edge of one scissor blade. "I can make press coverage."

Ava was staring into space. "I just don't understand. How?"

Sophia shook her head. "I don't know."

Ava was pale. "The only people who have seen the work are in this room." She looked around at Lily, MM, the Contessa, Toma, and Sven.

"And the three seamstresses," Sophia said. "But they weren't with us in LA, and most of the designs they stole would have had to be taken then."

"Plus, I know these women a long time," the Contessa said. "They work for my father. They would not do this thing."

Sven raised his hand. "Perhaps the phone or the computer? They are turned into spies?"

Toma sat up. "Yes, this is possible," he said. "I have medium-level encryption only. I am thinking no big deal for the clothes, but maybe the system is breached. I will erect a firewall with a hypersensitive perimeter and set a jelly can trap—" He stopped and looked at all of them with narrowed eyes. "I will not disclose it. Give me your phones and computers, I will make a trap with the follow bots."

Ava leaned over to Sophia. "Is he speaking English?"

"With a hint of Operating System," she said. "Could Toma be—"

"My little *angelo* hacker." The Contessa said, beaming. "Of course you do this. But be careful, no? I do not want this to be like what happened in Spain. Such beautiful carpets the men from the security force destroyed during the raid."

"Do we want to know?" Sophia asked Ava.

Ava shook her head definitively.

Sophia's phone, which had rung at five-minute intervals for the last half hour, rang again. She was aware of the Contessa glancing icily at her every time but there was nothing she could do about it. Hunter had a routine he liked to follow, with boxes for everything—running at 8:00 A.M., breakfast at 9:15, meetings, golf, lifting—all precisely planned. When his schedule said Talk to Sophia, he wanted to Talk to Sophia, and would keep calling until he got her.

Which was nice, she knew. That he wanted to talk to her. That he called "just to hear her voice." Only a fool would complain that her boyfriend paid her too much attention.

The next time her phone rang, Sophia said, "Excuse me," and moved slightly apart to take it. But she and Hunter had barely gotten through the opening act—

HIM: Where have you been, princess? I missed hearing your voice.

HER: Sorry, in a meeting.

—when Ava began frantically waving Sophia back to the table. She promised to call him back in a few minutes and went to rejoin the others.

"What's wrong?"

Ava said, "Toma needs your phone to amp up the security." Her eyes moved, refusing to meet Sophia's. "And one of our models just pulled out."

By three thirty, when Harper Harlow, their PR woman, arrived, they'd lost four models to various infections that required them by doctor's orders to stay in bed until the day after the AS show.

Harper always wore the same thing, a gray dress, black

platform pumps, a large diamond on her middle finger, and her phone earpiece. Her dark hair was twisted into a chignon. She double kissed everyone and said in her cool English accent, "Well, children, this is clearly a disaster."

Ava nodded glumly.

"Which means, there's only one thing to do." She pulled three folders out of her shoulder bag.

"What?" Sophia asked.

"Go to parties. You two," Harper handed one of the folders to Sven and MM, "will be doing art parties with the big collectors and the hip after-parties to get the buzz going. The details are in the folder. Your job is to sell the story that the girls are being targeted because they're different, young and new, that it's jealousy of the old establishment because your girls are so good. Your second message is that their show is going on and is going to blow everyone's mind. Got it?"

"We just tell the truth then, yes?" Sven said.

MM pulled him close. "How I adore you."

Harper handed a folder to Lily. "You're doing the private house parties, society types, ladies who lunch, people on the board of the museum. You're there to reach the people who own and run the magazines, and start building sympathy for our side. Make them think of the girls as their daughters and nieces."

Lily scanned the paper. "Shouldn't be hard. I think I'm related to most of these people."

Harper handed the last folder to Ava and Sophia. "You're hitting the main parties. Your job is to say you're shocked and saddened by the allegations, you have only the utmost respect for Christopher Wildwood but you have never nor would ever steal anything in your lives, and you take what you do very seriously." She looked around. "Does everyone know their part?"

"And for me," the Contessa said, holding out her hand.

Harper pointed a finger at the Contessa. "You I am not speaking to. Do you have any idea what my phone looks like in the wake of"—she took it out, thumbed down—"scissorgate? Young Green has just had his braid insured for a million dollars."

"What is Young Green?" The Contessa made a face. "Sounds like the medicine for influenza."

"It's the name of the man you threatened."

"Not him, his hair," the Contessa corrected. "It is quite beautiful I will say. Would make a very nice scarf. But okay if you say to me not to take the scissors to a party, of course I won't."

Harper shook her head. "No, love, I'm saying you are going to sit at home and think about what you've done."

As far as Sophia and Ava could tell, Harper was the only person who could say things like that to the Contessa and expect her to listen.

Eventually.

The Contessa shook her head back. "I will not."

Harper nodded and chucked the Contessa under the chin. "Yes, you will. Because otherwise I quit."

Toma came over. He looked at Ava and said, "For you, I add some very special photos on the phone."

"I don't want photos."

He waggled his eyebrows. "You will sing a different number when you see them. In my tuxedo, I am just like 07," he said. "And out of it."

Ava held her phone with her fingertips, as though it might be contaminated. "What about her?" she asked as he handed Sophia her phone. "Doesn't she get photos?"

Toma shook his head. "No, only for you, *bebe*. Do not be jealous." He turned his attention to Sophia. "I could not finish with your phone, the boyfriend he calls every second. You give it to me later, yes?"

Sophia nodded, and, like he'd been listening, Hunter called at that moment. "Where have you been?" he demanded. "You said you'd call me back in five minutes and it's been two hours. Do you know how worried I was?"

"I'm really sorry, I just—"

"Couldn't pick up the phone for one second and call? Or text me?"

Sophia felt like the very last nerve she had was about to fray. "Someone is stealing our designs, we've been kicked out of Fashion Week, our models are dropping like flies, and we're trying to figure out how to put our show back together, okay? That's what I was dealing with."

Sophia felt the entire workroom go quiet at her back but she didn't care.

"Oh, babe," Hunter said, his voice full of compassion, his tone, everything exactly what she needed. "I'm so sorry. I had no idea. Tell me what I can do to help."

Sophia wanted to cry with gratitude. "Your being understanding is amazing."

"Of course," he said, his voice like a caress. "But what happened? Do you have any suspicion how—I mean, I don't quite know how to say this but—"

"Everyone who sees the clothes is a friend," Sophia supplied.

"Yeah."

"We don't know." She went and stood near one of the windows and pushed the shade aside to see out. There were banks of snow around the bottoms of the light polls but the sidewalks were clear, and the sun dropping into the clouds was turning the sky purple. "We think maybe a computer breech? We're setting up a perimeter to try to catch the guy. But even if we do, our credibility is tarnished and our models are disappearing and I'm starting to think we should just give up." She wouldn't have said that to anyone else, she realized.

Hunter said, "Are you crazy? This is when you fight hardest. You and Ava have been through worse than this."

Sophia wasn't sure they had, but she appreciated his confidence.

"You two are going to bounce back, I know it. I've watched you. A little bad PR is just fuel for an even bigger triumph. This is just the beginning for the London sisters," he said. "Remember, everything can turn on a dime."

"Thank you, sweetheart," she told him, her heart filling with gratitude for him. How had she been annoyed earlier? "You just said exactly what I needed to hear without knowing it."

"That's because I'm your soul mate," he said. "And it's why you should call me regularly. To keep up the dosage."

Sophia smiled as she hung up but it wavered when Daisy came in to say that another one of their models had contracted viral laryngitis.

"I thought they were having meningitis," Sven said.

"It doesn't matter, she doesn't have it," Ava told him. "How many models do we have left?" Ava asked MM.

"We're at eight. Of twelve."

Harper waved that away. "Don't worry. From now on, we control the press. After our charm offensive tonight they'll be calling to tell you about a miracle cure and begging for their places back."

That's the attitude, Sophia thought. And then Lily came over, talking in a very strange, loud voice.

She hung up and her eyes were sparkling. "I got us a venue. Graveswood House."

"What is it?" Ava asked.

MM was gaping at Lily. "One of the most stately mansions in New York City. It's been under restoration for—"

"Twenty-three years," Lily said. "But they're finishing the work this week."

"It's like Versailles," MM said. "Only better. How did you do it?"

"I saw my aunt Ruthie's name on my party list so I called her. It's her place and she said of course my friends could have a little party for up to five hundred people."

"It's perfect for the line," MM said.

"And it's a PR dream," Harper told them. "People would come just to see the house. Now your going to have models coming back from the dead to walk for you."

"I do not think those would be good," Sven put in. "A smooth gait is preferred."

"Of course, sweetie," MM said as they all cracked up. Suddenly things didn't seem so dire.

It took exactly four minutes from when Harper gave Ava the signal at their first party of the night to say—

"I mean, the space is amazing. Like Versailles but better for a fashion show. Especially after the restoration" for a reporter to come rushing up to Sophia and ask, "Is it true that you've landed Graveswood House for your show?"

Sophia put on the surprised look they'd practiced—eyes wide, lips slightly parted, tiny frown between the brows. "Where did you hear that?"

"It's all over the Internet," the reporter said. "Can you confirm it?"

She pretended to look around confusedly for Ava. Finally, as though resigned, she said, "I can. That is our new venue. But—"

The parties became much more interesting after that. MM called to say that first one, then three of their models had miraculously recovered and were available for the show. Sophia and Ava went from objects of curiosity to everyone's new biff.

"I'm exhausted," Ava said as they rode back to the apartment. "I've had enough excitement today to last me for at least four days."

"Six," Sophia said, checking her phone. "I have about a million text messages." *And three voice mails from Hunter,* she didn't add.

"Me too," Ava said.

Sophia's phone rang. "I've got to take this," she said, and answered, curling toward the window for privacy. "Hi, sweetheart."

"I can't believe it. She stoops to answer my calls."

Sophia laughed. "It's been a crazy night."

"Apparently. Since you've been too busy party hopping to answer a single call for six hours."

Sophia felt the first twinge of a headache. Sometimes Hunter got this way when she was busy and she'd learned that it passed if she just ignored it or managed to make him laugh. "It's not fun, it's work. Harper is so organized but she's a slave driver. We all had assignments for the parties and she made sure we kept on them."

"Did she. And what was yours like? Tall, dark, and handsome?"

Sophia laughed again. "Don't be ridiculous."

His voice was cold. "I'm not."

Sophia leaned her forehead against the cool glass of the car window. "I talked about you."

"Am I supposed to be flattered?" he said, like a challenge.

"No, you're just supposed to know that I tell everyone what a great boyfriend I have." Leaving out, Sophia thought to herself, the part about how he was a little nuts about communication.

"I'm glad I can be cocktail party conversation."

Her head was throbbing. Clearly, ignoring his mood wasn't working. "I don't know what you want from me," she said.

"I want you to call me when you say you're going to call me," he snapped.

"I was working. I was going to call when I got home." She looked down at her lap and saw that her hand was balled into a fist. "I hate this feeling, like I'm letting you down when I haven't done anything wrong."

His voice was full of contrition. "You're right. I'm sorry, babe. I don't know what came over me. I just miss you. I really really miss you. Like an ache. In the deepest part of me. And it's worse when I can't hear your voice."

His voice, his pain, made her wish he were right there so she could put her head on his chest and wrap her arms around him. "I really miss you too."

"I wish we were playing footsie on the couch."

Sophia smiled and felt warm despite the cold night and realized her headache had completely disappeared. "That would be amazing. I can't tell you how much I—"

She frowned, feeling Ava's hand gripping her arm. "What?" Sophia started to ask, turning to look at her sister, and then the words died, changed to, "I'm sorry, Hunter, I have to go."

"Wait, why—"

"*Now.*"

LonDOs:
Models who don't quit
Lily

Lily's aunt Ruthie
Boyfriends who want to play footsie
Graveswood House
Butterscotch-pudding lollipops at cocktail parties

LonDON'Ts:
Models who quit
Models who are zombies
People who make false accusations
People who eat other people's cookies when they are in
    the bathroom
Cocktail napkins that take your lipstick but leave your lip liner

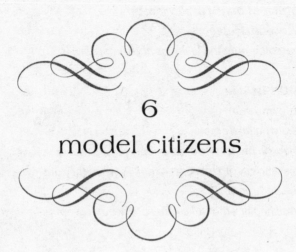

6

model citizens

This can't be happening. This cannot be happening. This isn't happening, Ava kept thinking as she watched the firemen putting away their hoses. It wasn't possible.

Her mind kept replaying it, as though maybe she could find a way to make the story line different. She'd found five voice-mail messages from Lily on her phone, which she concluded were all pocket dials since Lily never left messages. But then Sophia had gotten on the phone with Hunter, and even after Ava had run through several fantasy scenarios about the cute guy with the sleepy eyes at Starbucks actually talking to her, Sophia was *still* on the phone, so she'd decided to see what Lily's night sounded like from the inside of her pocket and pushed to play the most recent message.

It started off sounding like a pocket dial with incoherent noise and shouting but then Lily's voice was there, saying, "I can't believe it. It's—you can see the flames coming out the windows. All that work, the restoration and now. I'm so sorry. I wanted this for you so badly. I— There's a fireman—I'm going to ask him how bad it is. I'll be here if you want to find me."

By the time she and Sophia got to Graveswood, the fire was out. Now they were standing with Lily, MM, and Sven, talking to one of the firemen while the others stashed their gear.

"Definitely electrical," the fireman said. "Someone left one of those room heaters on full blast and it just overloaded. Happens a fair amount this time of year, not usually in a place like this, though," he said, looking at the mansion. "Must have been one of the workmen. Still, managed to contain it. The damage is minimal, some smoke, some structural. Your aunt was lucky."

"Can we go in?" Lily said.

He shook his head. "Got to get the fire inspector in first, make sure it's structurally sound. Then insurance. It's a whole circus. Probably can't be back in there for a month, three weeks at the soonest."

After that, none of them wanted to go home so they'd gone to an all-night deli around the corner from Graveswood. Ava had a cold cup of coffee in front of her and a plate of fries sat in the middle of the table, untouched. She stared into the coffee cup. "We're cursed. That's the only explanation."

"We're not cursed," Sophia said. "We're just—"

"Cursed," Ava finished.

"It's all relative," Sophia said. "We still have—"

Lily looked up from the brownie sundae she'd been dragging her spoon through. "That's it!"

"What?" Ava asked.

"This is it. My moment." She looked at them breathlessly. "I was born for this challenge."

"Why is the tall one so happy?" Sven asked MM.

"I'm not sure but usually when she's in this mood the best thing is to nod and move far away."

"Lily, what are you talking about?" Sophia asked cautiously.

Lily wolfed down a bite of brownie. "Don't you see? It's all about relatives. I have dozens of them, who know dozens of people, who own three-quarters of this city." She brandished her spoon. "I have the will. I have the connections. I will find you a venue or die trying."

"That seems a bit extreme," Ava said.

Lily tapped her on the nose with her spoon. "There is no cause for concern, little London. Obviously the fire was a sign. Graveswood wasn't the right place. We must be bolder. Smarter." She scarfed down another bite of brownie. "But don't worry. Everything I've ever done has been preparing me for this one moment. Trust Auntie Lily." She gazed across the table, her eyes shining with zeal. "And pass the fries if you're not going to finish them. I have to keep my strength up."

When they got to the showroom the next day, they found that the Contessa had been busy. She'd decided that they needed better protection, which meant there was a team of people putting up sensors everywhere, an intense-looking man who introduced himself as T, standing in front of the door to the workroom, and a cameraman named Sam, who was supposed to follow them around to document everything they did or made.

"So when they do blah blah blah we have proof to smash their noses in." The Contessa ground her palm into the tabletop to illustrate. Then she looked up and smiled at the camera. "And who knows, maybe we make a movie later. Is a possibility. We call it *Biffs*. Is good, no?"

Ava and Sophia nodded, neither of them having enough energy left to object.

The Contessa left then to, as Toma translated it, "Sharpen her claws," which they concluded meant get a manicure, and then Lily appeared, carrying two large canvas tote bags.

"What's in there?" Ava asked her, trying to peer in.

"I was in consultation this morning with my godmother, Lady—" She stopped, noticing the camera. "Who are you? What is this?" She indicated him, his camera, his boots.

"I'm Sam," he said, holding out his hand.

Lily didn't take it, just stared at him. "Are you wearing Doc Martens?"

Sam looked tongue-tied, like he wondered what the right answer was. "Yes?"

Lily rolled her eyes. *"Please."*

Ava looked anxiously from Sam to Lily. To Sam she said apologetically, "She's not usually like this," then turned to Lily. "The Contessa thinks we should have a record of everything we do in case anyone questions our process," she explained.

"I don't think he looks trustworthy. There's something around his eyes," Lily whispered to Ava. Putting her back deliberately in front of the camera, she began to pull things from the tote bags.

MM frowned. "Why do you have back issues of—"

"Shhhh!" Lily said, shooting a glance over her shoulder at Sam. "I don't want him to know. He could be one of *Them.*"

"I think he's okay," Ava said. "Plus, things can't get any worse."

"Maybe," Lily said skeptically. She turned to the camera and pointed from her eyes to Sam. "I'm watching you, New Dork City."

He grinned and gave her a thumbs up.

"Ugh," Lily said.

Sophia pointed at the tote bags. "You were explaining."

Lily nodded. "I spent the morning with my godmother. We'll call her Lady A," she said with a glance over her shoulder. "I learned a lot. Our objective is to find a fabulous venue with a wide open space that can seat at least two hundred people and accommodate a catwalk, is beautiful, elegant, and somehow representative of New York or sisters or both."

"Also the tall roofs," Sven said.

Everyone frowned at him but MM nodded. "He's right. You need a place with high ceilings because the models are so tall a normal space makes them look out of proportion."

"And that rules out pretty much all restaurants and most of the private clubs," Lily said. "But the biggest challenge is finding a place that isn't already booked. Anywhere anyone has held a show for the past twenty years was reserved months or even years ago. Which actually makes things easier because it narrows our task to thinking of places no one else has. The hidden gems of New York." She whipped around to look at Sam. "Did you make a noise?"

Sam shook his head, clearly trying not to laugh. Lily scowled at him for a moment, then went on. "I found a subway station that's been closed for two decades with great atmosphere and ceilings, but your guests would have had to enter via a manhole so I crossed that off. I looked into tenting the Brooklyn Bridge but there's some law about not blocking emergency access off the island. So Lady A lent me her archive of issues of *Town & Country Magazine* from 1952 to 1980. They document every major event and party held in NYC during that period. These old issues will help us find the hidden treasure everyone else has overlooked. I've already begun marking some." She pointed at a stack feathered with green Post-it notes.

Sophia took one and opened it. Her face lit up. "My god, this place looks perfect." She held up the magazine. "The Rainbow Room at Rockefeller Center."

"I love the name," Ava said, crowding next to her.

From behind them Sam said, "I'm afraid it closed in 2009."

Lily flinched, like a fly had buzzed in her ear, and said to Sophia, "Why is he talking? Is he allowed to talk?"

Sophia nodded. "I'm pretty sure."

Ava picked up another magazine. "What about here? Studio 54?"

"I have heard of this one," Sven said happily. "From my grandpapa. He was there I think maybe in 1981? And then it is closed by police?"

He glanced at Sam, who said, "Yeah, I'm pretty sure that's been closed at least twenty years."

Lily started pulling at the collar of her sweater. "Is it me, or is someone sucking all the creativity out of the room?" She began shoving magazines back into the tote bags. "This is just the beginning. We've got weeks and weeks before the show. Trust me. I'm telling you, this is my destiny. Has Auntie Lily ever failed to surprise you?"

Sophia and Ava exchanged looks. Sophia said, "No, you are always surprising."

Lily grinned. "Exactly."

Somehow that did not entirely lighten the mood. Ava slumped, with her chin resting on her hands. "So we have no venue, no credentials, no models—"

"We have one still," MM said, appearing to find something very interesting to look at near the ceiling.

Sven frowned. "I thought you say that is because she has the stomach bugs and cannot call."

MM brought his eyes down to shoot him a .22-caliber look and snapped, "What happened to raising your hand?"

"—Which means we have no show. It's over," Ava finished.

Sophia's eyes blazed. "But if we don't show, then everyone will think it was true and we're frauds. I hate the thought of that."

None of them had realized the Contessa was back but she burst in now, slapping the top of the table with her hand. "*Basta*! I will not let that Worm man—"

"Wormwood," Ava corrected.

"Wildwood," Sophia said.

"—Worm-faced pumpkin-head ruin my fashion line," the Contessa proclaimed. "I will fix this."

There was a cackle from the door, and over Daisy's babbling that she'd tried to stop the lady but she rolled right over—look, there was the mark on her boot—Lucille Rexford said, "Well isn't this a pretty picture? You look like one of those end-of-the-world cults the day after the end of the world doesn't come."

Lucille was pushed into the studio in her gold-plated wheelchair by a man wearing a dark blue coat with gold buttons, matching jodhpurs, and black boots, like an old-fashioned chauffeur. She was wearing all black, as always, this time a black fur cape with a black fur blanket over her legs, and her eyes were only slightly visible behind large, smoky-lensed glasses. The only color came from her silver helmet of hair, which was cut in a severe bob, and her pure red lipstick. A Pomeranian sat on her lap, growling at everyone despite Lucille's patting him and saying, "There there, Cuddles."

"Lucille?" Sophia breathed. "Charlie? Cuddles?"

But while Sophia was still trying to decide whether she could believe her eyes, Ava was on her feet, giving the chauffeur a kiss on the cheek and hugging the woman. "If you must you must, but just so we're clear, that won't be necessary again for the duration of my stay," Lucille told her.

"Of course," Ava told her solemnly, reaching out to scratch

Cuddles's stomach while his tongue lolled blissfully out of his mouth.

"I really don't know what comes over him around you," Lucille said. She tapped the dog's nose with her finger. "Traitor. I should have known even you were susceptible to the attractions of youth."

She raised her eyes from the dog to Sophia and said, "I suppose you need to hug me too. Very well if you must, let's get it over with."

Sophia wrapped her arms around Lucille and gave her a kiss on her surprisingly soft cheek. When she let go, she gave Charlie, the chauffeur, a kiss too, then stepped back and said, "What in the world are you doing in New York?"

In addition to being the millionaire owner of LuxeLife cosmetics, the company that produced Ava and Sophia's makeup line, Lucille was crotchety, snarky, hard as nails, and a confirmed recluse. Ava and Sophia adored her but were shocked to see her here since she had barely left her house in the Hollywood Hills for decades, let alone crossed the country.

"Charlie heard that someone was throwing a wrench into your plans. He got upset and then Cuddles got upset and between the two of them they wouldn't leave off pestering me and let me have a decent night's sleep until I agreed to come out here and see what was what," Lucille explained.

Ava and Sophia looked at Charlie, who nodded somberly. "Exactly how she tells it," he said.

Lucille scowled at them. "Got too much invested in you two to let your reputations slide, that's all. And besides," she nodded forward and Charlie pushed her toward the Contessa. "I wanted to meet this one. I liked the sound of you," she told her.

"I am honored," the Contessa said, and Sophia thought she genuinely meant it. "I have heard many frightening things about Lucille Rexford which has given me the utmost respect."

"Is Lucille *blushing*?" Ava asked Sophia

"Yes. She looks happier than Charming after he learned how to knock the cream container over."

Lucille turned to Ava and Sophia. "Now tell me what's going on." MM got up to make a place for her at the table but she waved it away. "I want to look at things. Where're the clothes?"

Ava and Sophia pointed to the door of the workroom and Charlie pushed Lucille there. As she reached it, T looked to the Contessa, who said, "Yes, move of course," adding, "*Idiota*," under her breath, and Lucille cackled again.

As Ava and Sophia took turns telling the story, Lucille went from one mannequin to the next, eyeing the clothes, fingering hems and details, and then turned to take in the rest of the space with her keen eyes.

Lucille said, "There's your problem right there," and pointed at the wallboard with the photos of the models all Xed out.

"Right," Ava said resignedly. "No models."

"No, ninny. Too *many* models."

"What?" MM asked.

"Why are you using *models*?" Lucille demanded. When no one answered, she shook her head and told Cuddles, "Bad as talking to a bunch of chickens." She cleared her throat and said, "Your entire line is about real girls, come AS you are, take us AS we are, be AS—blah blah blah." The Contessa beamed as Lucille used her favorite English phrase. "Who wants to see more models? You should be casting the girls you've designed the line for, AS girls. Not these *as if* ones."

"Real girls," Sophia repeated wonderingly.

Ava said, "Sure, but how do we find them? Do we just cast off the street?"

"We could," MM said. "It would take time but—"

Sven raised his hand. "Excuse me, but you have the Web

site with the very many followers, yes? Maybe they would like do it."

Ava grabbed Sophia. "A contest!"

"An essay," Sophia elaborated.

Ava nodded. "Yes! Tell us about yourself—"

"What you love—"

"What it means to you to be an AS girl—"

"And no photos," Sophia said. "Beauty is about the whole package."

"And being confident in who you are," Ava agreed. "Real girls—"

"As they really are," Sophia finished.

They were jumping up and down, completely forgetting that there was anyone else there.

"Real girls, real bodies, real lives," Harper said an hour later when they told her. "Underscoring that you're the real deal. I love it. And you know what this means?"

"More parties?" Sophia said.

Harper agreed. "More parties."

"And this time I come too," the Contessa insisted.

"Oh yes," Harper told her. "I have a special job for you."

"But we still have no venue, and no credentials," Ava pointed out.

Lucille said, "Leave the credentials to me. You just find a venue."

Lily patted the canvas tote bags. "Destiny."

LonDOs
Fire brigade
Real girls
Web contest

Lucille Rexford

Cute guy at Starbucks with the sleepy eyes smiling!!!

*Genius who thought to put extra whipped cream on brownie
    sundae*

Destiny

LonDON'Ts

Fire

Models who pretend to be sick

New security sensors that interfere with your phone service

Kitties who ate through the cord on Mommy's work-phone charger

7

snark avenue

The night's itinerary included five parties, each with a different, crucial agenda. This first one was on the roof of the Gramercy Park Hotel and would include a mix of people Harper called "string pullers," whom she wanted to introduce to Ava and Sophia.

"Tonight is all about making them aware that you exist, so tomorrow when they read about you, they'll feel attached, as though they were there at the beginning, and have a strange itch to help."

"'Strange itch'. I like this," the Contessa had said, beaming. "Yes, very good."

Harper had arranged for the Contessa to arrive ten minutes before them, explaining that her job was to "confuse and delight the press. Give them plenty to quote but nothing they will understand."

"But how do I do this?" the Contessa had asked, genuinely confused.

"You'll have no trouble," Harper had assured her. "Just say whatever comes to mind."

Ava had managed to stay calm in the limo and as they were escorted through the lobby, but in the elevator going up to the roof, where the party was being held, she felt herself starting to panic. After the debacle with the *WWD* reporter, she didn't trust herself to answer anything.

"Listen, think, respond," had been Harper's instructions to her at the studio. "It's simple. And when in doubt, watch Sophia, she's a pro."

Listen, think, respond, Ava repeated to herself, hoping that the ringing in her ears would subside enough for her to think, and the lump in her throat shrink enough for her to respond. She was terrified of messing up again. She remembered Sophia telling her that it wasn't her fault, but Ava couldn't help blaming herself, and she'd sworn then that wouldn't happen again.

"You'll be fine," Sophia told her as the elevator dinged at the eleventh floor. "You're great at this."

That set off a laugh that didn't sound like her. "Oh sure."

Sophia turned to face her. "Look at me," she said. "You. Will. Be. Fine."

They were at the fifteenth floor now, only two to go. "I will be fine," Ava repeated.

"Right. We rehearsed this. You know all the answers. Now let's go show the world that nothing will stop the London sisters."

The elevator doors opened and they stepped out onto the roof. It was beautiful, lush plants everywhere and the clear tent covered with a web of fairy lights that made the whole space seem almost magical. The Contessa, wearing a leopard turban and matching full-length leopard coat, was surrounded by a clump of reporters off to one side, but as soon as they spotted the London sisters, they left her and headed for them.

Before Ava knew what was happening, she and Sophia were swarmed by reporters. She saw Sophia being carried off in one direction and felt herself being pushed in another. *You're on your own*, she thought, then heard Sophia's voice again, saying, "You. Will. Be. Fine."

She would be fine.

Close to her someone barked, "What do you say to the rumors that you have no models to walk in your show?"

That was the first answer they'd practiced. Ava said, "They're wrong. We will have more than enough models."

The next question was an easy one also. "Who do you think is Christopher Wildwood's celebrity guest?"

"We're too excited about how our show is shaping up to spend time thinking about his," Ava told them.

A male reporter in a checked jacket muscled forward to ask, "What do you say to the people who maintain you're just publicity artists, hacks with no real talent?"

For a moment Ava's mind went blank, but they'd practiced this one, too. "Ask Christopher Wildwood. He wouldn't steal from talentless hacks," she said, and was rewarded with chuckling from a few of the reporters.

The circle of reporters wound tighter and the questions started moving beyond the ones they'd practiced.

"Is there any truth to the rumors that your boyfriend Liam was hurt in a train accident in Budapest?" a female reporter lobbed at Ava.

Budapest? Ava had thought he was in Moscow. She felt panic starting to creep into her and looked around for Sophia, spotting her partway across the room. Sophia looked so composed, leaning in to listen to each question, then smiling and nodding as she gave the answer. Like a princess, Ava thought, somehow part of it but above it.

Listen, think, respond, Ava reminded herself. *You can do this.*

"The last time we spoke, Liam was fine," Ava answered.

As though aware of Ava's attention, Sophia glanced over then and their eyes met above the heads of the reporters. Sophia gave her a smile and Ava was conscious of the strangest feeling of missing her. Which was ridiculous because they were together almost every hour of every day.

But they were always working, and when they weren't working Sophia was on the phone with Hunter. Ava wasn't jealous exactly, she understood that, but she wished—

Without explanation, the reporters began to peel away, at first one by one and then in swaths, as though they smelled bigger prey. Ava was perfectly happy to let them go. Their departure gave her a chance to sample some of the crispy maple bacon that had passed her by three times while she answered questions. As well as the mini tuna tacos. And were those tiny chocolate ice-cream cones?

She looked around to see if Sophia was free, too, but she couldn't find her among the well-groomed, perfectly dressed people at the party. She was struck by subtle differences from Los Angeles, the way the girls in New York wore dresses that seemed designed to showcase their cut and style more than their figures. Harper had explained that it was more important to look chic than to look sexy, and Ava definitely saw that maxim in action. The lines of the clothes and haircuts were a little more severe, the bras seemed less padded, the makeup was either more severe or nearly absent, and the focus was on a kind of aloof cool that made everyone, even the cocktail servers, seem sophisticated, like they probably listened to music in French and wrote dark poetry with lots of adjectives.

Ava was about to plunge into the crowd in search of Sophia when she heard a low, rumbling voice with a hint of southern accent behind her. She'd heard it before, on television, one of her favorite design shows—ex-favorite, she modified—and knew exactly whom it belonged to.

Turning, she saw the handsome face of Christopher Wildwood towering over the sea of reporters. He had a mane of white hair swept off his forehead and gray eyes in a tanned face. He'd been a model before he became a designer and he'd retained the height, looks, and, Ava thought, ability to pose.

At least now she knew where all the reporters had gone. Without consciously thinking about it, Ava found herself making her way to the group gathered around him. She stood at the back to be inconspicuous while she listened to what was being said.

The first thing she heard was her name. A reporter near the front of the group asked, "Are you pleased that the London sisters had their credentials revoked? Do you think justice has been done or will you be pursuing criminal action?"

Christopher Wildwood gave a weary—but practiced, Ava was sure—smile and said, "I've put this whole thing into the hands of my lawyers. To me, it's just an unnecessary distraction and I'd rather not discuss it."

I bet, Ava thought.

"Surely you have some comment," a female reporter pressed.

His expression grew thoughtful and his accent thicker. "I find it tragic that youngsters today have so little integrity they would be willing to take credit for someone else's work. But what can you expect?" He shrugged. "We've created a culture where a pretty face is more important than talent and hard work, where the ability to sell is more important than the ability to create. So I guess my comment would be that I pity these girls, and I hope they have a good investment adviser because fame built on lies will not last."

A chuckle went around the reporters but stopped as Ava said loudly, "I agree." Heads swiveled, and when they saw it was her the crowd parted, propelling her toward him. "It *is* a pity when people take credit for work that's not their own."

Christopher Wildwood smiled at her pleasantly. "I'm sorry. You are—?"

Ava was aghast. "Ava London. It's my work, mine and my sister's, that you are stealing."

His smile didn't falter, but his eyes, which had seemed bemused, changed. Ava had thought they were the color of pencil lead but they now looked like steel, and just as hard, and menacing. "There are many good things about being young, my dear. You have a long life ahead of you." He took a step closer to her and his gaze locked on hers. "But let me assure you that if you ever accuse me of stealing again, in public and in front of reporters, every moment of that long life will be filled with regret and pain."

Ava stared from him to the reporters, then back to him. "Are you threatening me?"

He grinned, amusement reaching only to the crinkles around his eyes, and stood up to his full height. "Of course not. I was trying to give you some advice. Stop this nonsense now, before it gets out of your control." Before she could answer, his eyes swept to the reporters. "Now that you bloodthirsty sharks have had your dose of ugliness, let's talk about beauty. I could not be more thrilled about my new line."

He moved off, trailing reporters in his wake. "We'll be proven innocent," Ava shouted after them, but no one seemed to take any notice. "You'll see," she said, a little more quietly.

She looked down and realized she was shaking. Partially out of rage, at the audacity of the man.

But it also came from fear. Not because of what he'd said. Because of what she'd seen in his eyes—or hadn't seen. There was no bluff there, no hesitation, not even the faintest glimpse of a naughty child getting away with something. He was acting like he hadn't done anything wrong, like he really believed the designs were his. If Ava hadn't known better, she could even have believed him. Given that, what chance could she and Sophia have of convincing anyone?

And what kind of person acted that way?

The kind of person who would stop at nothing to destroy his competition, was the unwelcome answer she came up with.

Wandering dazedly, she found herself in a little bar area at the far end of the party. It was dark and empty. *Perfect,* she thought, sliding onto the stool nearest her and ordering a bottle of San Pellegrino.

Although she was doing a boytox, there was a part of her that wished a knight in shining armor would come along and say, "You look like you could use a really good dessert. Let me get you out of this place," and carry her off. Only there were no such things as knights in shining armor and even if there were she imagined they rarely brought ice cream.

The bartender had just set her bottle of water in front of her when a voice said, "Excuse me."

Ava didn't look up. "I'm not answering any questions right now. I don't want to be rude, but please leave me alone."

"Sure. As soon as you get off my coat," the voice next to her said.

Ava looked down and saw that there was, indeed, a coat folded on the stool she was sitting on. She looked up at the guy who had spoken and her heart skipped a beat.

It was the cute guy with the sleepy eyes from Starbucks! Standing there, at the otherwise empty bar. Like she'd wished him into existence. Her knight in shining armor.

He was taller than she'd expected, well over six feet, but not skinny-tall, tall like an athlete. Up close his face looked like it had been chiseled from a block of something solid, with high cheekbones, a firm, square jaw, and deep-set, serious eyes. His skin was the color of a mochachino and his eyes were a few shades darker. Ava had thought he was cute but now she realized that she'd been wrong—he wasn't cute, he was handsome.

Definitely knight material.

Ava smiled at him and said, "What are you doing here?"

He pointed to the stool. "Trying to get my coat out from under you."

"Sorry." Blushing, she stood up and handed it to him. Their fingers brushed and she felt a shock, but she didn't know if it was from him or static. "I meant at this party. I—I'm surprised to see you."

His eyes came to her and he frowned more. He was wearing a blue-gray shirt with a heather-gray jacket over it. "Why? Do I look like I don't belong with the rest of you fancy people? Because my coat isn't hand stitched and I could use a haircut?"

That wasn't exactly the response Ava had been expecting. "No. I just—it's funny to see someone one place when you expect them to be somewhere else."

His frown became a squint. "Do I know you?"

He was not doing a very good job of fitting into her fantasy. Ava perched back on the stool. "Don't you recognize me?"

He went back to frowning. "Should I? Have you done something noteworthy? Found a planet? Cured cancer?"

"Not either of those—"

His mouth twisted into a wry smile. "So you're one of those." His tone made it clear that wasn't a good thing.

"One of *whats*?" Ava asked.

The bartender set a bottle of Coke in front of him. "A nobody who thinks they should be somebody. This party is full of them. Pretty girls here to 'network,' which is just code for land a rich, well-connected boyfriend." He tipped his Coke toward her, said, "Good luck," and turned to go.

"That's not me," Ava called after him. She knew she should just let him walk away, but for some reason she couldn't. She'd had enough of people underestimating her for one night. "You couldn't be more wrong."

He stopped and turned to face her. "Really? So you just came to have fun? Because if that's it, you don't look like you're doing it right."

"I'm here working," she said defensively.

He grinned. "As I was saying."

This wasn't going at all how she'd expected, and it was very unfair of him to be such a jerk, especially because when he'd grinned she'd discovered he had very nice teeth and a great smile. "You—you have to be one of the most frustrating people I've ever met."

The serious eyes studied her. "*Have* we met?"

"No."

"Good," he said, finishing his Coke and setting the bottle on the bar. "Let's not. I don't have anything to offer you, and I definitely don't need any more spoiled girls who are always looking over your shoulder to see if someone better is coming along in my life."

Ava stood. "And I don't need any more self-righteous, judgmental jerks who pretend they haven't been staring at me for the past two weeks at Starbucks in mine."

He tilted his head to one side. "What do you—"

"Ah, hello, my biff!" The Contessa broke in then, interrupting whatever he was going to say. "I have been hither and thither looking for you." A leopard arm looped itself through Ava's proprietarily. "Tell me, who is your friend? You have known each other a long time?"

"He's not my friend," Ava told the Contessa brightly. "We just *didn't* meet."

The Contessa smiled. "*Bene*. Because you know, the count he will be jealous if he hears you are talking to the other men. Even the"—the Contessa's eyes raked over him, taking in his clothes, and her face assumed a pained expression—"math teachers. And when he is jealous, perhaps he finds someone else to be interested in. We do not want to risk that the count loses interest, do we? So now is time for to say ciao. Besides, we have other people that require our charming."

Ava wished she were anywhere in the world other than there. The sleepy eyes came to her and now they appeared amused. "I can see I was completely wrong about you," the guy said to Ava. "You're not a pretty girl trying to snag a rich boyfriend at all."

"You don't know anything about my life," Ava answered. Her cheeks were burning with a mixture of anger and embarrassment.

He gave her a little salute. "And I'm glad to leave it that way. Have a nice night, Countess."

The Contessa, assuming he was talking to her, said, "Yes, you too, *istruttore*," and steered Ava away.

Over the sound of her stiletto heels tap-tapping the Contessa leaned her head close to Ava's to say, "There is no need for you to thank me for saving you from that." Before Ava managed to come up with a reply she wouldn't regret, the Contessa went on. "I hear that you put the Worm man in his place. I understand that must make you tired. Sometimes when we are tired we can act like a silly girl."

"I was not being silly," Ava objected. "I was just talking to—"

"Sleepy sleepy," the Contessa said, wiggling her fingers over Ava's eyelids. "Tomorrow you will be a serious girl again, like your sister."

Ava was near tears. How much more of a serious girl could she be? All she did was work seriously hard all the time. She couldn't even remember the last time she'd had fun.

And none of it mattered. Christopher Wildwood had only to lift a finger to destroy them, and the Contessa had only to think for one second that she was less than serious—less than Sophia—and it could all be over.

"Where is your sister?" the Contessa asked. "We have many more people to delight and confuse."

"I don't know," Ava snapped. "Where would you be if you were perfect?"

The Contessa tipped her head back and laughed. "Oh, you are going to be so *magnifico* with my nephew. I cannot wait for him to lay eyes on you."

Eye, Ava thought miserably. *Just the one.*

LonDOs
The Contessa delighting and confusing
Mini chocolate ice-cream cones
Turning a messy ponytail into a sexy loose up-do
24-hour shimmer eye shadow
Under-eye concealer
Lily staying home to work on finding a venue

LonDON'Ts
The Contessa threatening and terrifying
Boys with sleepy eyes who jump to conclusions
Boys with sleepy eyes who are smug
Boys with sleepy eyes who apparently did not notice you at Starbucks

Being told to be a serious girl
Not having time to shower before going out
Having four more parties to attend
Lily missing a chance to study the plastic surgery of NYC up close

8

fire and nice

Sophia didn't know why all the reporters had suddenly lost interest in her, and she hadn't bothered to ask. Instead, she'd stolen away from the main party and ducked around the side of a trellis covered in vines and twinkling tea-light candles, where it was quieter. The trellis was about three feet from the outer wall of the terrace, making a sort of corridor to a doorway that, judging by the trays filled with glasses lining it, must have been a back way to the kitchen. But there was no one going back and forth now, no distractions or other conversations, so she could actually think. And hear the person on the other end of the phone.

She'd hardly talked to Hunter that day—the new security the Contessa had installed was wreaking havoc with all their phones and they'd stopped at home only long enough to change and go to the first party—but she'd texted him from the limo on the way.

He had sounded upset in his replies, neglected and a little

angry, and the impact of it had lingered with her like a tight knot between her shoulder blades as she'd gotten out of the limo and talked to the reporters. She hated the feeling but knew that as soon as they could talk, everything would be fine, so she grabbed the first opportunity to slip away and call him.

"It's great to hear your voice," she said when he answered. "I missed you today."

"You could hear it more if you answered my calls more," he said, and she couldn't tell if he was angry or joking.

Sophia felt like someone was twisting the knot in her back tighter, making it hard to breathe. *How could I answer your calls more?* she wanted to ask him. She realized she couldn't even remember the last time she'd had a conversation without interrupting it to talk to him or write him a text. "Sorry, I was—"

"Working. I know." He sighed. "So, how is it going?"

Why was she suddenly near tears? Why did everything feel so hard all of a sudden? She stared out the clear plastic of the tent at the city beyond, twinkling under a gray sky. *Pull yourself together,* a voice in her head told her. She said, "It's going well, I think. I—I don't know."

"Babe, I hate hearing you like this," he said, his voice earnest. "Is there anything I can do to help? Tell me what you need from me and I'll make sure you get it."

Sophia was shocked to find the word *space* hovering on the tip of her tongue. That wasn't what she wanted. Where had that come from?

"I have to go," she said, not trusting herself. "I have to get back to the party."

"But you just called."

"I'm sorry. I'll call you back," she said and hung up.

She stood with her cheek against the plastic of the tent, looking down at the phone in her hand. She was just tired, she told herself.

The sense of not wanting to deal with anyone, of not having the energy to be responsible for anyone else's feelings, was just—

"*Stella?*"

It was like hearing a voice from a dream. Sophia's heart nearly stopped, her knees went weak, and she could have sworn the pavement dissolved out from under her. It couldn't be. *Could it?*

Taking a deep breath, she turned around and looked into Giovanni's bright, mystified eyes. "*Stella mia!*" he said, leaning in to kiss her on both cheeks and wrap her in his arms.

It was only after she'd let her head rest on his chest and smelled the slightly spicy scent of cologne at his neck that she remembered her unanswered texts and the calls that were sent right to voice mail and the long silence with no explanation. She stiffened and pulled away.

He looked at his arms, then at her. "But what is wrong? *Madonna,* you are more beautiful than ever before."

A smile tried to come out but she forced it back. "How are you?" she asked coolly. "You look well. Are you living in New York now?"

He shook his head and his mobile mouth turned down with sadness. "I am very sorry, *bellissima,* that I did not reply to your messages. The story I have to tell—"

"I didn't say anything about messages," Sophia bristled. She'd forgotten how he could do that, seemingly read her thoughts.

He smiled at her, laughing but not mocking, amused but not unkind. "You are the same and yet, I think . . ." He shook his head. "I have a tale to tell you which is long and—" His tone changed. "I'm sorry, I am afraid I must go now."

"Are you working here?" Sophia asked. "As a waiter?"

"A waiter, yes," he said, nodding somberly. "I am among the waiters still. And now I must go—do the waiting—elsewhere. Can we meet another time? You have still the same number? I will text you." He touched her cheek. "I promise. You have no idea how much I have missed you. How often you are filling my thoughts."

He disappeared as abruptly as he'd appeared, through the door to the kitchen, leaving Sophia staring after him, wondering if he'd really been there at all. Was it possible? It had felt like a dream. Looking into his eyes had felt exactly like the best dream.

She must really be tired to be thinking like that, she told herself. Hunter's voice, Hunter's eyes, Hunter's *reliable* chest and arms that loved her as she was, where she was, were the stuff that dreams were made of. She'd call him back and say—

"Why do you hide yourself back here?" the Contessa's voice interrupted, stopping Sophia mid-dial. She turned and saw her patron looking with distaste at what Sophia now realized must be a service corridor. "We go now to the next party. I have many people to confuse and delight with the blah blah. And your sister is too busy with math teachers."

"Of course." Sophia nodded, not even trying to make sense of the last part.

Ava appeared from behind the Contessa and took Sophia's arm. "I spoke to Christopher Wildwood," she said, almost casually.

"You did what?" Sophia goggled at her.

Ava nodded. "Talked to him. Calmly. Except at the end when I yelled at him. But here's what's weird: he acted like he'd done nothing wrong. In fact, he acted like he'd never even heard of us at all."

"So he's just trying to ruin our lives for no reason?" Sophia asked. She became aware that Ava's gaze was more than usually intense. "Why are you looking at me that way?"

"What foundation are you wearing? You're positively glowing."

"We're talking about Christopher Wildwood, not me."

"I disposed of him. End of story. Now back to you."

"There's nothing to say. I'm not glowing," Sophia told her.

"Superglowing," Ava confirmed. Her eyes got big. "Wait, I know that look. It's the look of love."

"Wha— No. You're—" Sophia stammered. Ava was seeing things. And the fairy lights hardly counted as good illumination.

Ava laughed. "I'm such a dope. I should have realized." Before Sophia could ask what Ava should have realized, she went on. "That's why we couldn't find you. You were somewhere on the phone with Hunter. Whatever he said made you adorably giddy. I love it. You two are so cute."

"Hunter," Sophia said. "Phone. Right." Any thought Sophia had had of telling Ava about seeing Giovanni vanished. Not that there was anything secretive to it. There wasn't *anything* to it. It wasn't worth mentioning. After all, she *had* been on the phone with Hunter.

And given his track record, Giovanni probably wouldn't text.

At the second party, a dejected Lily called to inform them that she wasn't able to get Yankee Stadium for their show but had a line on two other places.

At the third party, Sophia's phone died. The fourth seemed to go on forever, so it was nearly three in the morning when she got home, plugged in her phone, and saw the ten messages and fifteen texts from Hunter.

The texts started off asking about her night, then got progressively more annoyed, ending with, "Who the hell do you think you are? How dare you treat me this way? I will not be toyed with. You'll regret this."

She was shocked and almost didn't answer when it rang again. When she did, he barked, "Where have you been?"

"At parties," she said briskly. She was standing, frozen, in the middle of her room, still wearing her jacket and dress, her purse dangling from her wrist. The walls were covered with beveled mirrors, each sending back a sliver of her image from a different angle, none of them happy. "Working."

"And you couldn't reply to one single text in eight hours? I sent a dozen."

She watched the slivers of her step to the vanity to put her purse down and felt like it was her, not just her image, that had been sliced into pieces. "Actually you sent fifteen. My phone died and I just got them."

"You think I haven't heard that excuse before. Who is he? Reporter? Art dealer? Waiter?" he said with a sneer.

Sophia saw all the different pieces of her face lose color and her knuckles go white and she knew that was it. "You cannot talk to me that way," she said in a voice that sounded as broken as she felt.

"I can talk to you however I want."

The shock of his words sent her backward, until her knees hit the end of the mattress and dissolved, so that she was perched on the edge of the lavender-satin comforter. "No." She shook her head hard back and forth, closing her eyes to avoid her reflection. "You have to treat me with respect." She felt Charming leave the pillow he'd been sleeping on and come curl up next to her, as though sensing she needed moral support.

"What about you treating me with respect?" he demanded. "Instead of just disappearing, taking off with God knows what men behind my back."

"That's enough," she cut him off, surprised at the authority in her voice. "I have never once been unfaithful to you. My phone battery died while I was working. I'm sorry I'm so busy. I used to be sorry I didn't have more time with you but—" She paused, groping for words.

"Sophia," he said.

"No, let me finish." She felt a tear on her cheek and swiped at it. "You're making me feel stifled and I hate it. I can't breathe. And I can't take it anymore. I feel like you're making me chose between London Calling and you. And that's a terrible, cruel position to put me in." She took a deep, ragged breath. "You say you love me, but recently that seems to mean you want to control me. And—that's not what love means to me. It's not what I want it to mean." She put her forehead in her hand, waiting for the fallout.

It was silent for so long that she thought her phone had gone out again. "Hello?" she said.

"I'm sorry." The words were so quiet, and in such an unfamiliar voice, that at first she didn't think she'd heard him.

"What?"

"I said, I'm sorry." His voice got stronger. "I'm really sorry. I swore I would never do this again, and without realizing it, I'm doing it." He let out a long, noisy breath. "There's something I—I want to tell you."

Sophia opened her eyes. She sensed real pain in his voice, not like anything she'd ever heard from him before, and her anger vanished. "What is it?"

"I loved my mom. You know that, we talked about her."

"You gave me her camera," Sophia said. "You said she died when you were fourteen."

"Yeah. That's what I tell people because it's—easier." He got quiet.

"What do you mean?"

Silence and then, in a voice that sounded like it was being squeezed from him: "When I was eight, one day, she left. Said she was going to the store, and took off." There was a long pause and when he came back, his voice was tight with restrained emotion. "Took off and never came back. No phone call. No postcard. No message under a windshield wiper. Just gone forever. Gone like that."

"I'm so sorry," she said.

"When I was fourteen my father came into my room one day, picked up the baseball on my desk, and said, 'Champ, thought you should know, Mom's dead.' Then he asked if I wanted to do some batting practice." Hunter gave a tight chuckle. "That's my dad."

"My god, Hunter, that's terrible."

"That's why I get—a little anxious, when I don't know where you are," he went on. "Because ever since she walked out on me, I've been afraid of losing someone else. And I guess I'm extra afraid of losing you. Afraid you're going to walk out the door one morning and not want to come back."

Sophia sank to the floor and Charming crawled into her lap. "You won't lose me, Hunter."

"I never want to make you choose between London Calling and me. I love your work, your company, your passion for it. I want you to succeed even beyond your wildest dreams. Please believe that."

"I do." Charming nuzzled under her hand.

"I'm not trying to be controlling. I'm just trying to make sure you're okay. We're okay. I just want to know that what we have is real. That you're still there. That's why I call so much. For reassurance to keep me from spiraling to a dark place. Because once I thought something was real and it just disappeared and since then it's hard for me to believe in anything good."

"It *is* real," she said. "I'm real and we're real. And I'll work extra hard to be there whenever you call." In this position on the floor she could see only one mirror, and it just showed Charming's face looking blissfully up at her as she scratched between his ears.

"Maybe we could compromise and make it like every other time," Hunter said.

She smiled. "That sounds like a good compromise."

He let out another deep breath. "I can't believe I just told you that. I haven't told anyone that. Even Liam doesn't know."

Sophia felt like she'd been given a precious gift. "Thank you. I'm glad you did."

"Now tell me about your day. I want to hear everything."

Sophia shrugged off her jacket, which Charming promptly lay down in, and started telling him from the beginning, about the new security and her phone being on the fritz and Lucille and the contest and how it seemed like everything might finally be coming together. Again.

Only when they'd hung up and she was getting into bed did she realize she'd forgotten to tell him about running into Giovanni. She hadn't mentioned it to Ava, either, she reminded herself, because it was too insignificant. She and Giovanni had been friends, but he lived in New York City now and it wasn't like she would have time to see him while they were there. She had much more important things to focus on.

If he even texted her.

LonDOs
Cuddly kitties
Honesty
Compromise
Friends from the past
Makeup-remover cloths

LonDON'Ts

Kitties who think Wolford thigh-highs are for their clawing pleasure

Jumping to conclusions

Mirrored walls

Alarms that go off way too soon

People who say they are going to text but never do

9

textuplets

There was a cold wind whipping across the sidewalk the next morning as Ava and Sophia left for the studio, and the doorman who put them into a taxi said, "You ladies be careful. Predicting snow for this evening."

"Popcorn is going to be in heaven," Ava said as they pulled away. "He loves walking in the snow."

"Mmhmmm," Sophia answered, already texting. Or still texting. Ava was starting to wonder if Sophia texted even in her sleep.

"I'm so excited about the contest. I can't believe it goes live in two hours."

"Me too," Sophia said, which was the right answer, but something about her tone made Ava question whether Sophia was actually listening.

"I heard a news story about a woman whose phone merged with her hand," Ava said.

"Mmhmmm," Sophia answered.

"Soon she lost the power to interact with others and could only communicate with her phone," Ava went on.

"Me too," Sophia answered, typing.

"And later she gave birth to textuplets."

"Mmmhmm," Sophia said.

Ava sighed. The taxi ride was the only time the two of them had alone together most days and she found she'd started to look forward to it. Plus, she'd wanted to tell Sophia about running into the guy from Starbucks at the party the night before and how horrible that had been, and then tell her about the Contessa coming up and how horrible *that* had been. She really wanted someone to laugh about it with her because otherwise it felt a little grim.

Click click click. What could she be saying? What was so important that she couldn't stop even for a moment to talk to her sister?

She glanced over and saw that Sophia was smiling. It did seem to make her really happy, though, Ava had to admit, remembering the way she'd been glowing the night before at the first party.

"I do not think your friend is listening," the cabdriver told Ava.

"Thanks." Ava pulled out her phone and checked her messages. It contained the usual, "Sorry we didn't get to talk last night. Have a great day!" text from Liam, this time with the addendum, "The train accident no big deal. Cute of you to worry."

She deleted it, then typed, "Dear right side of the car. How's it going? Your friend, left side of the car."

She pressed Send, and heard Sophia's phone chime. Sophia frowned, looked over at her, rolled her eyes, and went back to texting Hunter.

You're right, Ava, she said to herself. *It's going to be a very exciting day.*

The "AS you are" model search launched at ten o'clock, and by noon the entries—and press queries—were pouring in.

"I've got a waiting list for VIP," Harper announced, meaning that more celebrities than they could accommodate wanted front-row seats. "A good waiting list," she added.

"We don't even have a venue," Ava reminded her.

"I'm getting close," Lily said. Her head shot up, looking for Sam. "I heard you laughing." She growled in his direction.

"That wasn't Sam, sweetie," MM said gently.

Lily growled at him, too.

Sophia looked up from her phone then, causing Ava to say, "My, what pretty eyes you have."

"All the better to glare at you with," Sophia answered. She glanced around the group. "Hunter just had an idea and I think it's worth discussing."

Ava had to work hard to keep from rolling her eyes. "What does Prince Charming say?" she asked.

Sophia blushed. "He suggested that we make another piece. Now that we have all the security in place and Sam filming, there's no way Christopher Wildwood—"

"Wormface," the Contessa corrected.

"Can get it, that would prove, definitively, that all the others are ours. Something that is like the rest of the line but new."

"That's a great idea," MM agreed. "And, Ava, that's no problem for you, right? You can come up with something new."

"Sure," Ava told them. "It's just like kindergarten."

Sophia's brows contracted. "Ava, are you okay?"

"I'm joking," Ava said, and she was.

Or she had been. She'd been sitting in the workroom for almost an hour, staring at the bolts of fabric she'd pulled, seeing no shapes, no colors, no drape. With Sam's camera hovering around behind her, recording the nothing, and Sophia poking her head in every fifteen minutes to tell her that they were now up to five hundred, then seven hundred, then eight hundred fifty entries, and finding out how it was going, Ava found herself feeling less like joking and more like being annoyed.

She was annoyed with Sophia for not taking even one minute to talk that morning, annoyed with Liam for not letting her break up with him—"Cute of you to worry," he'd written, like she was a puppy—annoyed with the Contessa for not letting her have her own life, annoyed with Hunter for suggesting that they make a new piece, annoyed with herself for not knowing what the piece should be, and annoyed that no one took anything she said or did or wanted seriously.

She got up abruptly and went into the other room. "I need a break. I'm going for a walk."

"Bring me a latte?" Sophia said to her with a wink.

"I'm not going to Starbucks," Ava told her.

"Right." Sophia grinned.

But as she left the building she was so busy thinking about how upset she was that she didn't pay attention to where her feet were going, and she found herself standing inside Starbucks without meaning to.

Stupid traitor feet, she told them. Out of the corner of her eye she saw the (formerly) cute guy with the sleepy eyes, camped at his regular table, but she wouldn't let herself look at him. She would get her coffee and go. It was freezing outside but a walk in the chilly wind would be bracing.

She took her mochachino—Sophia could get her own coffee— and was heading for the door when she found it blocked.

"You weren't actually going to leave without saying hello, were you?" the (ex)cute guy with the sleepy eyes said. Standing in front of her like that, he seemed even taller than he had the night before and, in his blue button-down shirt and jeans, even buffer. He was also wearing glasses with dark brown rims the same color as his hair, which somehow made him even . . . more annoying.

"Why should I say hello to someone I've never met?" Ava countered.

"Maybe because that person behaved like an idiot the night before and would like to apologize." He put out his hand. "Truce?"

Ava looked from the hand to him. When she was still hesitating he said, "I'm sorry I was a jerk. I was supposed to meet someone there and got stood up and it made me—upset."

"I'd say it was her loss but I'm not sure," Ava told him.

The door opened from the outside, sending a blast of cold air right into Ava's face, and he pulled her back into the store. "You look like you're having a really bad day."

"Wow, you are a real charmer. No wonder your girlfriend didn't show up."

"Don't change the subject," he said. "You *are* having a bad day."

"I'm having a bad two weeks," Ava admitted, not sure why she was confessing this to a mean stranger in front of a rack of Valentine's Day mugs.

"Do you want to talk about it?"

"With you?" Ava's eyes rested on a mug with I LOVE YOU A LATTE written in pink. *Sophia would like that,* she thought, and then pushed the thought aside. "Not a chance," she told him

"Okay. Let me guess then."

"Yeah, I think I'm just going to go," she said, starting to turn away.

"You don't have a boyfriend so it's not that—"

She turned back. "How do you know I don't have a boyfriend?"

He held up a finger. "One, you hit on a guy in a bar."

"I did not hit—"

He held up a second finger. "Two, you said you noticed me studying here."

"And you didn't notice me," Ava said, rolling her eyes as much at herself as at him. Why was she talking to the one person who had made her feel worse in the past twenty-four hours than anyone else?

He tapped on his glasses. "Without these I'm more or less blind beyond a foot in front of me. I can see fine close-up, like to read, so I keep them off when I'm studying to cut down on distractions. For example, if I'd been wearing them I would absolutely have noticed you when I looked up. And then I would have had a hard time getting any work done."

He smiled at her and Ava felt her pulse rate jump up like an ice skater doing a triple twirl. "You're just saying that because I'm having a bad day," she told both him and herself.

He looked serious. "I thought we established I'm not charming or nice."

"True."

Without realizing it, she'd let him lead her from the mugs to his table, which had a bunch of folders on it. "So not boyfriend troubles and for some reason I don't think it's parents. Your dog?" He held a chair out for her and she sat down in it.

She leaned across the table toward him, so surprised that she almost crushed her coffee cup. "How did you know I had a dog?"

"Hair on your boot," he said. "Small and white?"

Ava nodded, impressed. "But it's not him."

"So it must be job," he mused. "But you are kind of young to have a job."

Ava snorted. "I feel about twelve million years old."

"What's your job?"

She looked up at him. "I am designing a fashion line that's going to be shown during New York Fashion Week." Her voice sounded small and tight and afraid in her ears, with none of the pride she usually felt.

He leaned back and regarded her thoughtfully. "Really?"

"Really," she confirmed.

"Sounds like some kind of fairy tale," he said.

She felt like every muscle in her body was tense. "It's not."

"What about the count?" he asked.

She shook her head, standing. "Thanks for the chat. I have to go."

He bounced up as soon as she stood, and at first she thought it was just good manners but then he started putting his folders into a messenger bag. "Just give me a minute," he said.

"I said *I* was going," Ava pointed out.

"Right, but you meant we were going," he explained.

Ava shook her head. "No, I didn't."

"Yeah." He nodded, shrugging into his coat. "Pretty sure. Well anyway, we are."

"Where?" Ava asked, not sure why. There was only one place she was going and it was back to the workroom. Back to the bolts of fabric that wouldn't talk to her. To Sophia texting and the Contessa watching her like hawk and Lily chasing after venues.

He slung the messenger bag across his body. "You need a day off."

She laughed, and it sounded slightly hysterical to her. "Maybe, but a day off isn't going to happen for another month."

"An afternoon off, then."

"I really can't," Ava said, suddenly aware of how desperately she wanted that. An afternoon off. An afternoon away. "It's not possible."

"I know the perfect thing," he went on, ignoring her.

"Really?" she asked. "What?"

"Whenever the fairy tale princess is feeling the lowest, there's something that always cheers her up." He led her to the exit.

"I'm not a princess," she told him over her shoulder. "That's my sister."

"Countess," he corrected. "Although technically the sister of the princess is a duchess."

"Whatever it is, my life is no fairy tale."

"Maybe it is, but you're just stuck at the part where everything seems bleak. I think the cure will work anyway."

"What is it?" she asked and then shook her head. "It doesn't matter. I can't go." He pushed open the door for her and followed her outside.

"You'll see," he told her, holding out his arm to hail a cab. One swerved to the curb in front of them almost immediately. "You need it. You don't even remember how to have fun, do you?" He held open the door. "Come on. Your chariot awaits."

Say thank you and go back to work. You can't just turn your back on work and get into a taxi with a complete stranger, a voice in her head said. A voice that sounded a lot like Sophia's. *Even if he does have a nice smile and very good manners. You don't even know his name.*

As if he were reading her mind he said, "I forgot to introduce myself. I'm Jax."

"Ava," she said, shaking his hand.

"In or out," the cabbie called. "You're using up all my heat."

"In or out?" Jax asked Ava.

"I can't be gone long," she told him.

"I'll bring you back whenever you say."

"In," Ava said, feeling more like herself than she had for weeks.

LonDOs

AS-is model search

Cute guy from Starbucks (Jax!)

Guys who wear glasses

Feeling like yourself

Starbucks heart-shaped sugar cookies

Sorrel snow boots

Tinted lip balm

LonDON'Ts

People who don't have time for their sisters

People who can't stop texting for five minutes

Click click click

Leaving work with only enough money to buy a coffee

Being stuck in the wrong part of the fairy tale

10
central lark

While Jax gave directions to the taxi driver, Ava called to talk to Sophia but it bounced to voice mail, probably because she was on the phone with Hunter. Again.

Ava left a message saying she was walking around to get ideas for the dress and wasn't sure how long she would be.

It wasn't exactly true, but since she hadn't been making any progress on the new piece at the workroom and you never knew where inspiration could come from, it wasn't entirely untrue, either.

When she hung up, Jax was still giving the driver instructions, telling the guy which streets to turn on, what lights to avoid, and when he finally slumped back next to her he smiled. "That should do it."

"Do you know what you're talking about or did you make that up?"

"I grew up here. I know every pothole and slow light between Houston and Ninety-second street. And I work part-time driving an ambulance to help pay for school."

"What was it like growing up here?"

"Pluses and minuses, like any place. Plus, there's a lot going on. Minus, people can get distracted."

"Like your date last night."

"Yeah," he said, scratching the back of his neck. "Let's not talk about that."

"What are you going to school for?" Ava asked, indicating the messenger bag.

"I'm studying to be an EMT," he said.

"You mean one of the people who work in an ambulance? Saving people's lives?"

"Ideally saving them, yeah."

"Like a knight in shining armor," Ava said to herself.

Only apparently not only to herself, because he said, "What do you mean?"

"Nothing." She blushed. She went on, talking fast. "Just, um, something I was thinking about last night. Being an EMT sounds intense. How did you decide on that?"

"I wanted to be a doctor, but there's no way I can afford medical school. This seems like the next best thing. For now anyway." He turned to the window as he answered, and Ava sensed she'd touched a raw nerve.

"Well, I'm impressed," she told him.

He tapped the window and said, "Just in time too, because we're here."

Ava peered around him. "Central Park? My sister and I kept meaning to come here together on our day off, but we haven't gotten one yet."

He paid the cab and they got out. "This is even better than

Central Park. We're going to the Central Park Zoo," he told her, getting two tickets and piloting her through the entrance gates.

"I haven't been here before," Ava said as they walked past the gift store. "I never— *Ooh,* sea lions!" She rushed toward a large pool. As she approached, two of them turned and looked at her and started clapping.

She laughed and looked at Jax. "Did you see that?"

"I did," he told her. "And it just confirms what I was—"

"There are penguins!" She pointed at a sign with an arrow. "Come on."

The penguin enclosure was a series of pools carved out of what looked like ice floes, with a very strong smell of fish. They were lazing around on one of the icy parts as Ava and Jax walked up, but one of them spun its head around and caught sight of them and a group jumped into the water. They swam toward Ava and started squawking.

"They remind me of reporters at the parties we've been going to," she told Jax.

"And probably just as fishy," Jax answered dryly.

Ava laughed. "You're funny. I didn't think you would be funny."

He cupped his hand and pretended to be reading from a list. "Impressed her, check. Made her laugh, check."

Ava laughed again and gave him a sideways look. "What list is that?"

"My perfect-date checklist," he said, holding his hand close to his chest as though he were protecting an important notebook.

"Let me see that," Ava demanded, pretending to reach for it.

He took a step backward and she took a step toward him and he leaned back and suddenly they were standing nearly nose to nose. His eyes were brown and chocolaty and looked right into hers in a way that made her pulse beat hard in her throat. She bit her lip and his gaze moved there, then back to hers.

A shriek split the air between them, sending them flying apart. There was another shriek, from their left, and turning Ava saw a massive white peacock with his tail fully open, glaring at them from inside his enclosure.

"Looks like someone wants attention," Jax said.

"I bet you have that effect on all the ladies," Ava joked.

"Yes, I make them all shriek in horror."

"That's not what I—" Ava began to protest, then saw his lips curve into a smile and realized he was kidding again. As they moved on, Ava felt a lightness inside her that had been missing too long.

Next they visited the polar bears, who made a yodeling noise as they approached. The snow monkeys yelped and did loop-de-loops, the red pandas made whistling noises, a snake hissed, and the frogs all began croaking at once. As they walked, their fingers kept brushing accidentally, making Ava feel like there were fireflies darting around inside her.

"I told you that you were a duchess," Jax said matter-of-factly when they had circled back to the sea lions. "You just proved it."

Ava said, "What are you talking about?"

He looked serious. "In all the movies, the animals sing to the noble heroine when she's feeling low."

"This something you study in EMT school?" Ava asked.

He shook his head. "More like babysitting school. I have a six-year-old stepsister."

She said, "I'm sorry to disappoint you, but I've never had animals do that for me before."

"Maybe you've never been this down."

She looked at the sea lions. "Maybe."

A speaker announced that the zoo was closing in five minutes. "I guess that's our cue to go home," he said.

"Yeah, I guess," she agreed.

They stood side by side, looking at the sea lions.

"It hardly seems fair." Ava tilted her head to look up at him. "I mean, we can't have finished your entire perfect-date list yet, can we?"

He smiled down at her. "We've barely scratched the surface."

"You probably get a lot of use out of it." She was looking at their hands. As though it had a mind of its own, her pinkie inched toward his.

He cleared his throat and said, suddenly serious, "Actually, there hasn't been anyone I've wanted to impress in a while."

Their pinkies touched, and Ava felt a little spark leap between them. She peeked up at him through her lashes and saw that he was looking at her. Her chest felt tight and her knees felt wobbly and she found herself wondering what his lips would taste like. She said, "I guess I could stay out a little longer."

What are you thinking, she asked herself. *First of all, you can't stay out. Second of all, you shouldn't. Third of all, there are people counting on you. Fourth of all, there's no way that staring into a guy's eyes and hoping he'll kiss you is part of boytoxing.*

But she was so tired of being responsible. Of doing everything she should do. It felt like weeks since she'd laughed the way she had that afternoon. Years. Decades.

Okay, now you're exaggerating, she berated herself. *You haven't even been alive for decades.*

"A quarter for your thoughts," Jax said.

Ava laughed. "I thought they were only supposed to cost a penny."

"Haven't you heard, everything is more expensive in New York City."

She sighed. "I was just having a pity party for myself. Being silly. It's nothing." She bit the inside of her cheek.

"What's it like, launching a fashion line?" He asked casually.

"Exciting. Amazing. And overwhelming. If it was only the line that would be easy. But there are all these other things." And then without thinking she was telling Jax everything, about Christopher Wildwood and losing their credentials and the venue and the models, about the pressure of creating a new dress, about Sophia being all wrapped up in Hunter, even about Liam. The only thing she didn't tell him about was the Contessa's nephew. It was too hard to explain, she rationalized. And Dalton. She didn't mention Dalton, either.

But what was there to say about that except that she'd been completely and utterly wrong about him. That her heart had misled her? Besides, Jax couldn't have been less like Dalton. He was taller, more serious, more reserved than Dalton and he definitely had better manners. Like for example he wasn't a thief.

"It sounds like you're putting a lot of pressure on yourself to be perfect and please everyone," he said. "And that's making you feel trapped. By situations outside your control, and by other people's expectations."

Ava stared at him. She hadn't thought about it that way but she realized he was right. "I do feel trapped. In every direction."

"Maybe it would help to remind yourself that the reason everyone wants to be near you—the reason that guy won't let you break up with him—is because they see something special in you. And they still will, no matter what you do. So you don't need to worry about their expectations. You don't have to be perfect, you just have to be you."

"You're just being nice to me again because I was so upset," she said.

In a tight, almost angry-sounding voice he said, "We both know that's not true."

She stopped walking and tugged him to face her. "Then why?"

"Would you believe it if I told you it's because my mother

never would have forgiven me if she knew I'd spoken to a lady the way I spoke to you last night and I'm trying to work off the guilt?"

Ava said, "No."

"No, I didn't think you would." He said, "The truth is, since last night I haven't been able to think of anything but your smile and what I could do to bring it out again."

Ava's heart felt like it was too big for her rib cage. She reached for his hand and twined her fingers with his. "Thank you," she said. "For that. And for listening."

He slanted a smile down at her. "Thank you," he said. "For trusting me enough to talk."

His eyes held hers, warm and inviting, and his head bent slightly toward her, and Ava's gaze went to his lips, so soft-looking, and she thought, *He's going to kiss me.*

He stood up, suddenly formal, said, "We should be departing," and began to tramp down the sidewalk.

Ava blinked once and then jogged to catch up with him. What had just happened? She wanted to know. Had she done something wrong? The warmth she'd felt inside turned to tiny spots of cold. Wet cold. On her cheeks. She reached up to see what it was and a snowflake drifted onto her hand.

"Snow!" Ava cried happily, tipping her head back to let it fall on her face. "It's snowing!"

Jax looked at her and let out a little laugh. "It is."

Her eyes were huge and serious. "Let's stay out in it."

"Are you sure you have time?" he asked.

"I'm positive I *don't*," she said emphatically, "but I'm not going to miss my chance to be out in a real New York City snowstorm. Come on!"

Ava lost track of time as they wandered around Central Park, watching fluffy snowflakes fall and begin to drift. It got dark and the lights along the paths seemed to have halos. He showed her the Reservoir, named after Jackie Kennedy, and the Castle, and a pond that had turtles in it clustered near the edge where it wasn't frozen. There was almost no one else out and it was peaceful and beautiful.

"I have one more place to show you, but it's secret. Do you promise not to tell?"

"I promise," Ava said.

He led her from the road across an uneven snowbank, to a chain-link fence. He felt around for a minute, then said, "Got it!" and curled a piece of the fence away from the post. "Through here."

"Are we going to get arrested?" Ava asked him.

"Only if you're slow," he said, and his tone was serious but his eyes were laughing.

He held out his hand to support her, then shimmied sideways down a moderate slope toward an expanse of pure white snow.

"Close your eyes," he said as they reached it, gripping her hand more firmly. "It's a little slippery, be careful." They walked about a dozen steps and he said, "This should be good. Now open your eyes."

Ava gasped. It was like being in a winter fairy kingdom. All around her were trees covered in white with sparkling icicles hanging from the branches. The sound of the traffic outside the park seemed to have disappeared and it was perfectly serene. She looked up into Jax's face and this time, finally, his mouth sought hers.

His lips tasted like ChapStick and chocolate and their soft, lingering touch sent tiny flares of warmth spiraling through her. When he pulled away it took her a moment to remember where she was. She felt like she was in a dreamy daze. Her eyes began to open slowly, then flew the rest of the way open as she gaped at the astonishing vision that had materialized in front of her. Over Jax's shoulder, at the end of the snowy expanse where there'd been nothing but shadows before, there was now a building, hovering like some fairy's winter palace, spilling gold-tinted light onto the snow. Tiny lights twinkled around it and inside there were tables with tall candles in gleaming candelabra on them and a roaring fireplace, the whole place looking like it was set for an enchanted banquet.

"Magical," she whispered.

Jax smoothed his thumb over her lips. "Yes, you are. I've been wanting to kiss you all afternoon but I didn't want to be too forward."

She felt herself blush. Not knowing what to say, she gestured behind him with their twined hands. "What is that place? How did you make it appear like that?"

Jax grinned. "I can't tell you all my secrets." Ava gave him a pleading look. "Okay, I knew they turned up the lights at six, when they open, so I sort of tried to time it. That's the Boathouse. What we're standing on is a lake in the summer."

"It's beautiful," she said with a sigh. Then, as if just hearing what he'd said, she turned to stare at him. "Did you say *six* o'clock?"

"Yeah, that's when they open."

And just like that, reality intruded. Ava had only gone out for a coffee and she'd been out for hours, leaving behind all her responsibility, all her work. The stress of her life—her real life—settled back over her like a familiar coat. "I've got to get back. I can't believe I stayed away this long." She was alarmed at the tremble in her voice.

"Let's get you back," Jax said and sprang into action. He bent down, lifted her into his arms, and carried her back up the snowy embankment, not setting her down until they were on the street.

She gazed at him, a little breathless. "I think you just swept me off my feet. Literally."

"All part of the service," he told her.

She shook her head. "You're very strong."

His eyes moved away from hers. "In some ways." His voice had a serious note in it, but it was gone the next moment as he said, "The storm is going to make it hard to find a cab so we'd better hustle."

He was right; it took almost fifteen minutes to find a taxi that was free and even that involved some arguing on Jax's part. Since he had to get to a class on the other side of the city, he put Ava into the cab alone. As he was closing the door Ava heard herself say, "I liked kissing you."

She held her breath. For a moment he just stared at her. Then he grinned enormously. "I'm really glad you said that because I liked kissing you too."

"Maybe we could do it again sometime," Ava went on, amazed at her brashness.

The smile got even wider. Instead of answering he leaned into the cab and kissed her. Really kissed her this time, the kind of kiss that curls your toes and makes you forget your name. When he pulled away, Ava could only stare at him.

"I'll see you tomorrow at the usual place, Duchess," he said and shut the door.

The taxi had already pulled into traffic before Ava regained the ability to speak, and then what she said was, "Wow."

She'd gotten a message from Sophia saying they'd all headed home, so she gave the taxi the address of the apartment rather than the studio and spent the drive smiling and hugging herself and looking out at the snow-covered city. It looked beautiful, she thought. Everything looked beautiful.

She floated giddily through the lobby of the building and up the elevator, unable to stop smiling. She kept replaying moments from her afternoon with Jax, the penguins, the peacock, his saying that he liked her smile, the Boathouse floating over the snow-covered lake.

His kisses.

She couldn't wait to tell Popcorn about it on their walk. She wouldn't have minded telling Sophia, too, but she doubted she'd be able to free her from Hunter long enough to complete a full sentence.

She was surprised when she got to the apartment. She'd expected Popcorn to be at the door, waiting for her to take him out, but instead it was Sophia who greeted her. And instead of jumping up and down and looking happy to see her, she was curled in a chair in the foyer with a book.

"What are you doing here? Where's Popcorn?" Ava asked, peeling off her snow-covered boots and hanging up her coat.

Sophia carefully marked her place in the book and closed it crisply. "Sven took him for a walk a few hours ago. I suspect he's in your room."

Ava shook her head. "I think Popcorn slept for two days after the last time Sven took him out. I hope he didn't tire him out too much."

"Well, Ava," Sophia said in a weird, cold voice. "When you're not where you're supposed to be, you forfeit your right to say how things go."

"What are you talking about?" Ava froze with her coat halfway on the hanger.

"How you disappeared all afternoon without telling anyone where you were, or when you were coming back."

Ava felt anger rising inside her. With great care she finished hanging up her coat and closed the closet door. Struggling to keep her voice even, she said, "I'm amazed you even noticed, given how busy you are with Hunter all the time."

"I have no choice with Hunter," Sophia told her. "Otherwise he worries and that's not fair. Which is why I really don't have the time or energy to be wondering where you are."

"Then don't," Ava said, turning to Sophia. "No one told you that you had to wonder."

Sophia looked at her incredulously. "This is New York City. You can't just go off on your own with who knows what guys behind all our backs with no calls or texts for hours. You have to tell us where you are."

The two of them stared at each other. Finally Ava said, "Breathing. That's where I was. I didn't realize it until just now, when you said that, but I've been suffocating."

Sophia's face registered displeasure. "What are you talking about?"

"Do you have any idea what it's like to go through every day pretending to be someone else? Always second-guessing yourself? Worrying that with one wrong word you could let everyone else down?"

Sophia took longer to answer than Ava had expected. "Who are you pretending to be?"

"You," Ava said, realizing the full extent of it for the first time. "I've been trying to be you."

"Why would you do that?" Sophia asked and she sounded genuinely aghast.

"Because it's what everyone wanted," Ava answered. "I got us into this whole mess by being myself. You said so yourself. If I had been more like you in interviews with the press, we would still have credentials and a venue and models."

Sophia shook her head slowly from side to side. "I never said you got us into this."

"'*You were just being yourself*,' you told me after the interview broke."

"I meant it in a good way," Sophia said. "Not as an indictment."

"But it was true. So the less like me I could be, I figured, the less likely we'd have any more mishaps. The more peaceful it would be. The happier everyone would be."

"That makes no sense," Sophia said. "The Christopher Wildwood fiasco would have happened no matter what you told the reporter. And no one ever said you should be like me."

"Really? *Follow Sophia's lead. Just watch Sophia. Be a serious girl, like your sister*," Ava said, quoting the voices that chased one another inside her head like Popcorn chasing his tail. "And just now when I came in and you told me I needed to check in more. Tell you where I am going and with whom and when I'll be back. That's your way of wanting me to be like you. Like you with Hunter. Maybe you like it but I don't."

"It is—" Sophia began to protest, then stopped herself. She was staring into space, as though listening to a conversation only she could hear. Her hand came to her mouth and when she spoke it sounded like she was talking to herself. "It's true," she said. "I was doing what he does. I even used the same words." Her eyes went to Ava. "I'm sorry. I never meant to transfer that to you. And I'm sorry you felt like you had to be someone else. I don't understand how it happened but I hope you'll stop now."

"I felt trapped and miserable because I thought I had to be something other than myself, because it was safer, because I was afraid I would mess up. But the trap was all in my mind."

Sophia looked at her, and Ava couldn't read the expression on her face. "I don't need to be trapped either. I can tell Hunter that he needs to trust our relationship. For both our sakes. Just because he's trapped in this old hurt doesn't mean our relationship has to be. And in fact, by acting the way he has been, he keeps that hurt alive." She stood and hugged Ava. "You're a genius."

"You should see my sister," Ava said. "I'm starving."

"Me too. I was too worried to eat. There's pizza in the fridge."

When they were in the kitchen with pizza in front of them Sophia asked, "So where did you and Mr. Starbucks go?"

"How did you know I was with him?" Ava demanded.

"If I hadn't known, the way you're blushing right now would have let me know."

Ava shook her head. "We went to Central Park. We walked around the park and went up to a castle and then he showed me this boathouse. It's on a lake but now it's frozen and it was beautiful."

Sophia nodded, nibbling on a piece of crust. "I love the Boathouse. Hunter and I went there for a drink when we came on our date. He has a friend who rows tourists around the lake in a gondola and he took us out at sunset . . ." Her voice trailed off and a wistful expression spread over her face. "It's one of the most beautiful restaurants in New York. The kind of place you can only make good memories."

"Stop," Ava said. "Go back."

Sophia edged her chair backward.

"No," Ava said. "Repeat what you just said."

"It's one of the most beautiful restaurants in New York?"

"That's it!" Ava said. "I can't believe we didn't think of it sooner."

Sophia eyed her with concern. "What are you talking about?"

"We couldn't use restaurants for our show because we needed a place with high ceilings to accommodate the tall models. *But we're not using models.*"

Sophia's eyes lit up. "You're right," she said breathlessly. "And the Boathouse is—"

"The kind of place you can only make good memories," Ava finished for her.

"It would be the perfect spot," Sophia said. "But how could we book it on such late notice?"

"*Lily!*" they yelled in unison.

LonDOs:

Central Park Zoo

Boys whose kisses are magical

Lily's connections

Puppies who are so tired after their walk with Sven that they fall
    asleep with all four legs in the air

Falling asleep to a text that says, "Thanks for letting me be part of
    your fairy tale"

Waking up with an idea for a dress

LonDON'Ts

Letting yourself be trapped

Make your friends worry about you

Puppies who punish you for missing their walk by hogging the
    whole bed

Waking up on the floor of your room

11
uptown whirl

The Monday before their show, the Contessa scheduled their morning meeting at the apartment because she had a very special announcement.

It was preceded by the arrival of a very large object draped in black satin and guarded by a security guard who looked a lot like a ninja, presumably to keep them from peeking.

But it couldn't keep them from gathering around it.

"Do you think it's a sculpture of her?" Sophia asked.

"Of her, or her nephew," Ava said.

"Personally, I hope it's a punching bag," Lily said. "Or something else to help the Contessa vent her inner rage."

"I think we all do," MM agreed.

"I would like it to be a robot piano," Sven put in. "The kind where they play the music without the hands. I love those."

"You are a treasure," MM said to him.

The object had come with a note that said it would be unveiled at ten, which wasn't for nearly an hour, so Ava decided to take Popcorn for a walk. Lily had arranged for both him and Charming to have pet-spa appointments that afternoon—"because they have been under stress too,"—and Ava tried to make sure he had enough exercise to take the edge off his boundless energy.

"You should make the most of this," Ava said to Popcorn as he nosed from snow pile to snow pile down Riverside Drive. "Five days from today and it's all over."

Popcorn looked back at her with an expression of disbelief and Ava couldn't blame him. She herself could hardly believe that they were in the final stretch. But ever since the fire at Graveswood pieces had been coming together easily, rather than falling apart.

The Central Park Boathouse had received a cancellation just fifteen minutes before Lily called to secure it as a venue, allowing them to hold their show exactly two hours after Christopher Wildwood's show. The "AS you are" model contest had produced so much interest that the Contessa was already getting inquiries about the line from buyers even before they'd shown a single piece. And several celebrities had been quoted saying that they were just regular girls, too, and would give anything to walk in the show.

But for Ava the most exciting part was the new gown she and Sophia were working on. No one but them and Sam, the cameraman, had seen it yet, but she thought it was their best piece yet. It had come together almost effortlessly, as though it had been waiting inside them to come out. The Fashion Week opening-night party was that night, and they still hadn't decided if one of them was going to wear it, as a hint about what they could do, or if they were going to wait and debut it at their show.

Ava's phone buzzed in her pocket and she saw a text from Jax. "Sister still home sick from school. Not going to make it to Starbucks today. Miss you, Duchess."

Ava typed back, "Miss you too. Tell her I hope she feels better," and smiled to herself. She'd seen Jax at Starbucks the day after their trip to the zoo and even though it had started off a little awkwardly, with him pulling out her chair and jumping up every time she stood to do anything, it had ended with them joking and then kissing as he walked her to the door. The next day she'd been too busy even to break for coffee, and the day after, his sister had come down with the flu and he'd had to stay home with her. But they'd been texting regularly, and every time it made Ava smile.

"Do you think she knows she blushes every time she gets a text?" MM had leaned over to say to Sophia at dinner the night after Ava's date with Jax.

"I do not," Ava protested.

"I'm afraid you do," Sophia had said. "You seem to be pretty hooked."

Lily swallowed a bite of pizza. "What happened to your boytox?"

"Why are you ganging up on me?" Ava asked them. "I thought you'd be happy that I'm happy."

"Of course we are," MM told her. "It's just you're leaving New York soon. It wouldn't be geographically desirable to fall in love here."

"It is true," Sven said somberly. "The broken heart is not a good souvenir from a trip."

"Not to mention," Lily had said, pointing upstairs to indicate the Contessa while shooting an uneasy glare in Sam's direction.

But she might as well have spared him and pointed over her shoulder because the Contessa had appeared then, saying, "What is this I hear about a broken heart?" For a woman with such loud tendencies and noisy bangles, she had a way of sneaking up on you. She cupped Ava's chin in her hand and tilted her face up. "You are not going to break the heart of my nephew, are you? This would be most distressing."

"Of course not," Ava mumbled as well as she could.

The Contessa released her chin and patted her on the head. "That is good. We would all be very sad if this were to happen."

"I think that Ava should—" Sophia began, but quick as lightning the Contessa turned and put a finger over Sophia's lips, silencing her.

"It is so pretty when it is quiet," the Contessa said. "We all agree, no?"

Everyone else, even Sam, nodded.

"I have come here to discuss my entrance for the show," she said. "I have been working with a designer, and here is what I think." She snapped her fingers and Toma, who had been lingering behind her, stepped forward with a sheath of papers. The Contessa took them and unfurled them on the kitchen island.

"Is that a dog sled?" MM asked.

Sven said, "Those are not dogs. They are the wolf pack, yes?"

The Contessa beamed at him. "He is the smart of the group. Yes, they are the wolves. Dogs, I spit on dogs."

Popcorn, who had been hiding his head beneath Ava's arm since the Contessa had arrived, started to whimper.

"You're going to arrive at the show on a wolf-drawn sleigh," Sophia said, just to make sure she understood.

The Contessa nodded. "This way the Christopher Wildwood, he will know with whom he makes the mess."

"I bet there are rules against have wolves running around Central Park," Ava said.

The Contessa snapped her fingers. "It is a minor inconvenience. We will find a way. It's good, no?" Everyone stared at her. "Good. You leave it to me, I will make it all work."

"Maybe the thing in the living room is part of her sleigh," Ava said to Popcorn now. "I didn't think of that."

Popcorn was too busy sniffing a planter to pay any attention to her. As they progressed down the street, Ava's mind wandered to the essays they'd gotten for their contest. They'd decided to ask each person to describe a very good day, one they'd had or one they'd fantasized about. The entries had ranged from hilarious to heartbreaking—a picnic with friends; getting locked in the library overnight; butterfly catching; a family dinner with no fighting; seeing a parent who had been deployed in Afghanistan for the last eighteen months; graduation; a lunch with no bullying; dusk filled with the sound of croaking frogs; a tea party; a first kiss; a goodbye kiss; singing karaoke; baking bread with a grandmother; not having to share a bed with two sisters; visiting Mars; having a chance to say sorry. . . .

They'd known their viewers were talented but they'd been blown away and humbled. They had planned to pick ten girls but even Lucille had agreed that was "completely out of the question," so they'd upped it to fifteen, with each girl wearing two looks instead of three.

Ava couldn't wait to meet them. She and Sophia had been chatting and e-mailing with all of them and they already felt like friends. They'd arrive on Wednesday for initial fittings, do follow-ups and a press meet-and-greet on Thursday, and then walk in the show on—

Ava's arm was suddenly wrenched hard and she found herself being dragged down the street at the end of Popcorn's leash. He made a sharp left at the corner, then plunged diagonally into traffic. Ava's life flashed in front of her eyes as a taxi came barreling toward her. She heard a screech of brakes on the slick, icy road, the yelp of Popcorn being crushed, and felt herself flying through the air before landing with a thud on the ground.

A ground that was strangely soft and a little squirmy. And also licking her face.

Ava opened her eyes and saw Popcorn on the pavement, unharmed, next to her. And below her, the slightly dazed, impossibly-better-looking-than-she-remembered face of Dalton. His green eyes sparkled against his winter tan and his lips were chapped and his body beneath her felt like a slab of marble.

"I should have known," she said, thinking that Popcorn wouldn't have performed those tricks for anyone else.

"Me too," he told her. "I thought you would have learned not to let your dog loose in traffic by now. You almost got him killed."

"Me? It's your fault."

He looked at her like she was crazy. "How is it possibly my fault?"

"The only reason he ran into traffic in the first place was to see you."

"Incredible," Dalton said. "You haven't changed at all."

"Neither have you," Ava shot back.

He grinned, a dazzling ear-to-ear one, and said, "Ava London, I want to kiss you so badly it's making my head spin."

Ava felt a heart pounding against her rib cage but she wasn't sure if it was hers or his. It was like none of the past few months had ever happened, not the theft, not their meeting in the park, not her kiss with Jax. Here, right here, with him, was where she should be. Where she should always have been. "Then why don't you?" she said.

"Because our legs are sticking into the middle of a busy Manhattan street and I'm afraid someone is going to run over them," he said.

Better-looking than she remembered, but still completely maddening.

LonDOs
Central Park Boathouse
Girls AS they are
Being rescued from near death
Tarte blush stick by Flaunt
Puppies who know their own minds

LonDON'Ts
Mysterious large objects in the living room with bodyguards
Saying anything you don't want the Contessa to hear
Wolf-drawn sleighs
Puppies who don't know the rules of the road

12

upper west byes

Ava had been so distracted by Dalton's presence that she'd completely forgotten they were still lying on the ground where they'd landed after the close brush with the taxi.

"You're exaggerating," she teased, scrambling off him. "You're only halfway into the street. We were also half on the sidewalk. I think you just didn't want to kiss me."

"That must have been it," he agreed, standing up and moving his neck around.

"Are you okay?" she asked, not joking now.

He looked at her in a way that made her heart slow and let her know he felt it, too. "No," he said. "I haven't been since the way things ended with you."

That brought back all the hurt and betrayal and confusion, all the reasons—pages and pages of them she kept in a secret file on her computer to remind herself—that she was glad she wasn't with him.

But she would not get emotional. She would be cool and mature about this. As cool and maturely as she could she said, "Yes, losing you was hard for me as well. Especially with the way it happened—"

"That's the worst part of it, Ava. That you believe I'd not only steal from you but set you up. At first I was so angry at the way it happened. But after some time went by, I realized I was looking at it all wrong."

Popcorn's jumping up and down around Dalton's knees, trying to get his attention, refocused their attention. "I'd better carry him," Ava said to Dalton, and bent to scoop Popcorn up. But as soon as she got him into her arms the dog squirmed into Dalton's.

"It's nice to know someone missed me," he said, cradling Popcorn in one arm and taking Ava's hand with the other.

Even though things were far from perfect between her and Dalton, she couldn't deny how good it felt to be near him again, or the jolt of electricity—not a little spark like with Jax—that shot up her arm the moment his hand touched hers. "What are you doing here?" she asked tentatively.

"Coming to see Popcorn," he told her.

Ava laughed despite herself. *Cool and mature!* a voice in her head called out. "You flew all the way to New York to see him?"

"Well, there's also this gig my band agreed to do. A favor for someone at the label. It's supposed to be good exposure, and I was hoping to reconnect with you and get a few things off my chest."

"Why now? Why not before? Why were you so"—*Cool and mature!*—"standoffish that day at the park?"

"Because my lawyer told me that you and Sophia were the ones who had accused me of stealing the money, and you were the ones pressing charges." He bent to let Popcorn jump down onto the street, but kept his leash, and didn't let go of Ava's hand. "Based on everything I was told, I thought either you two had set me up, or were covering for whoever did."

Ava was chilled. "Why would we do that? You knew how I felt about you. That makes no sense."

They paused while Popcorn sniffed a fire hydrant. "When they presented the evidence against me, it was like all reason went out the window," he said, looking at her. "Nothing made sense anymore. Because based on what they had, even I would have thought I had taken the money, except I knew I hadn't. But it looked like someone had gone to a lot of trouble to frame me. I felt like I couldn't trust anything. Or anyone."

Their fingers were twined together and they were walking next to each other as if they'd done this a dozen, a hundred times. Like this was how it was meant to be.

"I got a letter," Ava said, getting excited. "An anonymous letter delivered to our house in LA. It said you were innocent and to ask about Xavier. Who is that?"

Dalton shook his head. "Xavier? I've never heard that name before."

Ava's excitement diminished. "Why would someone frame you?"

"I don't know, and since the DA dropped the charges against me, I have the luxury of not thinking about it anymore." He glanced at her. "That just happened last week, by the way. And you were the first person I wanted to see. Listen, Ava, I can't prove I didn't steal the money, though the police seem to think I'm innocent since they dropped the case against me. But the one person whose opinion matters the most still doubts the kind of person I am, and I can't accept that. So even if this is the last time we see each other, and some other lucky guy gets to call you his girlfriend, then I guess that's the way it's meant to be. But you need to know one thing." He continued to stare into her eyes with even more intensity than usual. "I would never, *ever* steal from anyone, especially not from you. I just need you to know that."

And she did. Looking into his eyes, she knew in the deepest part of her that he was telling the truth. "I believe you, Dalton. But why didn't you call? Or text?" she asked.

He smiled sheepishly. "I missed you too much for that." His arm came around her waist and her head rested on his shoulder. "And I guess I was also a little afraid that if I called or texted, you'd tell me to get lost. Or that you were seeing someone else. Or that you changed your mind."

"Even when I tried not to, I couldn't get you off my mind," Ava told him, tugging at a thread in his scarf. "I've missed you more than you know."

He pulled her closer and she felt his lips on the top of her head. They walked on that way, back toward the apartment, not talking, just being together, and Ava felt like she was floating on a sea of pure happiness.

"There were nights when I was in prison that I dreamed of the way your hair smelled," he told her. "That's how I got through it."

She pressed closer to him. They were approaching her door and she tipped her face up to say, "You said you and your band were playing a gig. Can I come?"

"I'm not sure of the protocol but I assume you can," he said. "It's a weird thing. We're doing the music for some designer's show. Christopher Wildman?"

"Wildwood," Ava said, pulling away from Dalton.

"So you've heard of him," he said.

Ava gaped.

"Did I say something wrong?" he asked. When she didn't talk but just kept gaping, he appealed to Popcorn. "What did I say?"

"Christopher Wildwood is the man who is trying to ruin our lives," Ava told him succinctly. "The number-one enemy. He who shall not be named."

"We'll pull out of the gig then," he said. "That's no problem. I really took it only for the excuse to come to New York and see you."

That made Ava gulp. "But you said it was good exposure for the band."

"We can expose ourselves some other way. I know how it feels to have someone trying to ruin your life. No way am I helping out your arch nemesis."

Ava said, "I can't ask you to pull out—"

"You don't have to. Consider it done."

"No," Ava told him. "If you really want to help, keep the gig and let us know what he's doing. We still haven't been able to figure out how he got our designs. Maybe having someone on the inside—"

"Say no more. I'll be your eyes and ears." They stood facing each other, noses nearly touching. "Although right now I have to say, I'm more interested in your lips."

"You still haven't kissed me," Ava reminded him. "Was that all just talk back there?"

He brushed his nose across hers and their lips touched.

It was like a lightning bolt went off between them, pulling them slightly apart. "I've never—" Dalton said.

"Me either," Ava agreed, bringing her fingers to her lips.

"Let's do it again and see—" Dalton broke off, frowning. "Your bottom is vibrating."

"The meeting!" Ava said, slapping her hand over her mouth. "I completely forgot." She pulled her phone out and saw it was five after ten. "I have to go," she told him. "The Contessa is crazy about promptness. But we can pick up here, where we left off, soon, can't we?"

He was laughing at her. "We can."

"Right. Good. Um, 'bye. Nice seeing you again."

"Nice seeing you too," Dalton called as she ran toward the entrance of the building. "Wait a second, aren't you forgetting something?"

"I told you I'll kiss you later," she yelled over her shoulder and heard him laugh.

"I meant your dog," Dalton said, coming up and handing her the leash. "I'll wait on the kiss."

Her cheeks were already burning and she felt them get even redder when she passed the doorman and saw him trying not to laugh. Riding up in the elevator, she glanced at Popcorn and could have sworn he was smiling.

But Ava worked hard to repress her smile as she walked into the living room. Everyone was gathered around the large, draped item, except the Contessa.

"She wanted to make an entrance," Sophia explained.

"I'm sorry," Ava said. "I ran into an old friend on the street and got distracted."

"By 'run into,' do you mean literally?" MM asked, pointing to the smears of dirt on her knees and on Popcorn's face.

"Yes." Ava nodded.

Sophia's face went white. "Are you both okay? Are you hurt? Was there an accident?"

"I'm better than okay," Ava said. "And we now have a spy inside of Christopher Wildwood's studio."

Suddenly the Contessa was there, dressed in a gold pants suit.

She clapped her hands for silence, then looked from one to the other of them to make sure they were all paying attention. "We have come the long way," she said. "We have survived many cruel twists of fate. And to commemorate now I present to you—" She whipped off the cloth, revealing a six-foot-wide, four-foot-tall clock set to four days, five hours, and forty-nine minutes. "The final countdown."

When the Contessa was finished, Sophia turned to Ava. "What did you mean about a spy in Christopher Wildwood's studio?"

"It's Dalton," Ava told her.

"*Your* Dalton?" Sophia asked.

"In *New York*?" MM followed.

"On the *street*?" Lily said.

"Who's Dalton?" Sam asked from behind the camera, but Lily glared him into silence.

"Yes, yes, and yes," Ava answered. "And his band is playing at Christopher Wildwood's show."

"What is this interesting person you speak about?" the Contessa asked them. "*Your* Dalton. I want to know all. I am, after all, a biff." She smiled at Ava winningly. "And for your protection. So close to the day of the fashion show it would be *tragico* if the count, he had the second thoughts."

LonDOs:
Dalton
The DA dropping the charges
Boys who take gigs just to see you
Puppies who smile

Puppies who are going to the groomer
Chests for leaning heads against
Lemon-peppermint conditioner

LonDON'Ts:
Put off kissing someone until later
Make pacts with the Contessa
Countdown clocks that tick loudly enough to be heard in your
    bedroom
Counts
Muddy paw prints on the black carpeting

13
bright lights, big party

The limo drove from the apartment down Broadway, through the middle of Times Square on the way to the Fashion Week opening party. Sophia, curled on the seat, stared out the window and found herself smiling at the lights and the sheer energy of it. The sounds of Lily's, Ava's, MM's, Sven's, and Sam's voices were a soothing backdrop to her thoughts.

How long had it been since she'd just sat and thought? she wondered. She looked down at her hands and was surprised, again, to see them empty. No phone. Nothing to check. There would be no messages. No texts. Hunter had—

Hold yourself together, she cautioned. *This is not something you want to share.*

She saw the Hershey's store, an ad for the national parks, a billboard showing people standing across the street waving, a butterfly turning into underwear, and the Naked Cowboy with his guitar, every surface pulsing and blinking and clamoring for her attention. Attention she was only too happy to give.

It wasn't just Hunter who wouldn't be texting. She still hadn't heard from Giovanni. Which was only what she'd expected. And completely fine since she'd decided she would have to tell him she was seeing someone else and couldn't continue their friendship. She'd composed the text a dozen times in her head, hating the sound of it, but given where things were with Hunter, it had seemed like the correct thing to do.

Seemed, she repeated to herself. *Correct thing to do.* With ideas like those, no wonder Ava had hated being her so much.

And no wonder Giovanni hadn't texted her.

She glanced down the limo toward her at exactly the moment that Ava looked in her direction. That happened when they were in sync, and for the past few days, since Ava's afternoon in Central Park, they'd been completely in step, finishing each other's sentences, filling in blanks. It was an amazing feeling, having a real partner, someone you knew you could trust without reservation.

It made what had happened with Hunter that much more jarring.

Don't think about it now, she told herself, shifting her attention back to Ava. She didn't want to spoil her sister's good mood.

Because when Ava had come in from walking Popcorn she'd appeared—happy, Sophia thought. Simply, blissfully, completely happy. In a way she hadn't seen for months.

And Sophia had known, even before Ava said a word, that it had to do with Dalton. No one else came close to making her look that way, not even the guy who'd perked up her mood at the zoo. She seemed happier that afternoon, but Dalton made her positively glow.

"So he came to New York just to see you," MM had summarized after Ava finished telling them about her meeting with Dalton. "As soon as his name was cleared. Adorable."

Sophia couldn't have agreed more. Even the Contessa seemed moved. "Not only is he in New York but he comes in and swoops, like the hero, saving your life," she'd said. "Wow. It is like something from a movie."

"It really was," Ava had admitted.

And then the Contessa had put on her most serious face and said, "Of course we are not fooled."

"Fooled?" Ava asked. Sophia had seen the flutter of panic in her eyes, the way her brows contracted.

"But yes." The Contessa looked at all of them incredulously. "It is so obvious this is all part of the plot." When none of them said anything, she went on. "You do not see? Even you, the smart of the group?" She pointed at Sven.

Sven shook his head.

Sophia had felt desperate to stop whatever the Contessa was doing. "Dalton is a friend. He would never do anything to hurt us."

"Yet, as you say, he was convinced you had been hurting him?" The Contessa gave her a frank, open gaze. "And what was it, this very moving line you related? 'I know what it is like to have someone try to ruin your life.' Very exciting." The Contessa nodded. "Only ask yourself, what would he not do to punish the two people he thought tried to ruin his?"

"But he doesn't think we ruined his life," Ava protested. "He said he knew that wasn't true."

"Blah blah blah." The Contessa waved it away. "He would say just this if he were trying to win your trust, no? And did it not strike you as too smooth as silk, him announcing he does not care who put him into prison? Now that it is over, he wishes only to move on with his life. *Pfui,*" the Contessa said. "No one is that good at forgiving."

"Maybe you're not," Sophia had insisted. "But Dalton could be."

The Contessa turned up a hand. "Also, he is already accused of being the thief."

"And let off," Lily pointed out.

"Not to mention, we were arrested for the same crime," Sophia said. "So if you're going to hold it against him, you have to hold it against Ava and me as well."

The Contessa raised her arms in a gesture of surrender. "Perhaps you are right. Perhaps he is the saint in wolf's clothing. But me, I do not chose to take this chance. And I know also that Ava, she is a serious girl. A serious girl would not take this chance."

For the first time her eyes moved to Ava. "I know you know what to do. I know I do not need to watch you with the eye of a hawk to make sure you do not see him. Or put the little bug on your phone to make sure you do not talk to him. Or have the camera in your room to make sure you do not see him on the computer. Of course I can do all of these things, but why would I need to? You are serious girl." She patted Ava's cheek. "I can trust you, no?"

"No—yes," Ava said. "You can trust me."

"You are thinking now only of Fashion Week, but I see more. I am confident you will fall the head over feet for my nephew and him for you and all will be well. The manufacturing, the licensing. We will have much happiness together as a family. We do not discuss now the future, we only mention it so you can think a bit."

"Think a bit," the Contessa had prescribed. And Ava had, all afternoon. Sophia had seen it as they went over the order of the outfits for the show, observed Ava half there but half somewhere else as Lily made sketches of the stage. Ava had momentarily snapped out of it as she watched the whole thing in motion, and when she'd rushed to hug Lily and tell her it was brilliant, Sophia had known that there was no Dalton, no trace of the Contessa's injunction to think on her mind.

But it was as they were getting ready she had said to Sophia, "It's obvious that what I have to do is let Dalton go."

Sophia heard the ache in Ava's voice, saw the pain of her heart breaking all over again. "There must be another option."

Ava shook her head and Sophia made out the tears there, waiting to fall. "If I don't, I'd just be stringing him along for who knows how long while the Contessa played her games—with us, and, worse, with him. But if I don't see him or talk to him, then he'll be safe." She took three quick breaths and tried to muster a smile then. "Besides, when I'm with him I can't think straight, and we don't have time for that right now."

Go think about it. The words echoed in Sophia's mind, snippets from a different conversation, but interchangeable in the pain they caused.

"That's what I'm going to do. Go think about it," Hunter had said in a strange, manic-sounding voice right before hanging up on her. Two days earlier. Forty-eight hours. The last time she'd heard from him.

The conversation hadn't started any better, but she'd been expecting that. It was natural that he'd be defensive at first when she brought up changing patterns of behavior he was comfortable with. It would be hard for him to hear how finding them creeping into her relationship with Ava had made her realize how toxic they were. But his defensiveness would wear off as they talked, as he saw she wasn't attacking him, she thought.

Instead they'd just gone around and around in a circle, making no progress, his position becoming more rigid and his tone more brittle with each rotation.

He'd said with a sneer, "So you're saying you want to hear from me less. Fine. I know what that means."

"No, sweetheart," she'd answered. "I want to hear from you whenever you have something to say. But I don't want either of us to feel tethered to a schedule. Or to your past. I'm sorry your mother left. But by trying to work that out through our relationship, you risk pushing me away."

"That sounds like a threat," he'd said.

"It's not. It's my attempt to make things between us stronger."

"By talking to me less?" he demanded, sarcastic. "Interacting with me less? Are you going to improve our romantic life by making out with me less? Or your attractiveness by wearing push-up bras less?"

"You're taking this the wrong way and being mean."

"Tell me how I'm supposed to take it when my girlfriend says she's going to stop answering my calls," he'd said, snarling.

"That's not what I said. I said that I'm not helping you by playing into your fear of abandonment," she told him. "I'm just letting that fear continue. I'm nurturing it. I'd rather help you get over it."

"You don't know what you're talking about."

"Maybe not," Sophia said. "But I know I'd be a better girlfriend if I could spend more time thinking about you, and less time thinking about *calling* you."

"That doesn't even make sense," he'd said.

"It would if you stopped to think about it."

And then his final foray: "You know what? That's what I'm going to do. Go think about it."

She'd left him alone the first day. But she'd called him that morning and been bounced straight to voice mail. Her texts had gone unanswered, too.

He was just taking time to think about things, she told herself. Because when she thought about it, really considered that it might be the end for them, she became shaky and felt like the world was tipping.

It's not, she assured herself. *This is just a bump. It's healthy for him to think. You'll come out the other side stronger.*

But there was part of her that wished she'd never brought it up. That cursed herself for not being able to just stay safely in the box he'd put her in.

MM's voice saying, "Places everyone," pulled her from her thoughts. Harper's assistant, who was riding up front, would be on the ground, shepherding them through the press gauntlet on what Harper referred to simply as The Rug, while Harper directed her through an earpiece from an elevated observation spot she'd staked out hours earlier.

The Contessa had already been there delighting and confusing the press with her *blah blah* for the last hour, "so they're primed for you," Harper's assistant reported.

"It's 7:07," Lily announced as the limo made the front of the line. "Synchronize your watches."

"Why?" Ava asked.

"Because you never know," Lily said leadingly as she opened the car door, letting in a blast of sound, and plunged into the crowd.

MM went after her, then Sven, then Sam.

"You will never experience this—knowing as little as you know, being as unscathed and unsuspecting as you are—again," Lucille Rexford had called to tell them earlier. "Cherish it."

She was right, Sophia thought. And no thoughts of any guy were going to get in the way of that.

"Ready?" she asked Ava.

"No." Ava shook her head. "You?"

"Nope."

Ava looked at her and winked. "Let's leap."

They stepped out of the limo and into a bright flash of bulbs that seemed to freeze the moment in time, etching it into Sophia's mind. The two of them, smiling at each other, every kind of adventure ahead of them.

It was 7:08 when they stepped onto The Rug.

At 7:29 their world shattered.

LonDOs:

Synchronize your watches

Cherish what you don't know

Lily's sketches of the fashion show

MM's styling for the party

Leap before you look

Eat before you leap

Mini hot dogs wrapped in puff pastry

MAC false lashes

The Rug

How cute Popcorn and Charming will be when they get back from the pet spa

LonDON'Ts:

Crying in limos

Staying trapped even if it's easier

Defensiveness

Offensiveness

14
meanpacking district

Pinkies linked, Ava and Sophia walked up the main red carpet, then went left to The Rug, where all the reporters were arrayed against the long step-and-repeat backdrop.

It was like some kind of crazy forest, microphones and cameras and lights making little groves around each reporter. Celebrities passed through, guided by their publicists, toward one crew and away from another, while reporters would sometimes avert their gaze or turn to reapply their makeup if a guest they weren't interested in appeared.

Sophia and Ava were sought out by everyone, because everyone was excited to discuss—and possibly expedite—their demise. They had dared to go up against Christopher Wildwood, an icon in the fashion world, and they were going to be made to pay.

The first question from their first reporter was, "Aren't you embarrassed to be here when everyone thinks you're frauds?"

"We're excited to prove them wrong," Sophia told her.

The same reporter followed up with, "Isn't it madness to cast models without seeing them?"

This one was Ava's. "Only if you're afraid of what your clothes look like. If you think they'll only work on models and can't stand up to the challenge of being worn by real people."

That pretty much set the tone for the first interviews, but Ava and Sophia were prepared.

"Ninety seconds per interview is the maximum," Harper had explained to them earlier that day. "They'll never use more than thirty-five seconds tops, so anything else is a waste. When you're done, you have thirty seconds to get into position for the next one. So two minutes total, per reporter. No matter how bad it gets, it will never last longer than that. The Rug can be brutal, but it's also quick."

"It always reminds me of miniature golf," Lily had said.

Harper had laughed. "If only it were that civilized."

They'd run questions as they dressed, practicing timing with a stop watch. "My sister and I are so excited to share our collection with the—"

"Too long," Harper had said, her eye on the watch.

Sophia started again. "Ava and I are so excited to show our—"

"*Beep.*" Harper cut her off.

"Sophia and I can't wait for people to see what we can do," Ava tried.

"Four seconds," Harper had reported. "Perfect, love."

Their second interview was nearly a carbon copy of the first, except the reporter this time was a man, and at the end he added, "I just got done talking with the ridonculous Whitney Frost. She disclosed in an Exclusive"—here he made an E with his fingers—"that she is *the* celebrity model in Christopher Wildwood's show. Does that stir any strong feelings given your shared Liam history?" He tipped his head to one side and looked at Ava expectantly, and Sophia found herself thinking that if this had been miniature golf, he would have been a gnome.

"As a fan, and a friend, I'm just glad Whitney is getting work," Ava told the gnome with a big, genuine smile.

From behind the reporter's cameraman, Lily gave her a thumbs-up.

Whitney Frost, Liam's ex-girlfriend and Hollywood alternative it girl, had decided months earlier that Ava and Sophia were rivals and had gone out of her way since then to create drama where there wasn't any. When they started on The Rug she was one person ahead of them, but by the third interview the other person had dropped out and they ended up right behind her.

Ava and Sophia were doing their best to ignore her, even though, as Lily pointed out, she was wearing the dress Ava had shown the oversight committee, but Whitney spotted them during her interview and began pointing in their direction.

Sophia was answering the question about what insanity it was for them to use real people instead of models for the third time, when Whitney pointed in their direction and said loudly, "Those two. The Londons. They're precisely what I mean about the death of fashion, and what I'm trying to help dear Christopher to remedy. If I can do one thing in this life, I hope it's save fashion from the likes of them."

As they waited for their fourth interview to begin it took all of Sophia's self-control not to laugh when she heard Whitney say, "No, *glam*ifarian. That means I consider fashion the prime material, the meat, the very marrow of self-expression. Fashion is the asterisk where art meets design, beauty meets courage, a true scholarly medium that can really only be grasped by the cognoscenti."

"I wonder if those words make sense even to her," Sophia mused.

Ava sighed. "It wouldn't be so bad if she weren't wearing a dress we designed."

"It would still be bad," Sophia said.

"Yes, but all her blah blah Glamifarian"—Ava shuddered—"wouldn't be as hard to stomach."

"I beg your pardon?" the reporter said. "Did you say the dress she's wearing is your design? Because she told me it was part of Christopher Wildwood's new line, the one we'll be seeing her wear on the catwalk."

Sophia and Ava's eyes locked, each of them asking the other the same question. Sophia raised her eyebrows, which Ava knew meant, *If you want to.* Ava smiled, which Sophia knew meant, *You bet I do.*

Ava turned to the reporter. "I did. The dress is our design. Only our version hangs better because—do you see, Sophia, how they didn't get the back quite right?"

The cameras all swiveled to Whitney, who shot them a quizzical smile over her shoulder, then went back to her interview.

"The photos they stole the design from must not have shown the back," Sophia said.

"That's quite an accusation to be making here," the reporter told them.

"Then you must be very lucky to have gotten it first," Ava said.

The reporter asked them for more details, forgetting entirely to humiliate them or wonder aloud if they were crazy.

Their next interviewer opened with, "You've been referred to as frauds, hacks, and even thieves. Why should—" but stopped halfway through when she noticed that Ava's eyes were somewhere beyond her. "You seem distracted, Miss London. Am I boring you? Is there somewhere you'd rather be?"

"I'm sorry," Sophia stepped in to say, looking as contrite as possible. "My sister is just upset about Whitney Frost. Or I should say what she's wearing. "

"It's from the collection Chris Wildwood is showing this week," the reporter said.

"But it's our design," Ava chimed in then. Only slightly—" She paused, looking for a word.

"'Off'?" Sophia offered.

"Exactly." Ava leaned close to Sophia and, apparently forgetting the reporter, said, "For one thing, they didn't understand the placket. See? They just made it a pleat, totally missing that there is actually a pocket there at the waist."

Before Sophia could answer, the reporter put in, "That's one of the most common differences between an original and a knockoff. Things like pockets are hard to see in a photo, which is usually what the copies are based on. If someone has their hand in the pocket, okay, but if the dress was on a dummy when it was photographed, you'd never know it was there."

"You're right," Ava said with keen interest.

"If you could locate a photo of your dress where that detail isn't clearly shown, you might be able to trace how the design was poached," the reporter went on enthusiastically.

"That's a great idea," Sophia told her. "Thank you." She wondered if the reporter realized she'd essentially just told her audience that Christopher Wildwood was a thief.

The woman glanced at her questions and frowned. "Most of these don't seem very relevant." She thought for a moment and then said, as if paraphrasing, "Some people say that you are taking a risk casting unknowns without seeing them. I can tell you two have your own point of view. What would you say to your detractors?"

In their sixth interview they drew attention to the fact that the trim on the dress had been moved from the waist to the hem. "Just like we moved it three weeks ago," Ava mused.

"But when the oversight committee showed us the pictures of Christopher Wildwood's version, the trim was still in the old place," Sophia reminded her. "Do you think one of them could have leaked our idea?"

"Are you accusing the oversight committee of impropriety?" the reporter asked, and Sophia had the uncomfortable idea she was licking her chops.

"Of course not," Ava said earnestly.

Sophia gave the reporter a worried smile. "Sometimes we forget everything is on the record. It just seems strange, doesn't it, that Mr. Wildwood would move the trim to exactly the place we have it, after they'd been to see it?"

"It's sort of brave," Ava said, "devil-may-care. He clearly thinks he's going to get away with it."

The finger-pointing went back and forth, Whitney saying in louder and louder tones that it was her responsibility as a style icon and Glamifarian to save fashion from the London sisters, Ava and Sophia meticulously documenting the mistakes in the dress she was wearing, acting more confidential with every reporter, letting each one feel like he or she was getting scoop.

"This is amazing," their seventh interviewer said as she looked at a photo of their design on Sophia's phone. "You're right—every difference you're mentioning could have come from copying a picture just like this. Do you mind if we film the image? I want to get this on camera."

At 7:24 Whitney stalked off The Rug, saying she had a head-ache, but as if by some unspoken signal everyone had decided Ava and Sophia weren't the enemy after all, and even without her dress to comment on, their next interviews were much friend-lier than their first ones.

In their ninth, the question that had started off as, "Isn't it madness to cast your show without seeing the models?" had be-come, "I know everyone is excited about your decision to cast your show blind, based on essays from your viewers. What would you say was the biggest challenge of that process?"

"Picking," Ava answered, glad finally to have something in-teresting to talk about. "We got over five thousand entries and nearly all of them were outstanding."

"When you say nearly all, which ones weren't?" the male re-porter followed up.

"The ones with headshots," Sophia told him. "And the ones offering us money."

After their tenth interview, Sophia turned to Ava and said, "Just to be clear, did that reporter refer to us as the future of fashion?"

"I think he did. Amazing what a difference"—Ava checked her phone and saw that it was 7:27—"nineteen minutes can make."

The eleventh reporter was probably the most even-handed. "There was a lot of talk initially about the challenges of using real-girl models," he said. "What do you see as the pluses?"

"Our entire approach is about teamwork," Sophia told him. "Since we first started putting up vlogs, input from our follow-ers has played a part in all our decisions. It's like having a really big—"

"Opinionated—" Ava put in.

"*Smart* family." Sophia gave Ava an amused glance. "Incorporating the people whose input has helped us into the launch of our line just feels right. Ava and I have designed all the clothes and made every prototype by hand, but we would be nowhere without our friends and supporters. Unlike other designers who promote themselves as if they are the brand, we know we are only as good as our collaborations, and we want to honor, not hide, their impact."

Behind the camera, Lily made a heart with her hands

"It's also going to make our show fun," Ava said. "Real fun, not smile-for-the-cameras fun. Because when your models *are* your customers, the line between the show and the audience gets blurry. So we have to make sure that being in the show is as fun as watching it."

"And vice versa," Sophia said. "Although that might not be possible."

The reporter said, "I've heard that from many designers over the years but with you two I'm— What the *hell*?"

A low rumble came from the direction of the main red carpet, a combination of shouts and shrieks, and the crowd splintered, scattering to either side of the carpet.

The commotion rolled toward them on a wave of screams and crashes as people threw themselves into the thicket of cameras to avoid the blurry object rocketing down the center of The Rug. Sophia dragged Ava to one side, but the object skidded to a stop in front of them. It was a bike messenger, who glanced at a notepad attached to his wrist and then at them.

"London, A or S?" he asked with a growl.

Sophia nodded. "Yes."

He shoved a white business envelope into her hands and, without waiting for her to sign a receipt, took off.

A security guard barreled through the cameras and dived to

grab the back of the bike, was dragged three feet, and let go, yelping as his chin caught the back tire before hitting the floor.

"Someone stop him," a reporter farther down The Rug yelled, but the messenger was already catching air over a planter and gone before anyone had even given chase.

An uneasy silence was followed by a smattering of applause, as though people weren't sure if that had been a piece of performance art or guerrilla marketing, and the regular babble of voices started up again.

The security guard limped to Ava and Sophia. "You responsible for that?" he demanded. "Can't just stage stunts without prior approval."

Sophia shook her head. "I have no idea what that was about."

"Try opening your letter," he told her.

Sophia looked at the envelope as though she'd forgotten she was holding it. There was a slight bulge in one corner, as though someone had written a note and taped a key to it, but there was no address on the outside or other marks of any kind.

The reporter they'd been in the middle of the interview with ordered his cameraman to zoom in on the envelope and every other crew within earshot crowded around.

"Maybe it's the credentials for Fashion Week that Lucille was working on," Ava said.

It seemed a bit showy for Lucille Rexford, Sophia thought, to have them delivered by bike messenger in the middle of an event on the red carpet, but you never knew.

Sophia tugged the flap open. Inside was a single piece of paper and two strips of leather that looked like—

Sophia glanced at the paper, held it toward Ava, saying, "I'm afraid it's not our credentials," gasped, and turned away from the cameras.

Pet collars.

"No!" Ava cried, staring from them to the letter. "Oh my god, someone has kidnapped Popcorn and Charming."

LonDOs:
Keeping your answers short
Honoring real people
Paying attention to what others are wearing
Paying even closer attention to bike messengers
Airbrush foundation
911

LonDON'Ts
Fashion only for the cognoscenti
Supercilious interviewers
Stealing
Cruelty to animals
Cruelty to animal lovers

15
furryous

"IF YOU WANT TO SEE YOUR SPOILED RATS AGAIN, HAVE \$100,000 READY AND WAIT FOR FURTHER INSTRUCTIONS," the laser-printed note said.

The Contessa was in consultation with the police while Sophia and Ava went from one news crew to another, showing the note and making impassioned pleas for the return of Popcorn and Charming.

Ava's mind was racing with questions but she tried to stay focused and sound sane when talking to reporters. She pulled up a picture of Popcorn and Charming on her phone and showed it to the cameras, but she couldn't bare to look at it herself.

Her phone had been bouncing in her pocket like a living thing with texts and tweets and Facebook messages of support but she felt it jiggle differently now and realized it was ringing.

She looked at it and saw that it was Jax. She hesitated for a moment, then sent him to voice mail.

Almost immediately it rang again. This time Dalton's name flashed on the screen. Without thinking, she answered.

"Ava, I just heard. I'm so sorry," he said.

Hearing his voice made her feel like someone had wrapped strong arms around her. She felt herself relaxing, felt her breathing slowing down. "Thank you. I know it's—I can't even put it into words."

"Of course not. Listen, I can be there in twenty minutes. Will you still be there or should I meet you at your apartment?"

Every inch of her wanted to tell him to meet her at the apartment. Every part of her longed just to be next to him, to feel his palm against hers, to be able to look up into his eyes. The Contessa would have to understand, she told herself. At least for tonight.

And what about tomorrow? When you say thanks for the support, I can't see you anymore, let's never speak again?

You can't do that. You can't see him. You shouldn't even be talking to him.

"I—I'm not sure," she said. She felt like someone was sucking the breath out of her. "It's probably better if you—" she had to squeeze her eyes shut and force the words out. "If you don't come by."

There was a long pause. "Okay." Another pause. "Are you sure?"

She nodded violently, not able to trust her voice, but she realized he couldn't see her nod. "Yes," she bit out. "Sure. I . . . gotta go, bye."

"Ava, I—"

She hung up and, wrapping her arms around her middle, turned away from the cameras and felt tears on her cheeks.

Dammit, she thought. *I should not be crying.* She should never have answered the phone, should never have let herself hear his voice. The thought that under other circumstances he could have been with her, would have rushed to her side and stood close, waiting to wrap his arms around her and support her and hold her and let her cry on his sweater, made her stomach crunch into a knot and her chest ache.

Enough, she told herself. *No more pity party.* She was just drying the tears off her face with the sleeve of a jacket someone had put over her shoulders when she heard a man behind her say, "Those London sisters have to be the two luckiest girls in the world. You can't buy publicity like this."

Ava swung around, fists clenched to punch the guy, but before she got there a familiar voice said, "And you wouldn't want to, moron," and Hunter appeared, pushing his way through the crowd.

Ava may have envied how much of Sophia's time he got, but she still adored him, and seeing his strong, decisive face made her instantly feel better. She didn't even think to wonder what he was doing there when he was supposed to be in LA. They hugged, he said, "Don't worry, we'll find them," and then went to where Sophia was giving an interview.

Ava watched as Sophia's interview ended and she turned and saw Hunter for the first time. Her face lit up even through the tears and she threw herself into his arms.

"You came," Ava heard Sophia say. "My Prince Charming."

"Always," Hunter answered. "I just missed you too much."

Ava approached them. "If you want to go home and spend some time together, I can finish the interviews," she said.

Sophia shook her head. "Absolutely not." Her hug with Hunter had made her hair come loose, and between that and the fiercely determined gleam in her eyes, she looked like an ancient goddess of revenge. "I won't rest. I'm going to find them. And they are going to pay."

"No Kitten Around, Sleeping Beauty Says Petnappers Will Pay."

"Fur Flies at Fashion Week Opener."

"Fur-or Over Furry Friends."

"This City Is Going to the Dogs! Petnapping at Prestigious Party."

Lily read each of the headlines from the New York morning papers aloud in a different voice, then pushed them across the kitchen island toward MM and Sven. "Not bad, but it's the photo that really makes the story."

Pretty much every article featured the same picture of Sophia looking gorgeous and furious simultaneously. Their parents in Georgia had called that morning at eight, worried that their daughters were in trouble and that New York City just wasn't a safe enough place for them. Ava spent the next hour reassuring them that she and Sophia weren't in serious danger and were confident about getting Charming and Popcorn back.

Only they weren't. When they'd gotten home the night before, the Contessa had revealed that she would be happy to give them the ransom money, except that she didn't have it. "After the show, yes, this will not be a problem, but today, right now, we are, as you say, at the bottom of the bank account." And there was no way Ava and Sophia could get the money on their own. Which meant their one chance was to figure out who the kidnappers were and rescue Charming and Popcorn themselves.

After getting off the phone, Ava had padded to the kitchen and found everyone but Hunter already there, having breakfast.

She was halfway through a bowl of frosted flakes when her phone rang again.

"Unknown number," Ava announced, and Sophia, Lily, MM, Sven, and Sam froze, all wondering the same thing: if it was the kidnappers with instructions about getting their pets back. She hit Speakerphone. "Hello?"

"Ava? It's Dalton."

Everyone got very busy with their breakfast again.

"Oh," she said, trying for a relaxed, what-no-you-don't-make-my-heart-pound tone as she took him off speakerphone and slipped from the kitchen to the long, formal dining room that adjoined it. "We thought you might be the kidnapper. I mean, we didn't think you were, but this came from an unknown number so it seemed like it could be them calling."

"I completely understand," he said. "Have there been any new developments?"

Ava wondered if Toma had done something strange to the wiring in the room because Dalton's voice sounded kind of strange and nasal. "No," she said.

"I felt really bad not being able to support you last night."

Ava felt like a piece of her heart had chipped off. "That is the nicest thing you could have said."

"It just means you have to let me help today. When can I come by?"

Looking down at Popcorn's favorite toy lying sadly on the rug, she wanted to say, *Right now. This second.*

But that was impossible. She glanced through the door back into the kitchen and saw that everyone was busy with their own thing but she was still standing on the phone with Dalton in the middle of the Contessa's territory. That was like putting a bull's-eye on herself and thinking she could pass as a spectator at a darts contest. She needed to get him off the phone.

"That's really kind of you to offer," she said, trying to sound nice but not too nice. "But I think it's probably better if you don't. And I'm afraid I have to go now."

"Wait, Ava." He sounded confused and short of breath. "Is there someone there? Is that why you seem so—"

"Bye."

Her insides ached when she hung up, as though she'd eaten broken glass, and she realized she would rather have done that than treated him that way.

You have no choice, she told herself. *This is kinder than the alternative.*

She went to her room to wash her face and when she came out she found everyone in the living room. The countdown clock had been pushed to one side and in its place was a whiteboard.

"We need a board that we can put pictures on and write on and run pieces of red thread around," Lily had said the night before when they got back from the party. "Since the police have made it clear they're going to be useless."

"Is that something you learned from reading *Town & Country*?" Sam had asked.

"No, New Dork City, it's according to Lily van Aden."

"I stopped wearing my Doc Martens," he'd said. "Do I still have to have the nickname?"

"If the shoe fits."

"But that's the point—" he had started.

"What is the red thread for?" Ava had asked.

"I don't know. We'll see when we get there, won't we?"

Now Lily was standing in front of the board, red thread, magnetic tacks, and a box of markers neatly laid out next to her. She uncapped a pen and wrote "IT" and "NOT IT" at the top of the whiteboard. Under "NOT IT" she wrote, "Present company because we were all together at the time of the kidnapping."

They knew exactly when that was because the Contessa's building had an extensive closed-circuit camera system as well as three doormen. Both the human and electronic monitors had recorded a man in a Pet Sanctuary windbreaker entering the building at 2:03 P.M. Lily had told the doorman that someone from Pet Sanctuary was coming to pick up Popcorn and Charming, so they'd let him up. Twelve minutes later he'd been back with Popcorn and Charming.

All three doormen agreed that he was young, Caucasian, a little overweight, and wore glasses and a baseball cap. If he'd been trying to make himself hard for the security cameras to capture, he couldn't have done a better job. The cap meant it was hard to see more than the lower half of his face, and if you did, the glasses reflected the light, blurring the image.

"I called the spa and they said no one matching the description I gave works there. They also told me the appointment I had made was canceled," Lily said now, sniffing the tip of the marker.

"Don't worry," MM whispered to Ava, "I bought the child-safe ones."

Lily looked at the marker. "These used to smell much better."

No one was sure when the Contessa had arrived but she was suddenly there, one hand on her hip, standing next to Lily at the whiteboard. She was wearing brown trousers and a brown cowl-neck sweater, both of which had red hearts printed all over them.

"It is a very good thing I am here," the Contessa said. "We have fun making the scribbles on the board of course. But now we will be the serious people." Ava groaned but the Contessa ignored it. "Of course it is obvious who did this thing."

"It is?" Sophia asked.

"I think this over all night. To take pets, it's very personal.

This is not a thing you do for money. This is done to distract you. Destroy your confidence."

"How does assuming it's personal make everything obvious?" Sophia said.

"It means we are not asking, 'Who in all New York City would take our pretty babies?'" the Contessa explained. "It means we are asking, 'Who in all New York City would like to rip our heart out and watch us suffer?'"

"I really can't think of anyone who would go to all that trouble," Ava told her. "All anyone who wanted to hurt us would have to do is go online and make an insulting video about us, or even slam us in our own comments section."

The Contessa rolled her eyes. "You're not thinking. It is your Dalton of course. He tells you practically, 'I am here to get revenge and rip your heart out.' And then he does it."

"He said the opposite, actually," Ava told her. "Pretty much word-for-word. And he would never hurt an animal. Especially not Popcorn or Charming."

The Contessa shook her head. "You are blinded by his pretty face. This is why it is so good I am here to save you from the unhappiness by fixing you up with my nephew. What you would do without me, having your best interests in my heart, it makes me shudder to think of it." She shuddered once, recovered, and pointed at Lily. "Write 'Your Dalton' for IT."

"It's not Dalton, Contessa," Ava said, sagging dejectedly against the couch. "He isn't overweight, doesn't stoop, and looks nothing at all like the guy who took Popcorn and Charming." She lifted her head and let it loll from one side of the couch to the other. "Would anyone besides me like a cyanide pill? I mean some coffee? I could use a break."

"Wait a second," Hunter said, breezing into the room then.

He slid onto the couch next to Sophia and wrapped his hand around hers.

"Where have you been?" she asked. "You were gone when I got up."

He nodded. "This morning I started thinking, How did this guy get the Pet Sanctuary jacket? Because that's the key to the whole thing, right? Without it he never could have gotten into the apartment or taken the kids. So I decided to pay the pet spa a visit."

Sophia's expression was a combination of amazed and impressed. "What did you learn?"

"That the person who called to cancel Popcorn and Charming's appointments was a woman," Hunter said. "And so was the person who offered one of the employees five hundred dollars to borrow his jacket for a few hours."

Ava stared at him. "Are you saying a *woman* kidnapped our pets?"

Hunter nodded. "And from the smell lingering on the collar of the windbreaker she borrowed, a woman who wears Parfum Celeste 123."

"But I wear that," the Contessa said. "Although really it is for the summer. *Bene,* this proves what I say, that the taking of the babies is not done for money. If you can afford this perfume, you are not going to do kidnapping."

"So it's not just a woman but a *rich* woman who kidnapped our dog and cat," Sophia elaborated.

MM said, "Which would mean the hat and glasses the kidnapper was wearing were a disguise."

"Yes, yes, I do this sometimes when I go to the Whole Foods," the Contessa told them excitedly. "Since they get so picky with their door policy. No you can't come in we have told you before blah blah. Who do they think it is, a nightclub?"

"This means it's not Dalton," Ava put in. "Since among other things he's not a woman."

But no one seemed to be paying any attention to her. Sophia shook her head. "None of this makes any sense. What woman hates us so much that she'd dress up like a man and kidnap a kitten and a puppy?"

Lily turned to write something on the board beneath "Dalton," then used the marker to point at it. "Whitney."

"Really?" Ava couldn't quite believe it. Whitney was a little nutty, for sure, but she didn't seem to be the one-hundred-percent certified authentic nut someone would have to be to kidnap someone's pets.

But the idea seemed to bolster Sophia. "Why not. Let's call Whitney and tell her we have proof she did it. We'll be bluffing, obviously, but she won't know that. We'll offer not to press charges as long as she just admits it."

Hunter shook his head. "Are you trying to get Charming killed?"

Sophia's eyes blazed. "What kind of question is that?"

"I'm not trying to upset you," Hunter said. "But if Whitney has gone completely off the rails and started kidnapping pets, what do you think will happen when you force her hand? Obviously none of this is the act of a rational person. We have no idea what triggered it, so we have no idea what would trigger its escalation."

"Then how do we get Popcorn and Charming back?" Sophia asked, and Ava heard a note of sad longing in her voice. "Don't tell me I have to sit and wait patiently because I really can't handle doing any more of that."

"Me either," Ava agreed, desperate to erase the grooves of tension between Sophia's brows.

The Contessa stared at them. "But you are joking, no? Surely there is plenty for you to do. I will make some calls about the moneys. But you two"—she pointed from Sophia to Ava—"you will go finish the last dress. The secret one."

"I don't think we can go work when Popcorn and Charming's lives hang in the—" Sophia began.

"*Basta*," the Contessa said, silencing her. Her eyes looked fierce, but not crazy. She made a fist and pounded it into her palm. "We will have no more giving up. Would Popcorn and the little Charming want you to stop and sit around like lumps on logs? No. They would want you to fight. If we do not put on this show, whoever has done this wins. And that we cannot allow. You will go to the studio. You will work on the line. The car will pick you up in ten minutes. That is the end of the discussion."

"Is that what they mean when they say someone is gnashing their teeth?" Ava asked MM and Sophia.

They both nodded, too stunned to talk.

Ava was in her room dressing when she realized she must have left her phone in the dining room. She dashed in there before meeting Sophia in the foyer and walked in on Hunter gesturing broadly and saying to someone on the other end of his phone, "I don't care about money or papers. I care about getting it now, and getting it right. It needs to be big, but elegant. Something that makes an impression, you know, makes people say 'whoa' even from a hundred pac—" He turned and saw Ava behind him.

She waved and mouthed *sorry*, but he put up a finger for her to wait. "I'll call you back."

"I didn't mean to interrupt. I was just looking for my phone."

He smiled. "No problem." He got a little sheepish. "I'm trying to get something to surprise Sophia. You won't blow it for me and tell her what you just overheard, will you? Promise?"

"Of course," Ava said.

Lily, MM, and Sven had set out to do a walk-through of the Central Park Boathouse with Sam filming, and Hunter announced that he'd come later with the Contessa, so it was just Ava and Sophia in the car when it left a few minutes later.

Which was making keeping her promise to Hunter very hard. Big, elegant, makes an impression and a surprise? There was only thing that could be, and it was really hard not to mention to her sister that her boyfriend was shopping for it.

She tried to distract herself by thinking of Dalton, but Jax's face kept floating into her mind, too, making her feel even more discombobulated. She'd had a really nice time with Jax at Central Park, but as soon as she'd seen Dalton, and looked into his eyes and known he was innocent, as soon as she'd felt his fingers twined with hers, she'd known he was the one.

But then she'd listened to Jax's message and the low rumble of his voice made her knees feel a little funny, and made her remember the swoony feeling she'd gotten when his serious eyes lit up with his perfect smile. And when he'd swept her up and carried her—effortlessly—across the ice, she couldn't remember ever having felt so protected and cared for.

Not that it mattered, strictly speaking, both of them were off-limits.

A nagging voice in Ava's head whispered, *What if the Contessa was right? What if Ava was a lousy judge of character? What if Dalton really was bad, actually was behind the kidnapping?* She couldn't deny that he'd come back at exactly the right time—

Sophia's voice interrupted her thoughts. "How would Whitney have found out about Popcorn and Charming's Pet Sanctuary appointment?"

"I have no idea." Ava said. "You can add that to the list of questions we don't know the answers to. Like how the Contessa can enter and leave rooms without making use of the door. Or how did Christopher Wildwood get all our designs in the first place." Ava remembered something she'd meant to ask Sophia about. "Did you take any pictures of our new dress with your phone?"

"One or two," Sophia said. "Why? Do you want to see them?"

"No, I want you to delete them." Sophia gave her a quizzical look and Ava said, "Last night while I was busy not sleeping I kept thinking about how much Whitney's dress looked not like our *prototype*, but like the *photo* of our prototype on your phone. Right down to the mistakes."

"Got it. That *was* weird." Sophia pulled out her phone, flipped through images, clicked twice, and announced, "Deleted. Just try to copy us this time, Wildwoood," she said to her phone. She looked up. "Somehow that all seems so much less important now."

Ava avoided her eyes. Studying the seams on the leather seat, she said, "But it makes sense that whoever took them is trying to hurt us. Leaving our line unfinished lets them succeed. The Contessa was right." *About that, anyway,* Ava added to herself.

She felt Sophia's eyes on her but she didn't meet them, not even when Sophia said, "Do you want to stop at Starbucks?"

Ava hesitated. "I'm not—I don't think—I'm not sure—"

Sophia took both her hands and made Ava look at her. "What is going on?"

Nothing was on the tip of Ava's tongue, as though if she didn't talk about it her worst fear would just vanish. But Sophia knew her better than that. Like she was reading her sister's mind, Sophia said, "I don't think Dalton had anything to do with what's happened to Popcorn and Charming, Ava. I'm positive."

Now Ava looked at her. "Are you? Really? Why can't I be positive?"

Sophia gave her the most understanding smile. "Maybe you're afraid. Afraid of liking him too much. Afraid of getting hurt."

"Maybe," Ava agreed. "But I'm so confused. Because I really like Dalton. I mean *really*. But I also really like Jax."

"What do you like about each of them?" Sophia asked.

"Dalton makes me laugh. When I'm with him I feel—alive," Ava said. "Fizzy. In the knees. Well, everywhere."

Sophia grinned at her. "That's a great feeling. And Jax? How do you feel when you're with him?"

"Safe," Ava answered without having to think about it. "Cared about. Supported."

"Your feelings for Jax seem much less complicated than your feelings for Dalton," Sophia observed.

Ava nodded slowly. "You're right. I hadn't realized that."

"Good, then it's settled."

"What do you mean?" Ava frowned.

"Well, it's clear who you want to be with."

"It is?" Ava's eyebrows shot up. "Who?"

Sophia laughed at her. "Ask your gut."

"My gut says to ask you," Ava told her. "Not that it matters, because I have to date the Contessa's nephew."

"I've been thinking about that." Sophia nodded hard. "I think you should ignore it when she mentions it. She can't really mean it."

"Um, this is the Contessa we're talking about," Ava reminded her.

"And it's also your life," Sophia said. Her tone was earnest and serious. "That's more important than anything else. We'll find a way to deal with the Contessa."

The lump that seemed to have taken up permanent residence in Ava's throat since the night before threatened to overwhelm her again. "Thank you. That means— *Oh no*."

The last part came as the car pulled up in front of the workroom and was immediately swarmed by reporters. They pressed against all four of the side windows. Ava felt panic rising inside her. "Sophia, I don't think I can deal with this right now," she said.

"I have an idea," Sophia said. Her eyes became unusually mischievous. "What if we tell them we'll have a statement soon. That way they'll stick around until the Contessa comes. And then she can talk to them. And after, maybe we can talk to her about her nephew. You know she's always in a better mood after a session of confusion and delight."

Ava's panic turned to admiration. "That's a great idea. And since you're on such a roll, why don't you tell me who I've made up my mind in favor of."

"Nice try," Sophia said, getting out of the car.

LonDOs
Whiteboards
Not IT
Concealer
Benefit Eye Bright stick
Hairbrushes
Our models arriving tomorrow!
Sherlock Hunter
Child-safe markers
Guys who make you feel alight
Guys who make you feel like everything is going to be all right
Sisters who can read your mind

LonDON'Ts
Police who don't think petnapping is a big deal
Presuming guilt before innocence

Believing the Contessa has your best interests in her heart
The temperature dropping below freezing
Missing Popcorn and Charming
IT
Sisters who won't tell you what they read in your mind

16
forget-me-hots

Two hours later, Sophia slipped off her earphones, looked up from the sound file she was editing on her computer, and said, "Why yes, I'd love a latte, thanks."

"I was going to say that," Ava told her.

"Don't you think a trip to Starbucks would make a nice break in your day?"

"Are you saying that Jax is the one I've chosen?" Ava asked.

Sophia looked at her wide-eyed. "I can't tell you that. But maybe a walk will clear your head and help you figure it out."

"You just don't want to go outside because it's below freezing."

"Don't be silly," Sophia said, scoffing. "I love the cold."

"Tell me three things you like about the cold."

"Blazing fire. Cozy sweaters. Hot chocolate. A Yule log. Stockings hung by the chimney with care. That's five."

"You were describing Mom and Dad's Christmas card, not real winter," Ava said.

"I was only looking out for your well-being," Sophia told her with a mock huff.

"And I'm looking out for yours. I am positive if you go to Starbucks, something great will happen to you."

Sophia scrutinized her. "And if it doesn't?"

Ava nodded toward the kitchen area. "I'll let you have the last two Oreos."

"You're on," Sophia said.

Now that she was outside and past the reporters, Sophia had to admit that the fresh air felt great. And she wouldn't mind if something great happened to her. Because she was feeling a little out of kilter.

Ever since they'd gotten the ransom note, Sophia had felt like something was wrong with her. All her reactions were off, as though they were minutely delayed or shifted, so what had once been comfortingly familiar now felt strange.

She'd first noticed it on the red carpet, but it was even more clear when she and Hunter had finally gotten to be alone together. She'd put her head against his chest and felt his arms come around her and waited for the safe feeling to come. But it hadn't. It was like after what had happened to Popcorn and Charming, nothing could feel right. Not even Hunter's arms.

They felt good, just—different.

She really was fabulously happy that he had come. And obviously she loved him or she wouldn't have been so upset the day before because she thought he was bouncing her calls. When actually he'd been on the plane coming to see her.

"I realized all our problems were exacerbated by distance so I thought I'd come a few days early and take care of that," he'd said when they were curled up together, talking in her room the night before.

"Thank you," she'd said, letting her hand linger on the smooth planes of his chest. "That was really—"

"Necessary," he finished for her. "When we had that big discussion you said you thought we should talk on the phone less, that you'd be able to think about me more if you weren't always worried about calling me, and that you felt torn between your work and me. Obviously I never wanted you to feel that way."

"I know," she'd told him, marveling at how solid he was.

"You said you worried that my desire to know where you were and what you were doing was part of an old pattern that wasn't healthy for me or for us. And I realized, you were right about all of it." He shifted so that she was looking at him. "By coming, I solve both our problems: you can focus on your work and never think about calling me because I'm here, and I can avoid falling into a panic over being abandoned because I'll be right nearby all the time." He grinned. "It's a perfect solution, right?"

"Wow," Sophia had said. "Amazing." He'd clearly listened to what she'd said, but she felt like his solution addressed only the surface issues. It was like putting a fresh coat of paint on a crumbling wall, creating an illusion of progress while just covering over the cracks and dirt. His proposal seemed open-minded but really all he'd done was hide his overprotectiveness. There would be no reason for her to call him, and no reason for him to wonder where she was, because they'd be together all the time.

She could already imagine how further conversations would go. If she complained, he would look hurt and say isn't this what she wanted, less having to call him, having to let him know where she was. She'd point out that really nothing had changed, in some ways it was worse—

Then he'd jump on that. Worse? Was it bad, then? And de-pending on his mood, he'd pout or apologize.

Sophia pulled herself up short. What was she doing? He'd flown all the way there to be with her, to try to work on their problems. And all she was doing was shadowboxing in her head.

That ended now. Whatever was making her so edgy had noth-ing to do with Hunter, she suspected. She was just taking out on their relationship all her anxiety and stress and fear about the show.

The deep unfairness of it hit her hard, and she determined to make it up to him. In fact, she'd take him out for a romantic din-ner that night. Just the two of them, all her attention completely focused on—

Sophia felt like she'd walked into a solid tree. Only it was a tree with arms that came around her and a warm, honeyed voice that said, "*Stella mia.* It is destiny, no, that you walk right into my arms."

Sophia took a quick step backward. "No," she said.

Giovanni smiled at her, a different smile than any of the eleven variations she remembered and had cataloged in her head. This one was a little sad, a little serious, both of which were strange for him.

Something had changed inside him. She had the sense that he'd gone through something deeply painful or deeply harrowing.

He reached up to tuck her hair behind her ear and she grabbed his hand and held it between both of hers. "What happened to you?"

The new smile vanished, replaced by the flirtatious one she'd become accustomed to. "Why? Do I not make a good impres-sion?" He turned to the left and the right. "Have my looks suf-fered since the last time we met?"

She frowned. "This isn't about your looks."

"There is that in your tone which tells me that you are not completely delighted with me. Am I correct?"

"What are you doing here?" she asked, ducking his question.

The studio was just around the corner but the place where she'd run into Giovanni was a particularly sad-looking part of the neighborhood. One corner was occupied by a large construction site that looked like it hadn't been worked on in months, another had a deli that advertised cigarettes, candy, lotto, and gum, a third had a shuttered storefront, and the fourth held a pillar for the rusty elevated train tracks above them.

"It is a lovely spot, of course," Giovanni said, pulling his coat more tightly around him as a gust of cold wind ricocheted off the pillar and whipped past them, "but actually I came to see you. I hear you have your design studio somewhere near this place, so I plan to walk around until I find you."

"That's ridiculous," Sophia said. "That wasn't really your plan."

"How ridiculous?" He shrugged one shoulder. "Did you or no walk right into my arms? It is okay, you do not need to be embarrassed, I know my magnetism is impossible for you to resist."

"You were standing in the middle of a fairly deserted sidewalk," she said.

"Just so," he answered. "Where anyone and their cat could see me. And yet you alone do not see me. So you alone crash into me."

She laughed, despite herself. This conversation was as surreal as the one she'd had with Hunter the night before, Sophia thought, although at least this one was funny.

"Why did you come to see me?" she asked.

"Because I desire to speak with you? I hear about your small furry friend and I imagine how you must feel. And I wish to congratulate you."

"About what?" Sophia said.

"Often, I find myself remembering your face when he was small and you worried that you could not decide what name to call him." He reached out and touched her cheek with one finger. "So much worry for one girl. But now I see from the news-paper reports that you picked a name, so I wish to give you the congratulations."

"I was going to call him *Stella*," Sophia blurted.

"Yes?" His eyes momentarily widened and for an instant she caught that same sad, serious smile. "But then the friend who sug-gest this to you disappears, and you think, perhaps such a name is not good luck."

"Something like that." She looked past his shoulder, not want-ing to meet his eyes. "Why didn't you text me?"

"Ahh," he said, drawing out the syllable. "Yes. The text. This is a long story for another time. But not far away. Next week?" he said hopefully.

"Why can't you tell me now?"

"It has the many tiny, you say, fastenings?"

"Facets," Sophia guessed.

"Yes, exactly." He raised an eyebrow. "You see how still our minds beat as one? Many tiny facets that today will cause me pain but next week it will be like eating pie to speak of them."

Sophia worked to keep her tone flat. "I'm sorry I'll miss it. I'll be back in Los Angeles next week."

Giovanni tilted his head, a sad twinkle in his dark eyes. "'I go to Los Angeles,' she says, cool like gelato, as though the thought of leaving Giovanni causes her no pain."

She offered a polite smile. "It doesn't."

He took her hand and pressed it to his chest and she felt his heart beating. Fast, as though he was nervous. "A little? Do not, I beg you, say it causes no feeling, no pain at all. You char my heart."

"Char?" Sophia repeated.

"Maybe is not the right word? Burn your name upon it? So now I"—he made a face like he was tasting something unpleas-ant—"taste only ashes."

Sophia didn't want to laugh, she wanted to be angry, but she couldn't help it.

"Yes, this is much better," he said, slipping his fingers between hers. "Now I hear again the music of the angels. I propose this. I say we do not want to be hogs and not share this magical sidewalk with others, so let us leave and you show me the studio of Sophia and Ava London. When we are there with maybe less fresh air whipping around the face—though I feel very vitalized—I give you the taste of my story, and then next week, all is revealed."

Over Giovanni's shoulder Sophia saw the Contessa's dark blue Maybach round the corner a block to the south on its way to the studio. She was relieved that they were out of sight because she didn't want Giovanni to see Hunter. Or Hunter to see Giovanni.

But she could picture Hunter opening the door for the Contessa, a perfect gentleman. Imagine his straight back and broad shoulders, serious, firm, unwavering as the press engulfed the woman like a school of ants on a leftover cupcake.

Serious, firm, unwavering, Sophia repeated to herself, and added, *reliable.* Those were the attributes she wanted in a partner.

Through that lens, she told herself, Giovanni's charms dwindled. She thought about her conversation with Ava in the town car, how clear Ava's preference had been to her, and realized that hers was just as clear. Giovanni was funny and charismatic and entertaining. But he was also irresponsible, immature, impractical, and unpredictable. You could count on him to amuse you, but you couldn't count on him for much else.

Aren't you being a little unfair? her mind asked. *He said there was an explanation.*

Next week, another part of her mind said. *What kind of explanation has a Do Not Open Until stamp on it? A lie, that's what kind.*

Maybe he's waiting to hear about a new job, the first part pointed out. *And you did notice a new seriousness about him that could suggest—*

Whose side are you on? Besides, it doesn't matter, because you love Hunter. Who is waiting for you right now around the corner.

"Goodbye, Giovanni," she said, pulling her hand from his. "Be well."

"How will I be well with ashes for a heart?" he called after her as she walked toward the showroom. "And also my hand, which you stopped holding, now feels lifeless. Like a noodle hand. No more fingers, now I have only finguini."

Sophia couldn't stop the laughter that bubbled out of her then. But as if repenting, immediately afterward she pulled out her phone and wrote to Hunter: "You made a very sexy Sherlock Holmes this morning and an even sexier bodyguard now."

Hunter's reply was nearly instantaneous: "How do you know?"

"Can't you sense my presence?" she text-teased.

"You are cruel, *stella mia,*" Giovanni called right as she turned the corner. "But you will come around. This is not the end."

She watched Hunter's face light up when he caught sight of her and thought, *Yes, it is.*

He would never have facets or long, complicated stories he couldn't tell you until next week. He would just be Hunter. Always.

She began to walk to him but he put up a hand, so she stood off to one side, watching him and thinking about how seriously he took even the most basic duties.

Finally, when there was a pause in the questions, he slid away, reached for Sophia, and wrapped his arms around her. *It's starting to feel like home again,* she assured herself. This was where she belonged. This was what she wanted.

The Contessa turned and glowered at her. "You are making a distraction. Take your Hunter and go."

They laughed as they dashed around the reporters, through the lobby, and into the elevator, but as soon as the doors closed he pulled her to him and kissed her softly on the lips. A nice, friendly kiss, she thought.

"I am crazy about you," he said to her.

"I know. And I'm crazy about you." *Friendly?* she asked herself. It had been better than that. *Hadn't it?*

"Good." He grinned. "Just checking in."

"In fact I was thinking we could go somewhere special for dinner tonight." Their eyes met in the mirrored surface of the doors. "Just the two of us."

The look of pure joy that swept across his face made Sophia feel Christmas-card warm inside.

Sophia could tell as soon as she stepped off the elevator that something was wrong with Ava, and that Ava was working very hard not to show it.

Lily, MM, Sven, and Sam were gathered around a monitor in one corner, watching the footage they'd just shot at the Central Park Boathouse, that they would turn into a video to help the girls learn the layout for the show. Daisy was compiling stacks of photocopied packets on another table, and an assortment of strangers were putting exquisitely wrapped boxes and beautifully stitched silk sachets into cloth bags printed with one of their patterns that she'd never seen before.

She said to Hunter, "I'm afraid I need to leave you on your own for a while."

"That's why I'm here," he told her amiably and curved off toward the group watching the video.

Sophia leaned against the table next to Ava's seat. "What's up?"

"I had an idea I wanted to show you in the workroom." Ava said, her voice strangely flat. She grabbed her purse and held it open. "Drop your phone in here."

The oddness of Ava's tone surprised Sophia, and she was even more surprised when Ava dropped the purse onto her seat and left it there as she started toward the workroom.

"Do you need me?" Sam called from across the room.

Ava shook her head.

"What about me?" Hunter said. "Are you going into the famed workroom? Can I peek?"

"Not yet," Ava told him. "But I promise to return Sophia to you soon." She held the door open for Sophia, followed her through, then shut and locked it behind them. Without saying a word, they made their way to the corner farthest from the other room, where there was a small café table with two chairs. A chipped gold cupid vase stood on the table, with some slightly-past-their-prime yellow and pink roses in it.

"What's going on?" Sophia asked.

"Dalton called while you were out. I sent it to voice mail because I couldn't face having to tell him I didn't want to see him again, and he left this message."

Ava put it on speaker and leaned the phone against the cupid vase.

"The first part is sort of personal," Ava said as the message started to play.

"Hi, Ava. It's Dalton. I don't want to sound like a selfish ass, I know you're going through a lot so I'm just going to blurt it fast: I hope I didn't do something to upset you and that's why you've been so strange on the phone. But if I have, tell me and we'll figure out a way to fix it, okay? I lost months of time I should have been kissing you and I don't want to lose any more."

"That's really cute," Sophia said.

"Yeah, too bad I won't ever get to kiss him," Ava answered. She turned up the volume. "Here's the important part."

"I'm calling because something strange happened at the

Wildwood design space today. That's what he calls it, by the way. The guy is a moron. It's been pretty organized, low-key the whole time we've been practicing there, but today everything was hopping. One of the assistants told me Wildwood had gotten a great idea for a new gown in the middle of the night last night and he'd decided he had to make the dress for the show, which was why everyone was running around. There was something about the way Mikasa—that's the assistant—said it, though that made me think she didn't believe in Wildwood's 'middle-of-the-night inspiration' story. I'll try to get more information out of her, but I thought you should know. I asked her to describe the dress and she said it used multiple layers of tools? Does that make sense to you? Also it had a smocked bodice, is biased cut, and it bustled. I'm sorry if I got the lingo wrong, I was trying not to seem too interested. Let me know how I can help, or if there's something I should be trying to fix. Yeah, I guess I'll just—"

It cut off.

"He got our dress," Sophia mumbled through numb, shell-shocked lips. Both girls stared down the length of the workroom to a dress with a smocked bodice and a bias-cut skirt that bustled in the back over several layers of tulle. "We were so careful," Sophia said. "I even deleted the picture."

"It sounds like the dress only started production late yesterday or today," Ava said. "So we must have deleted the picture too late. But what I don't understand is that Toma said we shouldn't have to worry."

Sophia felt all the blood drain out of her body and into her feet. "*You* didn't have to worry. I never gave him my phone back to encrypt after he couldn't finish because of Hunter calling. *My* phone was the leak," Sophia said. Now not only her lips but her hands and feet felt numb.

"This time," Ava told her. "The leak could have rotated. And you're only seeing the negatives."

"There are positives?" Sophia asked.

Ava nodded. "First, we know not to use your phone for anything because someone's listening. Which means we also know *to* use your phone for anything we want someone to hear."

"Like if we were to change the design of the gown," Sophia said. "We could take a picture—"

"And make Wildwood jump."

Sophia nodded minutely to herself. "This has potential."

Ava agreed. "I wish we'd thought of it earlier."

"For so many reasons." Sophia stopped nodding. Her eyes flashed to the door, then back to Ava. "I don't think we should tell anyone what we're doing. Not because I suspect anyone, but this way—"

"We'll be able to test for sure if your phone is the source," Ava said. "And we wouldn't want to worry them."

"Right." Sophia was already up heading to the door. "I'll go get my phone."

"I'll get the shears. What do you think we're missing from our collection?" Ava asked.

"A micromini of course," Sophia said.

"With a bustle," Ava added.

Sophia laughed. "Hideous! And yet oddly perfect for celebrity guest Whitney Frost."

LonDOs

Turning adversity into advantage

Ava putting on one brown over-the-knee sock and one navy-blue one

Girl who asked Ava where she'd gotten her "totally cute" thigh-highs
Having an inside man
Boyfriends who take what you say seriously
Boyfriends who understand when you fall asleep during your
    romantic dinner
Finguini

LonDON'Ts
Irresponsible, immature, unreliable guys
Wonderful, loyal, smart, funny, cool guys in bands who give you
    butterflies not only in your stomach but in your knees that you
    want to date but can't
Making up fights in your head
Making up what a girl named Mikasa might look like in your head
Your own phone spying on you
Trying to get dressed fast on no sleep
Sisters who don't tell you your socks don't match until you are at the
    showroom
Sisters who won't help you unlock the secrets of your heart
Kidnappers who have yet to give Further Instructions

17

big slapple

"I think I'm more nervous for this than I've ever been for anything," Ava said to Sophia the next day just before noon.

Sophia looked skeptical. "Even more than when you had that solo in the third-grade Christmas pageant?"

"You're right, playing Tree Number One was very challenging," Ava admitted. "But this is right up there."

They were sitting at the café table in the far corner of the workroom, tying bows on the gilded boxes containing the custom-dipped AS scented candles that the Contessa had set in front of them. Boxes of lavish items had been deposited in the studio over the previous few days by the Contessa's chauffeur, all of which she claimed were for "gift bags."

So far their favorites were the custom sunglasses with the gold lenses that had the AS logo screened onto them so it showed up in the sun and the cashmere socks that came in their own little bag with BE COMFORTABLE AS YOU ARE embroidered on it. Or, as MM said when he saw them, "To die for"—pointing at the glasses—"and to live in"—with his fingers caressing the socks.

"I didn't even know we were having gift bags," Sophia said. "And don't you think it's odd the Contessa didn't ask our advice?"

"You just used the words *odd* and *contessa* in the same sentence, as though they were an unlikely match," Ava pointed out. "That is hilarious."

In the main area of the workroom the three seamstresses were setting up their sewing machines and supplies for the onslaught of alterations they'd be hit with when the first round of fittings on the AS girls was done. They talked in low voices, as if they were saving their energy.

Ava stretched out her hands and glanced at the door to the main showroom, through which a low babble of voices could be heard. "What if they don't like us?"

Sophia shook her head. "Impossible. They might not like me but they'll love you."

"Are you kidding?" Ava said, pulling another pile of sachets and ribbons toward her. "You're the charming, lovely, beautiful, classy-but-still-fun one. They all want to be you. I'm the one who obsesses about every tiny thing and makes people bored."

"I'm pretty sure you mean makes people adore you," Sophia said. "Besides, you're BFFs with practically everyone in the room already."

Ava's face looked pinched and she whispered, "Don't let the Contessa hear you say that, we don't want her to be jealous."

The door opened and the noise swelled for a moment, then retreated as MM shut it behind him. He stopped to give each of the seamstresses a hug, then made his way to Ava and Sophia. "They're ready," he said.

"Are you crying?" Sophia asked.

"No," he lied. "Okay, yes."

"Why?" Ava said.

MM took a deep breath and looked up toward the corner of the room. "Because they're better. Better even than we could have imagined. And this crazy thing you're doing?" He wiped a tear and his eyes came to them. "It's not just going to work. It's going to soar." He made a face. "Don't you two start crying too. We don't have time for more makeup."

Ava and Sophia each took a few short, quick breaths. At the door he stopped to straighten Sophia's collar and brush a crease out of Ava's skirt. "Ready?"

"Yes," they said together.

He opened the door. "Ava and Sophia," he said, "meet the AS girls."

The next three hours passed in a blur of hugs and laughing and jumping up and down and screaming and crying and trading outfits and trading accessories and more stories. By the end, without anyone knowing exactly how, all the outfits had been assigned, polaroided, and pinned for alterations, and everyone knew everyone else's name, secret dream, deepest wish, and pets' names.

Each girl had been told to bring a chaperone and one accessory that she particularly loved or that had special meaning to her. MM wanted to incorporate them into the outfits, to highlight the idea that there was no one right way to be an AS girl, no one tyrannical point of view. The chaperones were led by Daisy down the hall to a pop-up nail salon the Contessa had arranged and given manicures and pedicures, while the girls each presented her accessory and explained why she'd chosen it. Sam filmed the whole thing and MM recorded it, flipping through the Polaroids to note which accessories belonged to which girls.

Ava and Sophia felt like they were watching a machine at work, one they'd sort of dreamed about but barely recognized in its fully fleshed-out form, as if each of the parts had taken on a life of its own.

This is going to work, they said to one another as if they didn't believe it. Somehow, despite everything, it was going to work.

At four o'clock the AS girls and their chaperones were picked up by a double-decker bus for a tour of Manhattan, which was going to be followed by dinner for everyone at the Contessa's apartment. When Sophia and Ava had asked whether it was going to be a buffet or seated, and what they should expect, the Contessa had said, "Fire," and wandered off.

Sophia glanced around the room, saw Lily and Sam putting the final touches on the video to be shown that night at dinner, and heard MM and Sven in the workroom, making the seamstresses laugh. Ava was in the corner, thumbs flying as she texted the AS girls who had just left and—as predicted—adored her. Sophia had the sense that something was missing but it took her another few seconds to realize that it was Hunter. She hadn't noticed him leave, but she found a text on her phone that read, "I love watching you. You were so absorbed didn't want to interrupt but had to run out on a quick errand. Let me know if you are home or studio later (no pressure!) and I'll come see how I can help."

Nice, she thought. *Perfect.* She'd been wrong to think—

Ava's gasp got the attention of the whole room. "He texted me," she announced loud enough to bring MM and Sven out of the workroom. "He or she. The kidnapper."

"Read it," Sophia insisted.

"I almost deleted it," Ava said, her hand shaking. "I thought it was spam, you know, no phone number, I almost—"

"Read it!" Sophia urged.

"'If you value your pets' lives, go to the NE couch in the lobby of the W Hotel in Times Square at exactly 4:43 P.M. No Cops, No Press. Come ALONE!'" Ava looked up. "It's 4:11. What do we do? We don't have the one hundred thousand dollars demanded in the ransom note."

"We plan in the car," Lily said, marshaling everyone toward the door. "Take coats and any weapons you might have," she commanded. "You too, Sam. I think we're going to want to film this."

The Contessa had arranged for a fleet of SUVs to be on call for the next few days and they'd found one of them idling right outside the studio. "There's something strange about this," Ava said as the car pulled away from the curb.

"You mean everything?" Sophia said, typing on her phone.

"Who are you texting?" Ava asked her in a whisper. They were sitting together in the farthest-back row. "And what do you want them to know?"

"Only Hunter," Sophia said, "to tell him what's— Oh. Good point." She dropped her phone like it was contaminated. "Could I send him a text from your phone?"

Ava was about to hand it to her when she stopped herself. "Hunter's phone might be compromised too," she said. "Most of the designs were stolen while we were still in LA."

Sophia sighed. "You're right. We'll have to get Toma to look at it. Later."

"Later," Ava agreed. "What I meant about something weird is that up until now the kidnapper has been a total publicity hound."

"That's true," Sophia said, nodding. "Like having the letter delivered by bike messenger in the middle of a red-carpet event."

"Exactly," Ava said. "But now we're supposed to come alone."

"Which is our saving grace," Lily announced from the front of the SUV. She was twisted around to face them. "It means the kidnapper will hopefully be somewhere nearby. To watch and see that you're alone."

"Why is that good for us? Since I'm *not* alone?" Ava asked.

"Since we don't have the money, our one chance of saving Popcorn and Charming is to get to the kidnapper before he can get to them," Lily explained. "We do that by luring him out. You leave this bag wherever you are told to drop the money." Lily held up a bag that Ava knew contained a dozen small boxes with unbelievably cool cut-crystal rings with AS ALWAYS engraved on them, but no money at all. "As soon as the kidnapper has the bag it will be clear that we haven't paid up, so he will take action. Best case, we catch him picking up the bag. Less good, we follow them with the bag to Popcorn and Charming."

"And what if we miss on both of those?" Sophia wanted to know.

"We won't," Lily told her positively. "I have a strategy worked out. It's called divide and conquer."

"I don't think you want to use that name," Sam told her.

Lily rolled her eyes. "The way it works is, we divide up. And then we conquer."

"That's really not how the original went," Sam cautioned.

"God, I wish this car had a trunk so I could lock you in it," Lily said to him. "Here's how this is going to happen. Obviously Ava is going to be the one making contact at the hotel, and obviously we're not sending her in alone."

"But the text—" Sophia started.

Lily put a finger to Sophia's lips and said, "Shhh. Don't make me go Full Contessa and use the lip finger. Since we don't know who is behind this, but we're entertaining the idea that it's someone you know, the person least likely to be spotted by the kidnapper is Sam. That means Sam will shadow Ava at the hotel."

"She's actually good at this, isn't she?" Sam whispered to Sophia.

"Very," Sophia agreed. "She learned it from watching the movies her dad was in. But she gets a bit—"

"The next person I hear talking will be playing the part of the guy in the red shirt who always dies," Lily said.

"—Tyrannical," Sophia finished.

"Everyone except Ava will get out of the car two blocks from the hotel," Lily said. "We'll fan out there, each taking a different route toward the hotel to circle it, scanning for familiar faces as we go. Sam, you'll go the most directly because you need to get into the hotel, but we can't risk you being seen getting out of the car."

"What happens if we see familiar face?" Sven asked. "Do we grab them?"

"Use your best judgment," Lily said. "Probably the most useful thing would be to follow them. Remember, our priorities are Ava's safety, then Popcorn and Charming's safety, then revenge, then mayhem, then snacks."

"You should put the pets first," Ava said.

Lily went right past that. "The lobby of the W is on the fourth floor," she told Ava. "You can access it either through a long escalator or an elevator. Take the escalator, that will allow the kidnapper to observe you and see you're alone. Since we're assuming they're watching, it might give you a glimpse of them as well." She turned to Sam. "You take the elevator. There's a bar behind the elevator bank that looks into the lobby. Position yourself there so you can see Ava on the couch but not be automatically associated with her. I am certain you don't know how to look nonchalant, New Dork, but try."

"I'll do my very best," Sam told her.

Lily rolled her eyes again. "Gold Team Two—that's you, Ava—your primary job is to keep the kidnapper talking and get as much information about him or her as you can, especially clues about their whereabouts. If you hear traffic, if you hear an elevator ding, anything like that, make a note of it and try to tell Sam. He'll be able to relay it to us. We'll wait outside the hotel to watch for anyone with the bag, or respond to any instructions you convey as an extra precaution, I want you on the phone with Sophia the whole time. When the kidnapper calls, put it on speakerphone so Sophia can hear. She'll tell— Why are you shaking your head?"

"Not with Sophia." Then realizing how weird that looked, Ava scrambled to say, "Her phone battery is dead. Right?" She looked at Sophia.

"Yes. Can I use someone else's phone?"

Sven handed her his, which she'd never noticed was completely covered in white Swarovski crystals. "This is beautiful," she told him.

"My mother makes it for me," he explained.

"Okay, it looks like we're all set. Everyone clear on their job?" Lily asked, looking around fiercely. Then she smacked herself in the forehead. "I almost forgot the most important part. The rendezvous point is the Kiss section of the Hershey's store. Can everyone find that?"

Everyone nodded.

"Gold Team One, we have reached our disembarkation point." She turned to Ava. "Good luck, little London. May the force be with you."

"You're quoting *Star Wars* and I'm the one with the word *Dork* in my nickname," Sam said as they were getting out of the car. "Unbelievable."

"What I say to my special ops commandos in confidence is none of your concern, soldier Dork."

"Yes sir, Admiral Obi-Wan Kenobi."

"It's General or Jedi Master," Lily hissed. "Don't even pretend you don't know his correct rank."

Sophia turned from them back to Ava. "Good luck."

Ava pointed at Lily and Sam. "You too."

"Don't do anything risky," Sophia warned. "*Very* risky, I mean."

"Me?" Ava touched her collarbone innocently.

They were about to leave the van when Sven raised his hand. MM said, "This isn't the time—" but Sven's expression got serious and he said, "The question is important."

"Yes, soldier?" Lily said.

"What does it mean that the kidnapper did not mention one word about money in the text?" He looked around at them. "To me, it creates wonder. Such as, is this a big trap. To lure the little London. Certainly she would be worth more than the animals."

The others goggled at him. Sophia hadn't thought of that but now that he'd said it, it made sense. A lot of sense.

"I'm sure it's not a trap," Ava herself said, too brightly. "If anyone was going to kidnap a London sister they'd take Sophia. She's bound to be more cooperative."

It was clear that she was trying to keep her tone light but it wasn't working and the laugh she forced out was worse.

But everyone went along with it. They climbed out of the SUV. Sophia turned back just before the door closed and saw Ava sitting alone, forlorn, in the backseat. She looked so small. So fragile.

There was no way Sophia was letting her do this. "I'm going with you," she announced.

"You can't," Lily told her. "If you go—"

"Basta!" Ava said, mimicking the Contessa. She was smiling but it looked fake, strained. "Stop worrying. And get out of here. You're going to make me late."

Sophia jiggled Sven's phone, "Call me."

"Such a princess," Ava joked. "Always has to have someone else make the first move."

They were both laughing as the door closed, the kind of laughing that comes from fear and nerves and working hard not to cry, and they both stopped as soon as the other one couldn't see.

"I hate this," Sophia murmured under her breath as she watched the car pull away.

"Your road lies thataway, young Jedi," Lily said, pointing Sophia down Seventh Avenue. "She's going to be fine. I'm not leaving here without all my troops."

She hugged Lily gratefully and was turning to go when Sam's hand on her forearm stopped her. "I won't let anything happen to your sister. I promise."

Sophia smiled and thanked him, but deep in her heart she knew that was a promise no one could keep.

LonDOs

Have Lily plan your ops mission

Sisters who worry

(I'm talking about you)

(No, I'm talking about you)

Gold Team 1

Gold Team 2

The Force

Sven's mom

LonDON'Ts

Letting your sister go into battle alone

*Pursing petnappers in four-inch platform pumps (pawsitively
    painful)*

*People who do not bother to learn basic facts about important
    historical figures*

Texts that could be traps

18

this is a lipstickup

It was 4:35 when the SUV disgorged Gold Team 1 and only two minutes later when Gold Team 2 (Ava) reached the hotel, but Ava felt like she'd aged ten years in that time. She wouldn't have been surprised to look in the mirror and see a solid white head of hair.

The "money bag" in her lap was heavier than she would have imagined, but she hoped her difficulty with it would make the illusion more realistic, at least from a distance.

Assuming she was on her way to a ransom drop and not a trap.

Sitting in the back of the SUV all alone, she felt like she was floating outside herself, as though she'd somehow moved beyond fear to a whole other plane of existence. Ava had heard that right before you die your life flashes before your eyes, but no one had ever told her that right before you might be walking into a death trap things that had been confusing became very clear, and problems that seemed insurmountable suddenly appeared easily overcome.

She found herself thinking about Liam and how she really should just break up with him by text the way everyone else seemed to, and about the Contessa's nephew with the one eye and the hairy body. Sophia had said she didn't need to worry about that, but Ava found herself almost wistful, thinking of him now that she didn't know if she'd even be alive on Friday for their date. The messed-up situation wasn't his fault, she saw. No doubt he was charming.

If she was alive on Friday, she resolved, she'd be as nice to him as she could. Give him a real chance. Not because of the Contessa's threats, either, but because given what she'd heard about him, she would bet that a lot of people treated him badly, and everyone deserved a friend.

She thought about the conversation she'd had the day before with Sophia, about choosing between Jax and Dalton. Jax made her feel safe, and there was no question that the past few days— the past few weeks—had made "safe and uncomplicated" very appealing. Being with him was easy.

That's what Sophia had meant when she'd said Ava already knew who she was picking. Ava London would never take "uncomplicated and familiar" over a challenging new adventure. Playing it safe had never worked for her.

Dalton was the one, not because of the prickly feeling she got with him or the electricity of his kisses or even the way he made her laugh, although that was all part of it. Dalton was the one because he challenged her, pushed her, made her think harder. Because he thought her capable of all that. He was the one because her emotions with him weren't tidy, they couldn't be easily classified. Because when she was with him she felt more—more alive, more excited, more herself.

And just as she accepted the true depth of her feelings, she accepted that she had to set him free. She'd told herself that the reason she hadn't been open with Dalton about the Contessa and her nephew was that she didn't want to hurt his feelings. But that was just a convenient excuse.

The real reason she hadn't told him was that she was worried that if Dalton knew why she was being cold to him, if he understood the impossibility of her situation, he would lose interest and stop trying to date her. She didn't want to tell him the truth because she was too afraid of losing him. She'd been playing it safe.

But that was stupid and selfish. And it couldn't be scarier than the kidnapper she was about to go confront. So if she lived through this, she would tell Dalton everything, she resolved.

This was going to be a very busy week if she made it.

"This is the W Hotel," the driver said. "You want me to wait? You going back tonight?"

"Yes," Ava said, feeling optimistic. "Please wait."

Ava got out of the car and dialed Sven's number. For one horrible moment her mind played crazy tricks and she thought Sophia wasn't going to pick up, that she'd be there by herself, facing an unknown enemy—

Sophia answered on the first ring. "Where are you?"

"I just got out of the car and I'm heading for the escalator up to the lobby where the couches are," Ava said. "I don't see any familiar faces. You?"

"Some from my nightmares," Sophia said. "A man calling himself the Naked Cowboy is right behind me, for example, playing his guitar."

"I wondered what that noise was. So he's naked except for a guitar?"

"And boots and a hat." They were talking about silly, trivial things, because at that moment anything else would have overwhelmed them.

Ava got to the top of the escalator and looked around. There was a reception desk in front of her and a seating area with four couches to her right. Beyond that, separated by a mesh curtain, was the bar.

"Are you there?" she said to Sophia.

"Yes but I'm going to keep moving. Where are you?"

"I just found the couches. There are four of them. The message said to sit in the northwest one—" Ava went and sat down. "Okay. I'm here."

"Are you sure it's the right couch?"

"Sure-ish," Ava said. "The text message said to be here at four forty-three. What time is it?"

"Four forty."

"This is going to be the longest three minutes of my life," Ava said.

"Do you see Sam in the bar?" Sophia asked.

"No. Wait— No," Ava said.

They were quiet for a moment then. What did you say when you were potentially walking into a trap? What did you discuss while you waited for a kidnapper to give you orders?

Sophia broke the silence, saying in a quiet, almost plaintive voice, "What do you think the AS Girls are doing?"

"I bet the bus is in Soho now." Ava closed her eyes, trying to picture them. "They're amazing, Sophia. I was blown away."

"Me too. And can you believe we picked twins without knowing it?"

"We have to remember to tell Harper that," Ava said. "It will be a great story for the—" She faltered. "You'll remember to tell Harper, won't you?"

"No," Sophia said. "You're going to tell her yourself. Nothing bad is going to happen to you, do you hear me?"

"Of course."

"I mean it, Ava. If something happens to you, I— Do you see Sam yet?"

"No," Ava said.

"Where is he?" Sophia demanded, sounding as angry as Ava had ever heard her. "I'm going to go and call Lily and have her check and then I'll call you back—"

"No," Ava cut her off without even realizing it. "Don't hang up. Don't—please don't leave me alone."

The fear in Ava's tone seemed to calm Sophia. "Of course not. I'm right here. I'm not going anywhere."

Ava felt another wave of fear roll over her as she heard the metallic sound of a phone close-by. "The couch is ringing," she whispered to Sophia.

"Answer it," Sophia whispered back.

"Right. Hold on." Ava put her phone in her lap and groped around the couch. Her hands were shaking so hard that it took her a moment to pry the black flip phone out from between the cushions. "Hello," she said unsteadily.

"You made me wait for you to answer," a voice hissed. It was a low whisper, and Ava couldn't tell if it was male or female. "I don't like to wait."

"I'm sorry," Ava said. "I had trouble getting to the phone."

"You'll have bigger problems if you don't pay close attention to what I'm saying," the voice—the kidnapper's, Ava thought—said snappishly.

"I'm sorry." Ava stared at the flip phone, looking for a Speaker button. Nothing was obvious and she was worried that if she pushed the wrong one she'd hang up, so she put her own phone next to the earpiece so that Sophia could hear the conversation, too. "I guess I'm just afraid."

"Stop talking and listen. I'm taking a big chance by doing this." Ava was increasingly convinced that her caller was female.

"If you do exactly what I say, you and your pets will be fine. But if you make any stupid mistakes or stupid moves, I can't answer for what will happen."

"I won't. I'll do what you want."

"We'll see," the voice said, snorting. "Go to the reception desk and tell them you're Coco Chanel. They'll give you a room key and you'll find your little treasures there. And—" Ava couldn't make out what the kidnapper said next because she was suddenly getting a large dose of the Naked Cowboy's strumming. Sophia must have moved back toward him, Ava thought, wishing there was some way to get her to step away.

"I'm sorry, I'm having a really hard time hearing you," Ava told the kidnapper, hoping that Sophia would understand the message, too.

"Whose fault is that?" the kidnapper demanded.

Ava shifted Sophia's phone but the sounds of the Naked Cowboy's guitar didn't lessen.

Her mouth went dry and her heart began to pound. *She knew where the kidnapper was.*

The Naked Cowboy's guitar playing wasn't coming from Sophia's phone, it was coming from the kidnapper's. Which meant she could tell the others where the kidnapper was standing and that they could capture her. Provided Ava could get the kidnapper to stay there without letting on that she'd figured it out.

Out of the corner of her eye she noticed that the bar table nearest her was now occupied by a very nonchalant-looking Sam. She couldn't tell if she was being watched so she didn't want to approach him directly.

Keep her on the phone, she thought as she started looking furiously for a notepad. "Can you repeat that?"

"Are you an idiot?" the caller demanded.

"I'm just a little scared," Ava said, "and my mind isn't working as clearly as I'd like." She found a notepad next to a house phone and wrote, "Female kidnapper at naked cowboy alert all teams go," crumpled it into a ball, strolled back toward the couches, and as casually as possible lobbed it at Sam.

"I'm hanging up."

"No!" Ava cried. Her voice sounded even more desperate than she felt. "Please don't. Please. If you really want to help me, you'll at least stay on the phone with me until I have the room key."

"Are you almost at the front of the check-in line?" the kidnapper demanded.

Was that a test or did it mean she wasn't being watched? Ava wondered. "There are maybe five people ahead of me," she lied as she approached the completely empty reception desk.

She wasn't sure if Sam had even gotten her note until she saw him race out of the bar, fly down the escalator, and disappear into Times Square.

At the same moment, Sophia's voice whispered from the other phone, "Keep her talking. You're doing great."

Ava let out a deep breath. She scrawled, "Please give me the key for Coco Chanel, EMERGENCY IMPORTANT," on a piece of paper and pushed it across the reception desk to the clerk, gesturing toward her phone. At first he looked at her with naked fear and she realized that if she'd been trying to look like a psychopath who was going to hold up a cash drawer, juggling two phones, throwing paper, carrying a large, heavy sack, and pacing back and forth would probably fit the bill.

She wrote, "I AM NOT PSYCHOPATH. PROMISE," and pushed that across to him but that didn't seem to help. Instead he disappeared.

"You haven't told me where you want me to leave the money yet," Ava said into the phone.

"I don't want your money. I don't want anything to do with you. I just want this to be over."

"That's all I want—"

Ava heard a clatter, the words, "You moron. You're going to pay for this. You're all dead," and then the screech of breaks and a busload of people shrieking in terror.

The flip phone went dead.

She said, "Hello? Sophia?" into Sven's phone but it was dead, too, and when she redialed it went straight to voice mail.

She hung up and dialed Lily. No answer.

Sam bounced to voice mail.

She was completely on her own.

If Popcorn and Charming were really at the hotel they'd be safe for a few more minutes but she had no idea what had happened to everyone else. The sound of breaks squealing and people screaming echoed in Ava's mind. She had to go find them, go find Sophia. If the kidnapper had them, if she'd done something to them—

Ava had to find them. Now.

She backed away from the reception desk and was on her way through the lobby to the escalator when a hand reached out, grabbed her arm, and a female voice whispered, "Don't make a sound or you're done for."

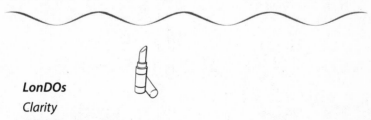

LonDOs
Clarity
The Naked Cowboy
Getting a chance not to play it safe

LonDON'Ts

Passing anyone a note that says I AM NOT PSYCHOPATH. PROMISE
People who do not answer their phones in the middle of an operation
Any sentence that ends with the phrase or you're done for.

19
midfrown

"I'm heading north on Sixth Avenue," Sophia shouted into her phone, following the girl in the gray hoodie through the crowd.

"I see the hoodie," Lily's voice said. "Sixth and Forty-fourth."

"Is it her?" Sophia asked

"Closing, closing— No!" Lily said. "Rats." Then Sophia heard her say in a much nicer voice, "I'm so sorry, ma'am, I thought it was a— No, there's no need for the police."

They'd pegged the girl in the gray hoodie for the person Ava was on the phone with while they were circling the Naked Cowboy. They had been creeping forward, ready to grab her, when she'd looked up, dropped her phone, and taken off.

The look had been brief, but enough for them to recognize her as Whitney Frost.

Sophia was still having trouble figuring it out. Had Whitney helped them?

Or had she been setting a trap? Because every time Sophia tried to call Ava, it went straight to voice mail.

Sophia had never before noticed how many people wore gray hoodies, but now that she was looking for someone in a gray hoodie, it seemed they were everywhere.

"I feel like I'm playing Where's Waldo in Hell," Lily said.

"She's probably left the vicinity by now," Sophia told her.

Lily put on a frowning voice. "That's not the kind of attitude I like to hear from my top squad leader."

"I don't have a squad," Sophia said.

"You're a unit of one," Lily told her. "Be all that—"

"I've got her," Sophia whispered. Her pulse picked up. "Seventh and Forty-fifth, heading west, north side of the street. She's strolling to look unconcerned. No idea she's being followed."

"You're sure it's Whitney?" Lily asked.

"Ninety-five percent."

"Stay on her. I'll try to conference in the others. If something goes wrong, converge around Forty-fifth and Eighth," Lily said.

Sophia hung back, dipping between parked cars and clinging to shadows. Which would have been easier to do in pretty much any other pair of shoes. She pressed herself into the side door of a theater.

Her phone vibrated and she answered without saying a word. "I've conferenced everyone in," Lily said. "Tell us what you see."

Sophia peeked her head around the edge of her hiding place and cursed. "She's speeding up. Heading west on Forty-fifth fast. Now she's cutting through to Forty-sixth, heading toward Eighth Avenue."

"I've got her," Sam said. "I'm east on Forty-sixth from Ninth."

"I'm on Eighth and Forty-fourth and I have seeing," Sven said.

"I see her too," Lily said.

"I've got her," MM reported. "Oh my—"

"Whitney!" Sophia shrieked, but Whitney was so preoccupied checking for traffic in the east–west direction that she ran right into a navy Porsche heading south.

Time seemed to stand still. There was a *thwack* and then the girl's body flipped high in the air like a rag doll, a flat pancake with arms and legs and hair and gray hoodie all splayed out. *She's so skinny,* Sophia thought.

She hung in the air upside down for a fraction of second. Then gravity took over and she was tumbling down toward the roof of a speeding yellow Camaro. Suddenly Sam came flying through the air, caught her a foot above the Camaro, flipped off of it, and landed on one knee like a knight bowing to a queen, with the girl's unconscious body draped over his lap.

Sophia goggled. "That was—"

"Unbelievable," MM said

"I never have witnessed such a thing," Sven said, his voice shaking with awe.

"I don't know why you're all making such a big deal out of what Sam did," Lily said.

They stared at her.

"What?" she said. "All he did was—"

"Leap over a car," MM said.

"Make a flip," Sven put in

"Catch a woman in midair," Sophia said.

"And land on one knee like he was proposing," MM finished. Lily shrugged.

MM said, "Lily, kitten, you are impressed by people who can tie their shoes in more than one way."

"You once you told me that doilies were manufacturing's miraculous gift to the world," Sophia reminded her.

"But a man flies through the air and saves a woman's life—" MM left off, staring at her.

Lily turned up a palm. "I'm sure when she wakes up she'll get all giddy over him and they'll fall in love, so there's no reason for me to get giddy too."

The phone in Sophia's hand flashed with Ava's number. "I'll get back to you about that," she told Lily, then said into the phone, "Ava? Is it you?"

"I've got them," Ava said. "They're fine. We're all fine. You?"

"We're all fine too. Or we will be. Where are you?"

"We're at the hotel."

"We'll be right there to get you."

"Take your time," Ava said. "We're having tea with the manager."

Sophia hung up and stared at her phone. The others had gathered around and were watching her closely. "Well?" Lily asked. "What happened?"

"Popcorn, Charming, and Ava." She looked up and there were tears in her eyes. "They're fine. They're—" She had to pause to wipe her eyes. She wasn't sure if she was laughing or crying. "They're having tea with the hotel manager."

There were tears in Lily's, MM's, and Sven's eyes, too. "Of course they are," Lily said.

MM nodded. "We should know by now, the Londons always end up on top."

"Especially Ava," Sophia said wonderingly. "My sister never stops amazing me."

"Did she say if there are lemon bars?" Lily asked.

By the time they were all in the car headed back to the apartment, filling in details for one another, the photo Ava had taken of Popcorn curled protectively around Charming in the corner of the armchair where she'd found them in their room at the W had already been retweeted over a thousand times.

Lily, Sophia, MM, and Sven told Ava about following Whitney, and Sam's miraculous rescue, and Ava explained to them how her behavior at the front desk had caused one of the reception clerks there to decide she was "unstable, possibly dangerous," and summon a security team to subdue her.

Luckily, the other clerk working reception was Sloan Lew, an aspiring designer and a longtime London sisters' viewer. She recognized Ava immediately, and having read about the petnapping, she figured the strange behavior was probably related to that. Sloan had put her job on the line by pulling Ava into a deserted office and telling her to stay quiet while the security team looked for her.

"Those goons would have held you for hours," Sloan explained when she introduced herself in whispers as they waited for the security guys to leave the lobby.

When they were gone, Sloan had looked up the room reserved under Coco Chanel and they'd found Popcorn and Charming napping quietly together in the corner of a chair. They had clearly been a little frightened, but that had just made them stick even more closely together.

"Like us," Ava said, grinning at Sophia.

"Except only one of us got to have scones," Sophia pointed out.

"And lemon bars. And tiny éclairs," Lily enumerated. "Explain how that happened again. And why were there no leftovers?"

"That was completely by accident," Ava told them. "I just wanted to tell the manager how grateful we were and what an amazing job Sloan had done, and we started chatting. Did you know Charming likes Earl Grey tea? He slurped it up. Popcorn was more partial to the finger sandwiches, weren't you?" she said, rubbing the dog's ears.

"I thought I heard several people say something about seeing you on Friday as they waved goodbye," MM said. "You didn't invite the entire staff to the fashion show did you?"

"Of course not," Ava said with a strange, high laugh. "Not the entire staff."

Lily gave her an odd, fixed look. "How many people did you invite?"

"Dkfjl," Ava told her, burying her face in Popcorn's neck.

"Was that six?" Lily said hopefully. "Because we can handle six."

"There *is* a six in the number," Ava said happily.

"Not sixteen." Lily blanched.

"No, no," Ava said, laughing.

"It's twenty-six," Sophia said. "How did you make twenty friends over tea? You were barely there an hour."

"Everyone was so friendly. Even the security guys, once we got everything straightened out. And they took amazing care of Popcorn and Charming. I had no choice. I mean, there was Sloan, who risked everything for us, and her four roommates, who all want to be designers, and the hotel manager and his wife and daughter and his daughter's best friend, and Mandy the housekeeper whose son has—"

Sophia put up her hand. "I changed my mind. I don't want to know. You can take this up with the Contessa."

Ava got pale. "You wouldn't make me."

Sophia just smiled and scratched Charming between the ears for the rest of the car ride home.

Hunter met them at the door when they got there, so overcome at Popcorn and Charming's safe return that he could hardly speak. He'd grabbed Sophia and hugged her and she had been astonished and touched to see that he was shaking.

"I know how much he means to you," Hunter told her. "I

couldn't bear it if something you loved got hurt. I'm just sorry I wasn't there to help."

"Where were you? What was this mysterious errand?" she teased.

"You'll find out soon," he said. "Now, I was told I was going to get to have dinner with a bunch of models. What's the holdup?"

Dinner with the AS Girls at the Contessa's involved not only fire, as promised, but four chefs from Benihana cooking at tables specially set up in her ballroom.

"I didn't even know there was a ballroom," Sophia had said.

"Mostly Toma uses it to stage his self-portraits," Lily said.

Ava shuddered. "I've seen those." She glanced at Sophia. "We have to remember to talk to him."

"Right." She nodded.

"Good luck," Lily told them. "I don't want to hurt your feelings, Ava, but I think he's found a new love among the AS models. Or a dozen. Last time I was out there he was surrounded by giggling girls."

"I don't know whether to be delighted or frightened for them," Ava said thoughtfully.

"I'm advocating delight on all fronts," Lily said. "And sake. We're celebrating the end of a reign of terror."

"It's hard to imagine Whitney as the mastermind of that," Sophia said. She was looking across the room to the table where Hunter was charming a group of the mothers and fathers who had come as chaperones.

"Really?" Lily sipped sake from a blue porcelain cup. "Not for me. But maybe that's because I knew her in junior high."

"Everyone is a criminal mastermind in junior high," MM said. "How much time did you spend sneaking out of the house or making out in bushes?"

"None," Lily said, looking aghast.

Ava stared at her. "You're telling us you were a perfect angel?"

"No, I just didn't waste my time on that stuff. I was too busy stealing cars."

They'd called the hospital every half hour until they were told that Whitney was out of the ICU. She still wasn't allowed to have any visitors, but the nurse assured them they would be contacted as soon as she could.

They were back from the Contessa's, eating ice cream in the kitchen, when Sam came in. Everyone stood and applauded and Sven made him a crown out of pieces of his *Men's Fitness* magazine.

"I do not easily cut into this," he said. "But for you, it is just."

Sam took it sheepishly. "Wow, thanks," he said. "It's really special."

"Is there any news about Whitney?" Ava asked.

"The doctor said she had some internal damage and they were still waiting on brain scans," Sam said. "No one seemed to think she was going to die, but there were questions about how long it would take her to recover. She did open her eyes once—"

"I'm going to bed," Lily announced, interrupting him. "I have a big day tomorrow and I can't afford to stand around the kitchen gabbing all night." She turned and stomped out of the room, leaving her ice cream unfinished.

Ava and Sophia exchanged perplexed frowns for a moment, but as if they'd simultaneously given a mental shrug and thought, *That's just Lily*, their attention returned to Sam.

"One of the videos of you saving Whitney that someone made on their phone and posted already has over thirty thousand hits," Ava told him. "Where did you learn to do all that stuff? Are you a superspy?"

Sam shook his head. "No." He drew the syllable out, then said, fast, "But I've played one on TV. Also a supervillian, a medium villain, and a lot of mid-level thugs."

"You're an actor?" Hunter said.

Ava's eyes got big. "No wonder Lily seems to be allergic to you."

"I'm not an actor," Sam rushed to tell them. "I'm a stuntman. Or I was—that's how I paid the bills while I was in film school."

"You mean like jumping off tall buildings?" Sven asked, fascinated.

"Those are the high-falls specialists," Sam told him. "I did that a few times, but those jobs usually go to the specialists. My focus was moving vehicles—trains, planes, motorcycles, cars—so I guess today instinct just took over." He shrugged, looking embarrassed. "It wasn't really that big a deal. There are hundreds of guys in New York who could have done it."

"I think it's a big deal," Ava told him.

"And it's definitely a big deal to Whitney," Sophia said.

"That's right, that's what I started to tell you." Sam nodded to himself. "Right after I caught Whitney, something weird happened. Her eyes opened for a second and she said, 'Tell them I couldn't let him go through with it.'"

"'I couldn't let *him* go through with it,'" Ava repeated, shifting the emphasis. "That means there really is someone else involved."

"And it's not over," Hunter said.

LonDOs

Boys who were stuntmen

Boys who fly through the air to save people

Whitney

Sloan Lew

Benihana for forty in your living room

Puppies who lick your face for hours

Kitties who want to sleep wrapped around your neck

Boys who also want to sleep wrapped around your neck

Breaking up with your boyfriend via text

Especially if his response is, "Bummer. Okay, babe. I understand.
   Gotta go run lines"

LonDON'Ts

Giving away all the VIP tickets

Puppies who eat the Contessa's hand-milled French soap
   and a washcloth

20
brokelyn-hearted

Ava woke up to Popcorn's kisses. "*Mmm*, lavender," she said to him. "I could get used to this."

Then Popcorn sneezed and she saw it wasn't the soap from the night before that she was smelling but the lose talcum powder she'd thought she had put far out of his reach, which he'd managed to find and get, well, just about everywhere.

"Very artistic," she told him.

He sneezed twice and looked up at her with sad eyes.

"Don't look at me like that. I thought you learned from the last time that you're allergic to talcum powder."

He made a sad noise.

"Were you this naughty with the kidnappers?" she asked him. "No wonder they wanted to—"

Her phone rang. The caller ID flashed DALTON. She hesitated. *You have to tell him everything,* she reminded herself.

But only in person, she answered herself back, picking up the phone and saying, "Hi there."

The happiness in Dalton's voice when she answered first made her heart soar, then deflate like a stomped-on I Heart U balloon.

That had been dragged through the mud.

And run over.

"Thanks for your messages yesterday," she said. *Cool and reserved,* she reminded herself. That was the way to act in this situation. "I'm sorry I was unable to get back to you."

"Based on the stories popping up on my phone, it looks like you've been busy."

"Yeah, it's been—"

"It's really nice to hear your voice."

Cool! Ava admonished herself. *Serious.* "It's the same voice as always. I just wanted—"

"I like it."

Ava closed her eyes and rested her head in her hand. Why did he have to be so awesome? Next time she was definitely falling in love with someone much suckier.

"How have you been?" she said. That was a reserved sort of thing to ask, wasn't it?

"Oh, you know, about the same as you. Nonstop excitement and press ambushes. Don't tell me you didn't see my tweets about how I thought I was coming down with the same winter cold everyone else has, but then it went away? Hashtag riveting."

Stop laughing, Ava ordered herself, but she couldn't. "I'm glad you're not sick," she said, which was not the impersonal, reserved thing she'd planned on saying.

"Thanks. And I have some news for you. I just got to the Wildwood place and everyone's in an uproar because apparently he had another vivid dream last night and this one told him to change the last dress they'd made."

Ava forgot about being aloof. "How, exactly?"

"Hang on, I wrote it down." He put her on speaker. "No wonder it's so cold up here," he said, and she heard the sound of furniture being moved around. "Sorry, I'm upstairs in our practice space and I just discovered something ate through the cord on the space heater. Let me just find a light that works." More furniture moving. "I swear this will be worth your while. And if it's not, I'll tell you some jokes."

"What kind of jokes?" Ava asked. She realized she was smiling stupidly at the phone. Which was not cool and reserved or aloof or mature or any of the other qualities she was supposed to be embodying. Also it was likely to end in tears.

"According to my sister Kiss, bad ones exclusively. When we were younger she used to fine me a dime every time I told a joke that didn't make her laugh."

"And you didn't stop?" Ava said.

"No way," Dalton told her. "Torturing her was totally worth ten cents." He paused, then said, "Okay, are you ready. The changes to the dress. First they slashed off the skirt but left the bustle. They used the extra fabric to make a bowling jacket?"

"Bolero," Ava said, adding in her mind, *with epaulets.*

"With epaulets," Dalton said. "Those are the military things on the—"

"I know what they are." *And I know exactly how they look,* she thought, *because I designed them.* She had to go tell Sophia. "Thanks, Dalton, that's great. I have to run now, bye."

"Wait, Ava," he said.

"Yes?"

"I—" He paused. "Nothing, I guess. I just feel like there's something strange going on and I wish I knew what it was. Sometimes you seem—"

You owe him the truth, the voice in her head said.

But not on the phone, she reminded it. *In person.* Besides, she needed to go tell Sophia—

Popcorn sneezed again.

"It sounds like I'm not the only one on trend," Dalton said.

Ava laughed and blurted, "I want to kiss you so badly right now."

The words popped out of her before she could stop them. They were true but they were completely, totally, 100 percent the wrong thing to say. If she'd been shopping at the Bad Idea Outlet for Girls, she could not have chosen worse.

And as if to rub it in he said, "I can't tell you how good it is to hear you say that. I want to kiss you too." But not in his fake sexy voice. In the nicest, sweetest, wrap you in his arms and make out for hours and laugh and whisper and giggle and maybe have caramel corn on the couch under a warm blanket voice.

She felt tears again, but not from laughing. "I've got to go," she said.

"Wait, Ava—"

"I'm late for something, gotta run, bye."

She hung up before he could say anything else.

She knew it wasn't cold in her room but she suddenly felt chilled and alone. Popcorn stood on his legs and put his face next to hers with his paws around her neck.

"Thank you, sweetheart," she said, hugging him.

There was a knock on the door and Sophia poked her head around the edge. "Charming ate through the cord on my hair—" She stopped. "Okay, that is like the cutest picture in the world." Then she must have seen Ava's face because she came around and sat next to her on the bed and hugged her from the other side.

"Don't ask," Ava said and Sophia didn't. Which was one of the excellent things about her.

When she pulled away, Sophia said, "Can I ask about the new

decorating scheme, though? Were you trying to get some of that dirty-snow feeling inside?"

"It's Popcorn's idea," Ava explained. "I like the energy, but I think we might need to work on the presentation."

Popcorn sneezed.

"I was just coming to see you," Ava told her.

Sophia rubbed a tear off her sister's cheek. "Really? Because it looks like someone was making you cry. Tell me who it was and I'll beat them up."

Ava laughed. "Remember Jackson Waters?"

"The school's serial braid puller." Sophia made a fist and fake punched it into her palm. "Not as well as he remembers the London sisters, I bet." She chuckled. "I still can't believe we didn't get in trouble for putting hydrogen peroxide in his shampoo."

"No one figured it out. He really believed it was the curse you put on him for touching my hair. You're that good."

"We are," Sophia said.

"And as proof I offer the latest dress in the Christopher Wildwood line, a micromini with a bustle, a bolero, and epaulets."

"They even took the epaulets? But we just drew those on."

"Apparently they didn't realize the bolero was paper either."

Sophia was staring into space, shaking her head. "I can't believe it. I can't believe it was so—direct."

"I know. I almost feel like someone is playing a trick on us." Ava stopped talking and gaped. "Why did you come in here just now?"

"To borrow your hair dryer?"

"Because Charming ate the cord," Ava said. "I think I know who the 'he' was that Whitney was talking about. When she said she couldn't let him get away with it?"

"The one who left the note," Sophia said.

"It's Christopher Wildwood. Popcorn and Charming were held in his house before she moved them to the W for us to find."

"What are you talking about?"

"I just got off the phone with Dalton. He was at Christopher Wildwood's space, upstairs, and he said it was cold *because someone had eaten through the cord on the space heater.* And he couldn't find a lamp that worked," she added excitedly.

Sophia shook her head. "That's a bit circumstantial."

"But it works. Think about it, Sophia."

Sophia said slowly, "If it's true, it means the motive *was* personal all along. Just one we didn't think of, to distract us."

"Remember when I talked to him and what frightened me was that he seemed completely convinced he'd done nothing wrong? I thought then that he was someone who would stop at nothing to destroy anyone who got in his way."

"And we would certainly qualify for that," Sophia said.

"What should we do? Call the police?"

"And tell them what? We think my cat ate through a cord at his house? I have to say, after how they acted when Popcorn and Charming went missing, I don't have a lot of faith in them. I think we should focus on putting on our show and making sure Whitney gets better."

Ava's eyes widened. "Do you think she's in danger?"

Sophia said, "If Christopher Wildwood is the one who kidnapped Popcorn and Charming and she's the one who freed them, then I'd say she certainly falls into the category of people who got in his way. And when I called the hospital this morning they said she'd woken up in the night and been hysterical and they'd worried she would reinjure herself so they sedated her. They said she won't be awake until sometime tonight."

Ava sighed. "Poor thing. She must have been so scared finding herself in the hospital alone."

"I'll take five to midnight," Sophia said as though they'd

already had the conversation about making sure someone was there with her when she woke up this time.

"I'll do overnight since I can sleep anywhere." Ava said. Popcorn sneezed. "Don't worry, you're going to have a big day too," she told him. "I promised to bring you to the studio and introduce you to our models."

"Lucky boy," Sophia said, patting him. "Lavender. Nice." She looked at Ava. "Speaking of boys, do you know anything about Hunter's mysterious errand yesterday?"

"No," Ava said, getting very interested in a thread on the edge of a pillow case. "Why would you think that?"

"Because Hunter asked me if you'd said anything to me." Sophia said. "And because you're about to unravel the edging on one of the Contessa's pillowcases now."

"No I was just looking at the sewing treatment and wondering if we might—"

"What. Is. It?" Sophia was using her the Obey Your Big Sister voice, a combination of menace and patience.

Ava cringed away, putting her hands up. "I can't."

"Ava."

When Sophia turned her Obey voice on, resistance was futile. "I heard him on the phone the other day talking to someone about getting you a ring," Ava said really fast. "At least, that's what it sounded like."

"Tell me the words he used," Sophia said in her terrifyingly patient voice.

"He said he needed something big but elegant that left an impression and would make people say 'whoa' even from a distance," Ava recounted. "And he told me it was surprise for you and made me promise to keep it a secret."

"Oh," Sophia said. "Oh my."

"Are you okay? You look pale."

"Yes," Sophia said. "I'm just really surprised."

"And maybe that's part of why he's so happy Charming is back," Ava said, warming to the idea. "Because he wants to use him in the—"

There was another knock on the door and Lily put her head around it. "Hello, Gold Team. Someone just delivered this." She wagged a large manila envelope at them.

Sophia put up her hands. "I'm not touching it. Not after what happened last time."

"This one came from Lucille," Lily said, "so I think it's probably safe."

Ava tugged the flap open and pulled out the paper inside. She took a deep breath and read: "'On behalf of the oversight committee and the organizers and sponsors of Fashion Week, I am pleased to reinstate the full credentials of AS by London Calling with all the rights and privileges accruing thereunto. Yours, Carlotta Shipley.'"

She handed it to Sophia, pointing to the notepaper clipped to the top. It was in Lucille's writing and it said, "The best revenge is making them cry."

Sophia looked at Ava. "I guess we have a show to put on."

"Looks like it."

"You know what that means?" Lily said. Ava and Sophia shook their heads.

"Screaming-and-jumping hug!" Lily declared. "And then waffles for breakfast!"

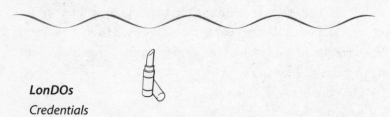

LonDOs
Credentials

Breaking up with your boyfriend via text
Especially if his response is, "Bummer. Okay, babe. I understand.
    Gotta go run lines"
#Boyswhocanmakeacoldfunny
Boys who are planning big, elegant surprises
Waffles
Quick-dry nail pens

LonDON'Ts
Christopher Wildwood
Forgetting how to be Cool and Reserved
Sophia's Obey voice
Puppies who redecorate with bath products
Kitties who eat the cord on Mommy's hair dryer

21
lash of the titans

Ava was still at the studio with Popcorn at eight that night, going over hems and edges and the programming for the show the next day. Sophia and Hunter had left at five to go to the hospital, and Lily, Sam, MM, and Sven were picking up the sets and then taking them to the Boathouse for installation. From the other room Ava could hear the clatter of the seamstresses doing the final alterations and she occasionally caught whiffs of the Contessa's perfume as the woman stalked around nervously, but otherwise it was quiet and nearly peaceful. Which gave Ava space to think.

Earlier that day she'd gone to Starbucks to see Jax. He'd looked as incredibly hot as always, but it was as though a switch had been flipped in her head and she saw him just as someone to talk to, not someone to kiss.

Well, mostly.

Which should have made what she was there to do easier. Instead, as she took her mochachino and sat in the seat at his table that he held out for her, she found herself feeling shy and awkward.

"How is your sister?" she asked him, blowing on her coffee to cool it down.

"Much better," he said. "Thank you for asking. How's yours? And your pets?"

"Everyone is a lot happier this morning than yesterday," she told him.

"Good." He smiled. "I like thinking of you happy."

This is it, Ava told herself. *The moment. Do it. Right now.*

Ava cleared her throat and said, "Jax, you're a really great guy but—" and at the exact same moment he said, "Ava, I think you're amazing but—"

They both stopped and stared at each other. And then started to laugh.

Still chuckling, Jax said to her, "So were you going to tell me—"

"That we should just be friends?" Ava nodded. "Yeah. I assume that's what you were saying too."

"Yep. That night we met, at the party? The girl who blew me off was someone I'd been dating for almost a year. She, um, called and we, uh—"

Ava reached across the table and put her hand over his. "I completely understand. Something similar happened to me," she said.

He smiled at her. "I hope he knows how lucky he is."

Ava felt a twinge inside her but she pushed it down. "I was going to say the same thing about your girl." She leaned close to him. "And what an exceptionally good kisser you are."

"Or you could just be very good inspiration."

After that, the conversation flowed easily and by the time they both stood so Ava could leave, she felt like she had a friend, whom she was going to miss.

Reflecting on it that night in the workroom, Ava had to admit that she was a little bit proud of how she'd handled it. She'd just said, "That just goes to show you that being mature and direct is a good policy," to Popcorn when his ears perked up and he got very attentive, as though she'd told him something particularly smart and he was dying to hear more.

But then the Contessa said, "Why, Ava, what a very interesting visitor you have." Although it was the tone in her voice that put Ava on the alert, she still wasn't ready for what she saw when she looked up.

Dalton was hovering uneasily in the doorway with a bouquet of flowers. The Contessa had taken up a stance in the opposite doorway with all the subtly of a tiger waiting for an antelope. In Ava's mind warning bells and Proceed Immediately to the Nearest Exit signs began to chime and flash and whirl.

"You brought flowers for Popcorn," Ava said, moving toward him. Popcorn was already there, dancing around his feet, and now she picked him up and held him toward the flowers. "Popcorn, do you see? That's right. Your first flowers."

Dalton frowned. "They're not—"

Ava put him in Dalton's face, cooing, "Give the nice man kisses."

Through the puffs of Popcorn's hair, Dalton stared at her like she might be possessed.

"I'll explain everything," she whispered. "Just go along with it."

Dalton gave a painfully fake laugh and said, "Flowers for Popcorn, yeah! Welcome home, buddy."

"I'm going to take my dog for a walk," Ava told the room at large. "I will return in ten minutes. We will be right outside the window the whole time if anyone wants to watch and see what we are doing."

The Contessa's eyes narrowed but she didn't say anything.

When they got downstairs Dalton stopped and put out his hand. "Hi, I'm Dalton. What is your name, miss?"

Ava bit her lip. "I owe you an explanation."

He stopped and turned her to face him. Her eyes went from his to his mouth and then back. His cheeks were pink from the cold but there was still a trace of his California tan and his eyes sparkled. He looked at her from lowered lids and said, "Actually, I'd rather just have a kiss."

She wrenched her gaze away from his, turning her whole body. She was short of breath and felt hot and cold at the same time. "I can't," she said miserably. "God knows I want nothing more than to give you a few thousand kisses. But I—"

"But?"

"I can't." She looked up at him. "Something happened before you—before—when you still wouldn't speak with me."

He stood up straighter and his voice had a slightly deeper tone. "Are you dating someone else?"

Ava gave a mirthless laugh, her eyes moving restlessly from one place to another, desperate to settle anywhere besides his face. "I wish it were that. That would be simple, I'd just break up with them. No. The problem is I'm *not* dating someone else. When we met the Contessa, Sophia was dating Hunter and I was single. Somehow the Contessa knew that I'd had my heart broken."

Dalton got very still. "You had?"

Ava closed her eyes and took a deep breath. She opened them and saw pain etched in his face. "You know that. You knew how I felt. How I feel—"

"Do you?"

Yes, she wanted to shout. Wanted to say it joyfully, wrap his face in her hands and cover it with kisses. Wanted to whisper *yes* in his ear, catch his smile with hers, taste happiness on his lips. She shook her head, swallowed. "It doesn't matter."

"It does to me," he said, and she felt like she could drown in his eyes.

"It can't," she insisted, her chest hot with frustration. "That's the point. We'd already put in so much work on our line, not just me and Sophia but everyone, and the first week we were here the Contessa called me into her den and gave me an ultimatum: either I agree to date her nephew, or she pulls the funding for our line."

Ava studied his expression, looking for signs of disgust or shame or disrespect, but all she saw was open, if slightly cautions, curiosity. He slid his hands into his pockets. "Did you? Are you dating her nephew?"

"No. Well yes. Yes I agreed to attend a few parties during Fashion Week with him. In exchange for keeping our line, that seemed a modest sacrifice. And he sounds like a sad sweet guy—he lost an eye in an accident or something so it can't be very easy for him to meet people." She sighed.

His hands seemed to be going deeper into his pockets as they talked. "How was it? Attending parties with him."

"I haven't done it yet. He's not even here. But what I learned along the way is that I'd made a terrible bargain. Because it wasn't just about going to a few parties with her nephew. The Contessa used it as a way to control me. Where I went, what I did. Who I talked to." She looked right at him.

"Me?" he said, and then as it hit him: "Me."

"She calls you my Dalton, because it was so obvious to everyone how I felt about you."

His hands began to come out of his pockets. "She knows about me? About us?"

"Unfortunately, she does," Ava said, not wanting to take the excitement out of his voice but needing him to understand. "She made it clear that if she thought something was going on between us, she would pull the funding for our line. I'm not even sure she's not up there right now trying to do it since you came over."

"That's why you were so weird just now."

"And all the other times. On the phone. It killed me to have to tell you I couldn't see you, you couldn't come over, when all I wanted in the world was to be with you. I knew I was confusing you and that wasn't fair, but I was afraid to tell you the truth."

He looked puzzled. "Why?"

"Because it meant admitting that it was impossible. It meant telling you goodbye for real. I hate having my life held hostage this way but I can't make this decision just for me. It's about Sophia and Lily and MM and now all the girls who are here helping." She looked up at him, willing him to understand. "And it's about you."

"And you." His voice was a low rumble she felt in her knees.

"If it was just about me, if I could choose for myself, I'd throw everything over for you. That would be worth it. I wish I could spend the day with you, doing all the things I've always wanted to do in New York City but didn't get to. I want to ride in horse-drawn carriages and eat bad pizza and walk through museums and go ice skating. I want to do everything with you. And I—" She closed her eyes. "I just hope you know how amazing I think you are." She pulled Popcorn's leash. "Come on."

"Ava, wait," he called, jogging after her.

"No. You can't see me cry."

His hand on her arm stopped her. "Why not?" he asked.

"It's not fair," she said, her voice anything but steady. "I only want you to see me when I'm pretty."

He turned her face to his and their eyes met and she felt a

spark through her whole body. His eyes were stormy green and intense and even in jeans and a parka there was something incredibly magnetic and powerful about him, like an ancient god visiting the mortal plane. His lips looked ready to curve into a smile and Ava ached to be the one that got to prompt it, day after day, week after week. He leaned close to her ear and whispered, "You're always beautiful to me, Ava London."

Ava didn't know how long she stood on the sidewalk staring after him, her heart beating, her body thrumming with his words, but it was long enough that he wasn't even a faint outline anymore, long enough that her toes were numb and even Popcorn was ready to go in.

The Contessa was the first person she saw when she walked into the showroom. She nodded and was on her way past when she stopped Ava. "I am proud to know such a serious girl," she said. "My nephew arrives tomorrow morning. You will meet him then." She took hold of Ava's arm and said earnestly, "Trust the Contessa, eh? I spare you much heartache and sorrow. My nephew is a very special boy. You will like him. You will be saved years of searching for Mr. Right."

If only I hadn't already found him, Ava thought.

LonDOs
Coming clean
Doing good
Popcorn
Making the Contessa proud
Boys who are friends
Boys who are amazing

LonDON'Ts
Saying goodbye
(it hurts)
(it hurts)
(it hurts)

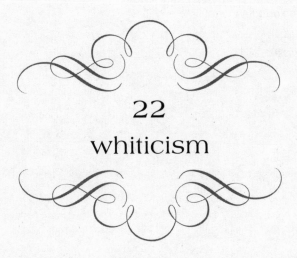

22

whiticism

The text arrived in Sophia's inbox at 8:01 A.M., right after Hunter kissed her goodbye and left for his 8:00 A.M. run. She was just going to see her sister when Ava appeared in her doorway saying, "Did you get it too?"

Sophia nodded and read aloud, "'Please come see me right away, it's vital. Whitney.'"

"It could be a trap," Lily said.

"It could be," Sophia acknowledged. "But for what?"

They were out the door by eight fifteen.

"You two are becoming speed-dressing champs," MM praised Ava and Sophia in the car on the way to the hospital. He, Sven, and Lily were going to drop them off and then head to the showroom to start prepping for the show that afternoon.

"What about me?" Lily asked.

"Sam's T-shirt looks better on you than it does on him," MM said. "If that's what you meant."

Lily turned five shades of pink. "It's not—"

"You and Sam?" Ava gawked. "Since when?"

"Since never," Lily said, tugging at the shirt. "MM doesn't know—"

Sophia looked pensive. "I actually think it's been going on a few weeks. Remember when we had the idea about the Central Park Boathouse and we went to get Lily and her door was locked?"

Ava's mouth fell open. "That's right. And it took her a really long time to 'find the key.'"

Sven raised his hand. "Why does she pretend not to like him?"

"For fun?" Ava said.

"For privacy?" Sophia suggested.

"So the Contessa wouldn't have anything to do with it," MM put in.

"You can feel free to chime in at any time," Sophia told Lily.

Lily peeked at them from around a pile of boxes. "Are you mad?"

"Oh furious," Sophia said.

"Spitting," MM confirmed.

"That's why the other day, after he did his superhero thing, you were truly upset," Ava said. "Because you and he were already together and you thought he was going to get together with Whitney."

"That's what happens in the movies," Lily said.

Sophia laughed at her. "But you know as well as anyone that real life is better than the movies."

Ava shook her head. "I can't believe that was going on under our noses the whole time."

"We have been a little busy," Sophia pointed out.

The car pulled up in front of the hospital and Ava and Sophia got out.

"Are you sure you don't want us to wait?" Lily asked.

"Go," Sophia told them. "We'll be fine. I can't imagine this will take more than an hour."

They went through the regular hospital to a special ward where linoleum gave way to wood floors and the waiting room had a butler. "This is our enhanced-privacy wing," Nathan, Whitney's "care coordinator," had explained the first time they went up there. "People who live in the limelight outside value their privacy in here even more."

As far as they could tell, that meant that it was basically a luxury hotel with a lot of medical equipment. It didn't even sound like a hospital, where the corridors always echoed with the sounds of compression machines and various tiny beeps, because every room was soundproofed.

"Your friend has two broken ribs and a slight concussion so avoid exciting her or causing any abrupt head movements," Nathan told them now as they reached her door.

"I'm not even sure I know what an abrupt head movement is," Ava said. "But I don't think it'll be a problem."

"Good." He tapped discreetly twice, waited for Whitney to say, "Come in," and pushed the door open. "Your visitors have arrived, Miss Frost," he said.

"Thank you, Nathan."

"I'll leave the door open in case you need anything," he said and left.

Whitney had almost no makeup on and Sophia thought she'd never looked better.

"How are you feeling?" Sophia asked.

"Is it true that one of you has been here much of the time I've been in the hospital?" she asked, and her tone was almost hostile.

Sophia shrugged. "We wanted to make sure you were safe."

"There's security for that," Whitney pointed out.

"And we also wanted to make sure that if you got up you weren't lonely. I'm sorry I wasn't here this morning," Ava told her. "I was here last night, but I left at six thirty to take a shower."

Whitney frowned. "Why? Why would you do that for me?"

"Because you were hurt and alone," Ava said as though it were obvious.

"I have hundreds of friends." Whitney spread her finger out and swept her hand through the air. "Look at all my flowers."

"Of course you do," Sophia said. "They're just not the kind who visit hospitals."

Whitney shook her head. "I don't understand. You two are too nice. Too really nice. You're not pretend nice, you're not going to go from here and tell everyone I looked like death without makeup on."

"You look amazing actually," Ava said.

"I was just thinking the same thing. Younger and prettier," Sophia said.

"Is that an insult?" Whitney demanded.

"Yeah," Sophia said. "And you know what else? You have really pretty hair."

"Stop, Sophia," Ava told her. "Don't be a bully. No more abuse."

Sophia couldn't stop herself. "Just one more thing. I like your eyebrows fuller."

"My god, Sophia, you're so mean," Ava said. "Stop compliment bombing this instant."

Whitney was laughing but it turned into a cough that brought Nathan in. "Are you all right?" he asked nervously.

Whitney signaled him away. "It's nothing. They were just making me laugh."

Nathan said, "Good. Carry on," and ducked back out.

Whitney's eyes went to the clock. "We've wasted so much time," she said.

"Wasted how?" Sophia asked.

"He'll be coming. As soon as he can he'll be coming to try to make me stop talking. But I'm not going to let him. Not this time."

"And neither are we," Sophia assured her. "We know about Christopher Wildwood. We know Popcorn and Charming were at his house and he's the one you rescued them from and we won't let him hurt you."

"Chris?" She laughed. "Chris wouldn't hurt a fly. Well, an animal. People are a different thing but this had nothing to do with Christopher Wildwood. It's Hunter," she said. "Everything bad that's happened to you is because of Hunter. And I helped him. I'm so ashamed. And so sorry. I know there's nothing I can do to reverse it but at least by telling the truth I can help it heal."

"Hunter?" Sophia repeated.

"What do you mean 'all of it'?" Ava asked. "You mean giving our designs to Christopher Wildwood?"

"That," Whitney said. "But that was easy. In LA he could just go and take pictures himself but he has also mirrored your phones and the phones of a few of your friends, so he could mine those for images. And of course kidnapping Popcorn and Charming."

"You remember their names?" Ava was impressed.

"My job is memorizing things," Whitney told them, smiling. "It's not like I just cured athlete's foot. Anyway, I helped him with that but it was his idea. They were all his idea. After the first one, he was just full of schemes."

"What was the first one?" Sophia asked.

"Your fund-raiser," Whitney said. "For the animal shelter.

All the money that was stolen. I thought you knew. He took it and framed Dalton."

"Why?" Ava asked.

"Because I like to," Hunter said, stepping into the room.

LonDOs

Lily and Sam!

Our show!

Our friends!

AS Girls

Dalton's innocence

Whitney

EVERYTHING!

LonDON'Ts

Finding out you're dating a psychopath

23
upper beast side

"It wasn't nice of you to start without me," Hunter scolded Whitney. "After all we've done together."

"I only did those things because you forced me to," she said.

Hunter sighed. "How completely uninteresting."

"Is this true? Did you do—everything?" Sophia asked.

Hunter grinned at her. "Babe, you don't know the half of it." He yawned. "God I'm tired."

Sophia said, "Why don't you take a nap and we'll—"

Hunter leaned against the heavy, soundproof door of Whitney's room until it closed. "I don't think you're going to go anywhere, my dear." He reached behind him and they heard the click of the lock engaging. "And I don't think we'll want any interruptions."

"You've got our attention," Sophia told him. "Let's see your show."

"You sound so bitter," he told her. "I don't understand it. I've been nothing but good to you. Great to you."

"I'm sure you think that's true."

"It *is* true," he said, his eyes getting a crazy look. "I don't just think it."

"Okay," Sophia told him.

"Forget about her for a little while," Ava said. "Explain it to me. What you've done."

"It's a good story," he said, chuckling to himself. He measured out the length of the room using his feet—heel, toe, heel, toe. "You know I've been playing in these very hush-hush, prestigious celebrity poker games."

Sophia nodded like she was bored but Ava put some enthusiasm into it. "Whenever you talked about the people you were meeting it pretty much blew our minds."

Sophia shot Ava a look but Ava pretended not to notice.

"I'm a pretty popular guy around Xavier," he said. "I can more or less come and go as I please. Not many people like me."

"Xavier?" Ava said. "That's the name—"

"Of the place where the games are held," Hunter said. "Xavier Mansion. In the twenties and thirties it was one of the fanciest houses in LA. But it was abandoned a few years ago and since then it's been used as this sort of private club for high-stakes, high-credibility games."

"And you're a bigwig there," Ava parroted.

Hunter smiled like he was glad to be understood. "Exactly. I won't lie to you—part of my popularity comes from the fact that I've been on a bit of a losing streak. Losing a lot. At first it was no big deal but after a while it was harder to get credit, especially when my dad started being such an asshole about everything."

"He didn't approve of the Xavier stuff, did he?" Ava said.

"Exactly. Thought I was wasting my time, called the people

there lowlives, said I was having another incident." Hunter's voice dropped to a lower register as he said, "You're spiraling out of control. You're headed for a deep valley if you don't apply some breaks. I know you think it's fun but there's a bottom and when you reach it, I'm not going to be there." Hunter shook his head and in his own voice demanded, "What kind of a parent is that? Says I know you're hurting, I can tell you're in pain, but take care of yourself? A selfish-bastard parent." He reached around and rubbed the small of his back. "Where was I?"

"Ask him about his mother," Whitney said.

"What about her?" Sophia asked.

"When was the last time you saw your mom, Hunter?" Whitney asked him.

"Shut up, you piece of trailer park trash," he said.

"See?" Whitney told her. "As soon as you get close he deflects."

Sophia frowned. "But he told me about her. At first he said she died when he was fourteen. Then he told me that actually she left when he was eight, and it was only when he was fourteen that his father said she was dead. For all those years his dad had let him believe she left because he wasn't good enough."

"That's a tragic story." Whitney sounded sympathetic. "Except it's all a lie. His mother is actually alive and living in Brooklyn. She has a photography gallery. Isn't that right, Hunter?"

"You're just a conceited pile of bones. Why are you even talking?" He swiveled his head around the room like a bird of prey alert to dinner or danger, and faster than a shot he lunged at Whitney.

But Sophia was faster and put herself between them.

"Hunter, get away from her," Sophia ordered in her sternest, most mom voice.

Hunter glared at her, his body just inches from hers. His jaw tightened and she wondered if he was about to attack her.

He disgusted her now, and standing this close to him was un-nerving, but she wanted to hold his attention. Behind his back, she saw Ava inching toward the door. If she could get it un-locked, they would be able to get help.

Hunter sneered at Sophia. "You hide it well but you have this real selfish streak."

Ava guffawed. "You have got to be kidding."

Sophia put up a hand to keep her out of it, subtly pointing to the door. Ava nodded, and Sophia returned her attention to Hunter. "Let's talk about you, then. You were telling us about Xavier and how popular you were."

"Because you were a loser," Whitney said.

"Shut up!" Hunter yelled at her. Ava froze three feet from the doorknob as he started pacing the room again. "I'm not a loser. I lost. Those are not the same thing." Whitney laughed mirth-lessly but he ignored it, looking from Sophia to Ava and back again as if daring them to contradict him. "I needed money fast. So I stole the money from your precious little animal fund-raiser. Whitney helped me, she got me the photograph with your sig-nature on it," he said to Sophia, "and she planted the page of fake signatures to frame Dalton. It was even better because he'd just sold all his precious surfboards to pay his sister's unsavory debts, but no one tracks surfboard sales so it was the easiest thing in the world to make it look like he'd come by all that honest money dishonestly."

"Why did you want to frame him?" Ava asked.

"He's a pain in the ass," Hunter said with a shrug, as if that explained everything. "He blames me for his sister's problems, says I'm a bad influence. But look at your sister." He pointed to Sophia. "Her life has gotten nothing but better since she and I have been dating. And that's all because of me."

"I'd say that's an exaggeration," Ava told him.

"You smarmy little cretin," he said to her, his face now inches from hers. He stared at her like that for a moment, then pulled away, relaxed again. "The pet-sanctuary money was okay for a while but it wasn't infinite—you really could have worked harder and raised more—so I had another idea. I invested in you." He used the pointer finger of each hand to point to Ava and Sophia. "The London sisters. After the crazy rich women you seem to attract like flies to a picnic, I am your biggest investor."

Sophia's head went to one side. "Thank you."

"You're welcome. I'm glad you realize how much you have to thank me for. I'm the only person on your team who was truly determined to do whatever it took to make you a success. Your PR people and your agent and the Contessa will all go so far. Only I would take it the extra mile."

"By kidnapping our pets?" Ava demanded.

"Exactly," he said earnestly. "Look how much publicity you've gotten from that. Free publicity. God, I set that up so beautifully. A bike messenger on the red carpet. The Red. Damn. Carpet. The whole spectacle. It looked great on TV by the way. I don't know if you've had a chance to watch any of your coverage."

Ava shook her head slowly.

"But that's just the most recent one. Lets talk about the theft from your fund-raiser. Can you honestly say that a single one of the opportunities you have right now would have come your way without that? You got your bedroom line because of it. And it was only because of the bedroom line that you started making clothes and"—he snapped his fingers—"presto!"

Sophia glanced at Ava, who was watching Hunter with morbid fascination. "You're right," she said. "When you put it that way, everything we have we owe to you."

"And now your show. You would have been nothing, some

average young designers lost in a sea of others in that big tent," he said. "Everyone knew it, I was just the only one willing to do something about it."

"By which you mean stealing our designs and giving them to Christopher Wildwood so that he'd call us out as frauds and get us kicked out of the main tent."

"'Give.'" Hunter scoffed. "Never give anything. People have no respect for things they don't pay for. But yes. I got your designs into his hands, and then started the action against you. You can't ask for better PR than a feud with an established designer like Chris. You went from being nobodies to prepping the most talked about show of Fashion Week. I'm—I'm actually very proud of you two. You took my groundwork and ran with it. This has turned out to be a great partnership."

"But it's your last one," Whitney said.

Hunter's face creased into a broad simile. "What can you possibly mean by that?"

Whitney sat up. "I'm ready to tell. Not just Ava and Sophia but everyone. The police, the district attorney. I'll tell them everything you did, and everything you made me do for you."

"Why would you do that?"

"Because I'm tired of being afraid of you. You've had that— accident—hanging over me for four years and I'm tired of looking at it every time I close my eyes."

"What accident?" Ava asked.

Whitney swallowed. "I made a mistake once, four years ago. I let someone record me while I was being intimate with someone else."

Hunter cupped his hands around his mouth and boomed, "It's called a sex tape. Whitney made a sex tape, and little Hunter found it and told her what to do."

Whitney nodded but avoided Ava and Sophia's eyes, as if she was embarrassed. "I know I have this persona," she said, "but I come from a very conservative family and the thought of them—my mom or dad but especially my little brothers or sister—seeing it, ever." She hugged herself. "It makes no sense, I know," she said. "All the strangers in the world could look at it. But my little sister?" She swallowed hard and there were tears in her eyes.

"That doesn't sound weird at all," Sophia told her, but she was looking at Ava.

"You two are so open about your mistakes," Whitney said.

"We have no choice with Hunter over here digging holes everywhere so we fall on our faces," Ava pointed out.

"I was so worried about tarnishing what my siblings thought of me that I got obsessed with making sure they never saw the tape. I ended up doing things I'm far more ashamed of just so Hunter wouldn't show it to anyone." She looked at him. "I'm done with that now. I don't care what you do with the tape. Sell it. Burn it. I'm done letting you use me. And you're done destroying other people's happiness and pretending you're helping them."

"I'm really sorry you feel that way," Hunter said to Whitney and for a moment he looked normal again. "I thought I was protecting you. I thought you enjoyed what we did together. All I ever wanted with you and Sophia and Ava was to help."

"That's a lie," Whitney said.

"Don't call me a liar," Hunter said in a tight, even voice.

"Why not?" Whitney taunted. "What are you going to do to me? You can threaten me but you have no power over me anymore. Because you're a liar," she jeered.

"SHUT UP!" Hunter roared, pulling a gun from the small of

his back and holding it against Whitney's head. "Now let's all just take a minute and calm down," he suggested. "No one is turning anyone in. No one is a liar. We're all friends here. Look what I've done for all of you." He was smiling but it looked strange, malformed. "Without me you'd all be nothing. Weeds. I'm the genius behind all of your success. Whitney's just tired, she didn't mean what she said." He looked at her. She was shaking but the gun in his hand was completely stable. "Right? You didn't mean a single thing you said."

Whitney stared at him. "Go ahead and shoot me. I meant every word."

His eyes got very strange, then he lifted the hand holding the gun and brought it down hard across Whitney's head, knocking her out.

He stood looking down at her. From where she was standing Sophia saw a line of blood forming on Whitney's forehead. And she saw Ava stretching toward the lock on the door.

Her fingers were millimeters from it when Hunter whirled around. He brought the gun up and pointed it at Ava's forehead. "You're not thinking of being crafty are you? Why don't you come over here." He nodded to a place by his side.

Sophia put herself in front of Ava. "You can't have her. You can only have me."

Sophia heard the click of Ava undoing the lock as Hunter said, "I don't think you understand how guns work. I can have you. And then I can have her." He stepped toward her and pressed the gun against her forehead. "Is it clearer now?"

The door to the room opened at that moment and a silver-haired footman in an impeccable gray suit stepped officiously in. Hunter's back blocked his view of the gun so he gave a little bow, held open the door, and announced, "Il Conte di Bellevista."

The count walked in, reeking of money and privilege in his beautifully tailored navy suit, took one look at the situation, picked up Whitney's breakfast tray, and slammed it edge-first into Hunter's head.

Hunter's mouth made a sound like *ho!* and his eyes rolled back in his head. He dropped the gun and went sprawling into unconsciousness, ending half in and half out of the doorway.

Hospital personnel began to pour in through the open door. The count made a slight bow, and had started to say, "My apologies for intruding. My aunt ordered me to come here. I am il Conte di . . ." when his eyes registered whom he was talking to and he changed it to a breathless, "*Stella mia*? But what are you doing here?"

LonDOs
Footmen announcing your arrival
Men of action
Men in traction
Giovanni is a count???
Giovanni is the count
Getting your life back
Owning your mistakes
Owning your own vineyard

LonDON'Ts
Finding out that the big, elegant, impressive-at-a-hundred-paces
    object your (ex) boyfriend was shopping for was not a ring
        but a gun
Which he pointed at you

And your sister

Riding in a car with two people who are blissfully in love with each
other and spend the entire time kissing and whispering too
quietly for anyone else to know what they are saying

Even if that car is a Rolls-Royce limo

24

empire fate

The Contessa's sled arrival was witnessed by the hundreds of people who had taken up positions along the fence that enclosed the boathouse lake, hoping to catch a glimpse of the show from the outside. The line of people who actually had wristbands to enter snaked down the carriageway in the other direction. Harper and her team were carefully checking everyone against the guest list after they'd discovered a brisk market in counterfeit wristbands. Hunter might have been nuts but he was correct about one thing—the Londons' show was definitely the show of the season.

Those lucky enough to get in were seated in rows that wound around an unusual catwalk, not a straight line but more like a curving river, to take advantage of the shape of the Boathouse and maximize the number of seats.

The beginning of the show was signaled by the room falling

totally dark. Through the windows, the flicker of flashbulbs from the spectators around the lake looked like fireflies. Over the sound system, a girl's voice said, "Once upon a time there were two sisters. They had a dream. It looked something like this—"

There were two beats of silence and then the deep, resonant tones of Big Ben struck six times. A female voice announced, "You're now on London time," and a spotlight appeared on three large beds done in fabrics and sheets from the Live Love London homeware line that had been the jumping-off place for their fashions. There were five girls lying "asleep" in each bed, and one by one they slid out, stopped in front of a mirror to pretend to check their makeup, and made their way down the catwalk. The way it was set up, it wound through the audience, as though they were as much a part of the show as the models. While the girls walked, their voices reading parts of the essays they'd submitted to be chosen were heard over the music, as a tribute to their individuality and uniqueness.

When all fifteen had walked from the bed the spotlight shifted to the other side of the room, which had been transformed into a picnic. The girls sat on blankets and pillows and lounge chairs covered with the Londons' fabric with a big picnic hamper in front of them. This time when they walked the catwalk, their voices talking about which accessory they'd brought with them and what it meant to them played over the music.

The room went dark again when the picnic set was empty and the last girl had walked. The lights came up moments later and all the girls reappeared, now carrying butterfly nets. Holographic projections of butterflies flitted around the Boathouse, seeming to hover in midair. The girls' voices saying, "I dream of . . ." were layered over the music, as though their dreams were filling the room. As they circled through the audience in a line, the layering of sound grew denser and the number of butterflies increased, until a brilliant cloud of them massed at the front of the room. The line of models seemed to march through it and then the cluster shimmered apart and Ava and Sophia were there in floor-length gowns they'd designed, glowing and resplendent.

"Once upon a time there were two sisters who had a dream. It looked something like this," the voice said again, bringing the show full circle, and as Ava and Sophia walked the catwalk the room erupted into wave after wave of deafening applause.

The applause didn't end with the show. Within an hour the reviews were up, and they were, as Lucille Rexford put it, "satisfactory."

"I would like to propose the toast," the Contessa said, clinking a glass as she rose to her feet. She was standing at the head of one of the three long tables loaded with silver and crystal that had been set up in the middle of the Boathouse after the show was over. "To," she glanced at a paper in her hand and read, "a grand show in the style of the greats . . . A joyful spectacle that served as a true showcase for the amazing design . . . A collection that manages to combine the girly with glamour in the manner of Coco Chanel's best early work . . . A tour de force that won't soon be topped—from the makeup to the sets to the soundtrack and their decision to use their viewers as their models, the London sisters' show was organic in the broad sense of the word, made from elements they cultivated and nurtured themselves. Every piece of it showed their talent, imagination, and heart . . . the first new designers in a long time to make this critic excited." She looked up and raised a glass of golden champagne. "Congratulations, Ava and Sophia. I knew what you could do but now, now the whole world knows."

The glasses of the hundred guests all clinked and a cheer went up and Ava turned to Sophia and said, "Is this real? Because I don't think I've ever been this happy in my life."

"Me either," Sophia said. She bit her lip. "We should toast the Contessa. I can't believe we didn't plan ahead."

"Do not worry, *stella mia*," Giovanni said from Sophia's other side. "That is a toast I will happily make." He kissed Sophia's hand and stood.

Sophia looked at him, marveling at the revelations of the last twelve hours. The Contessa had been responsible for his mysterious appearance in Whitney's hospital room, having sent him there to pick the girls up and bring them to the studio to prep for the show.

He'd whisked them into his Rolls-Royce, and on the way from the hospital to the studio, between kisses, had explained to Sophia that his father had died and he'd inherited the title.

"All at once, I have lost a parent, and my life as I had it," he'd said. "I do not complain. It is fun, eh, to be the count? Of course. The houses, the vineyard, the boat, the tinier boat, the horses," he'd said. "Nice. But also I must tell you, it is a lot of work. I think maybe we sell them all but first you come and see and then we can decide." Ava told Sophia afterward that she'd blushed when he said that, but Sophia didn't remember. Didn't remember his words exactly because he'd been looking into her eyes as he spoke and all she was aware of was the feeling that a piece of her she'd been keeping locked away was suddenly free. A piece she hadn't even realized that she had been hiding, but which now she knew was the crucial, vital piece. The part of her heart that Giovanni had taken months earlier and that was now fluttering like a baby bird just learning to fly.

He smiled down at her now as he clinked his glass for silence and began his toast.

"Five months ago, I met the woman of my dreams. Incredible this one was, you can't believe it. And also not hard on the eyes," he said. "But then I was very fast forced by sad circumstances to leave, without saying goodbye. My father in Italy, he dies, and for months afterward my life is upside down. I become the count, something I hoped would happen only when I had gray hairs growing out of my ears." He shook his head. "So I go to Italy, I lose the girl, my father, my life, everything. I am very sad. And one day I get a phone call from my father's favorite sister. He always called her Zuzu so for me she is Aunt Zuzu. Even when he is dying, my father talks about Zuzu and almost his final words to me are, 'When Zuzu calls you to service, you go and no questions. She is crazy like an entire asylum of lunatics, but she has her reasons. Not once has she ever sent me wrong.' I say, 'Yes, Father—I mean, to one who is dying that is what you say. And also I figure Zuzu has never called me, why would this happen now? But . . ." He shook his head ruefully.

"Of course she calls and orders me to New York on such a date at such a time because she has the girl for me to marry, and I say, Auntie, I do not wish—and she says none of the blah blah, you will come. I will fix everything. And if you do not come you will regret it for the rest of your life, I swear on your father's soul." He hit himself on the forehead. "What am I supposed to do? So I say, Yes of course, Auntie, my father's soul, but tell me about this girl. And she says, You will find out about her when you come and meet her. All you need to know now is that she is perfect girl for you, and you two will be very happy couple."

He leaned forward. "Meantime also I am thinking my father must have been nuts."

"So here I come to New York to meet the girl. And this morning I go to the appointment and I see a girl and I think my aunt is right. She is perfect. She is the girl for me. Because in fact, she *is* the girl of my dreams from before. The same one. But"—he put a finger in the air—"she is not the girl my aunt has picked."

A noise like a tiger growling came from the Contessa's end of the table. "So I make the tiny error. Tiny." She held up her thumb and forefinger a millimeter apart.

"It is just important to point out that you are not always correct," Giovanni said. "For my future happiness."

"Bah your happiness. Look at you." The Contessa whipped a hand toward him. "There is no question of it. Please stop talking and kiss her already, it is what we want to see."

"Maybe that I can obey," he said, and did.

As the rest of the room resumed their conversations, Giovanni put his arm around Sophia and said in a low voice, "I think you will like being the girlfriend of a count very much. I am glad I have something to share with you now. If I was still in my old life, I would not be such good boyfriend material."

"What do you mean?"

He smiled sheepishly and shrugged a broad shoulder. "I have always had deep feelings for you, *stella*. I could not bring myself to tell you because I was . . ."

"Because you were what?"

"You know, just a bartender."

"Wait a minute—*just* a bartender? Is that really what you thought, Giovanni? That it made any difference to me whether you were a count or a bartender or an astronaut or a sheepherder?"

"You don't seem to understand. Perhaps I say it wrong. What I mean is that you are a very beautiful woman, and you deserve a man who will give you a good life."

"But a good life has nothing to do with money, Giovanni. I always liked you for *you*. Love has nothing to do with money or someone's title or what they do for a living. It's about the person, and I've always loved the person you are. We just had some very bad timing."

Giovanni put his hand to his heart. "*Stella mia,* I didn't think this would be possible. But I have just fallen even deeper in love with you." He leaned in and gave her a soft kiss on the forehead. "Now I know you are beautiful both inside and out."

It was a half hour later, after the toasts were done and people were mingling, when Sophia saw Ava waving to her urgently. Excusing herself from the group of AS girls she was talking to, Sophia crossed the floor to see what was so important.

"Lucille is here," Ava said, taking her by the hand. "She watched the show on the webcast at home, but she came here now. She's in the manager's office and she's demanding to see us both."

"Is she angry?"

"It's Lucille," Ava said. "How can you tell?"

They found her at the front of the restaurant, her wheelchair parked next to the wide fireplace with a crackling blaze in it. "We didn't think you would come," Sophia said when they reached her.

"I'm only here for a moment, I'm not staying," Lucille answered sharply.

"It's Cuddles, isn't it?" Ava said seriously, scratching the dog's head. "He made you come."

Lucille smiled ruefully. "No. Not this time. The truth is—I wanted to introduce you to someone."

She sounded almost nervous, not like any version of Lucille they'd ever encountered before. She gestured behind her and Ava and Sophia saw that there were two women standing there, one about Lucille's age and the other closer to theirs. "This is my sister, Carlotta," Lucille said, pointing to the older woman. "And this is my great-niece, Francesca."

Carlotta put out her hand to shake theirs and then said, "I'm sorry, I need to hug you," and did. When she pulled away there were tears in her eyes. "Thank you. If it weren't for you, Lucille would never have called me."

"They haven't spoken in forty years," Francesca, said.

"Why?" Ava asked.

"I was stubborn," Lucille said, patting Cuddles. "I was waiting for Carlotta to apologize for something and when she didn't, I wrote her off."

"What was she supposed to apologize for?" Sophia wanted to know.

Carlotta gave a small smile. "Being happy."

"Running off with a scoundrel I didn't approve of," Lucille elaborated. "Against my better judgment." She cleared her throat and said in a slightly quieter voice, "Which turned out to be wrong."

Francesca leaned toward the Londons to confide, "I think that was the real issue. Aunt Lucille did not like being wrong."

"Bah." Lucille waved that away. "When did you young people get so smart, that is what I want to know." She growled it, but her eyes were sparkling.

Ava gave a little giggle but Sophia worked to keep her smile back as she asked, "How did we bring you back together after forty years?"

"Carlotta is the person who gives out accreditations for Fashion Week," Lucille explained. "I wanted to help you—"

"So she swallowed her pride and called me," Carlotta finished her sister's sentence, the way that Ava and Sophia finished each other's. "Finally."

"You did that for *us*?" Ava said. "Why?"

"Because you two bring out what is good in people. You make everyone want to be better versions of themselves. Even an old cynic with a heart as black as pitch like myself." Lucille leaned forward and both her voice and her expression softened. "It's a rare gift. Don't lose it, and don't squander it." Then she leaned back and said in her regular gravelly voice, "And of course it was good for my business. Your line is selling like hotcakes."

"Of course." Sophia nodded seriously. She bent to hug Lucille, taking advantage of the proximity to whisper, "There's a tear on your cheek."

"Don't you dare tell anyone," Lucille whispered back.

Sophia pulled away and smiled at the woman. "You know me far better than that."

"Thank you," Ava said when she'd hugged Lucille, too. "For saving us again."

Lucille looked at Carlotta and Francesca. She took a deep breath and said, "Actually I think this time you saved me."

They refused to stay, but everyone else did, and it was nearly midnight before Giovanni was able to get Sophia alone. He grabbed her on her way between two tables and said, "I have to tell you a secret."

He led her onto the patio, where heaters had been set up. It was beautifully still and the pure white expanse of the snow-covered lake glowed in the moonlight.

"What's your secret?" she asked, laughing.

"I want to tell you my favorite part of today," he said. "Besides, when I knocked Hunter out with the tray."

"That was very exciting," Sophia granted.

"And the part where you got so angry with me for leaving and not telling you that you stamped your foot and your hair came lose and you looked like one of the Furies."

Sophia made a face. "That wasn't my favorite part."

He spent a moment gazing at her, his hand on her cheek. "My favorite part," he said, "was when you and Ava walked out on the stage at the end of your show. It was amazing. Of course you do not need me to tell you, the applause, the reviews, the orders, say this alone. But I look at you, so beautiful and talented, so wise and kind—" He stopped.

"Yes?" Sophia asked.

"Madonna, *stella mia,* how you make my heart roar to deserve you. I think a lot about what you said, that you would have loved me even if I was not a count. And I realize that even though I am a count now, that is still not enough. I must still work every day to be worthy of you."

The breath caught in Sophia's throat. She had just heard words she had been longing for her whole life without knowing it.

"So that was my favorite part of the show. Knowing I would spend the rest of my life working to be a good man, because that is what you deserve."

She felt like someone had just tapped her on the shoulder and shown her an entire world of possibility that had been right inside her all along but invisible. There, waiting for her to see it.

She was ready.

There was a knock on the glass door behind them and Lily appeared, pointing at her wrist. "It's time," she said, grinning. "Let's go."

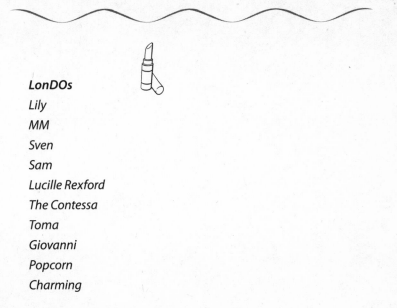

LonDOs

Lily

MM

Sven

Sam

Lucille Rexford

The Contessa

Toma

Giovanni

Popcorn

Charming

My sister
My sister
The AS Girls
Whitney Frost
Elnett Hairspray
Pomegranate Mocktinis
Warm little cheese puffs
Boys who make you feel like you're breathing for the first time
Midnight surprises

LonDON'Ts
Listening to doubters
Being too stubborn
Forgetting to breathe

epilogue
i'll take madhattan

"Why do I have to be blindfolded?" Ava asked. "Where are we going? You know it's cold outside. This coat isn't very warm."

"Do you want me to get a gag?" Lily asked. They were in the backseat of Giovanni's Rolls, with Ava sandwiched between them. Everyone else had gone ahead because they were a little late.

"No," Ava said. "I—"

"I wasn't asking you," Lily told her.

"Not yet," Sophia said. "We'll see if she improves."

"Wait, Sophia, you're here too? What's going on? Where are we—"

"We might need a gag," Sophia said.

"I'll be quiet," Ava said. "Although if you'd just— Never mind."

The car stopped and Ava felt herself being led down a pathway and through some doors. There was noise, a bunch of different voices, but nothing she recognized. Then Lily sat her on a hard seat that felt like it had been covered in carpet.

"Take off your shoes," Lily ordered.

"If I do I probably won't be able to get them back on because my feet are so tired so, unless—" Suddenly her mouth was full of something that tasted a lot like chocolate cake.

"Keep talking, toots, and next time it will be socks," Lily said in her ear. "I'm not messing around."

Lily pulled her shoes off and she felt her feet being bent into . . . ice skates?

"You know, it's not safe to ice skate blindfolded," she said. No one answered. "Hello?" Nothing.

Was she supposed to do something? Had they forgotten about her? Maybe she should take off the blindfold. She was reaching for it when a voice said, "Hands down."

So there was someone there. But not anyone whose voice she recognized. "Hi, my friends kidnapped me and I should really be getting—"

"The tall one left me some socks and said to put them in your mouth if you started talking."

"Right," Ava said. "Being quiet. Could I have some hot chocolate?"

"Yes."

She heard her guard step away and quickly glanced out the bottom of the blindfold. She was in a skating rink and—

"No peeking," he said, pushing her head back down and wrapping her fingers around the hot chocolate.

Apparently she was just going to have to wait. She hated waiting. Waiting meant time for thinking and even on pretty much the best day of your life thinking could lead to all kinds of knotty places. Like how looking at Sophia and Giovanni and Lily and Sam and MM and Sven and Ava and no one was a little depressing. Especially since now that she was free to date—with the Contessa's official dispensation—just exactly after she'd told Dalton she couldn't be with him.

He was probably with Mikasa right now at the Christopher Wildwood after-party.

She heard Sophia's laugh and then Lily's voice saying, "How was she?" to the guard.

"A little curious but fine. Didn't have to use the socks or the cuffs."

"Cuffs?" Ava said.

"Good girl," Lily told her. "Come on." Lily took one hand and Sophia took the other and they went from the cork floor of the inside out into the cold night and then they were on the ice.

"It sounds like it's crowded," Ava said.

"It's a special night. Invitation only," Sophia said. "Hottest ticket in New York to get tonight."

"Ticket to what?"

There was the sound of a guitar being tuned and then people clapping in unison the way they did at the beginning of a concert.

"Is it time, doctor?" Lily's voice said.

"Yes, doctor," Sophia agreed.

Ava's blindfold came off and she was standing in the ice skating rink in Central Park. They were at the front of a crowd that was pressed into a U shape around a stage set up in the middle of the rink.

"Ice skating," she said. "How did you know I wanted to do this?"

"I'm your sister," Sophia said. "I know things."

"And I'm your not-quite-sister," Lily said. "I know other things."

"I'm both comforted and frightened by that," Ava said happily.

"But this isn't just ice skating," Sophia said as they were

joined by Giovanni and Sven and MM and Sam. "There's a concert too."

The crowd started cheering then as five guys skated up to the stage. Two of them had guitars, one had a drumstick, and one had a trumpet. They got onstage, and Ava tried to place them. They looked familiar. This was . . . *Dalton's band,* Ava realized. And there, approaching the stage last was Dalton himself.

The crowed went nuts. Ava felt like she was curling up and dying inside. She glanced around the crowd, wondering which of the pretty girls was Mikasa.

Dalton walked to the front of the stage looking confident and charming and cheerful. There was no sign of the sad guy she'd seen when they said goodbye. He'd moved on. He was happy.

She needed to get out of there.

"This is really cool, you guys, but I have to go," Ava said, starting to turn.

"What's wrong?" Sophia asked. "I thought you liked Dalton."

"I do." God, she didn't want to go into this now. Couldn't they just let her go? "I did. I—I think I *love* him. That's the problem. He— It's over between us."

"What are you talking about?" Sophia said, not letting go of Ava's arm. "He—"

The rest of what she was saying was drowned out by Dalton. He picked up the mic and said, "We want to start with a new song we've just been working on, how long has it been, guys?"

"A day," one of them said.

"Ten minutes," the other shouted.

"Not long. Recent inspiration," Dalton told the crowd. "In the spirit of out with the old, in with the new."

Ava didn't want to hear a song for his new girlfriend. She didn't want to see how happy he could be. It was great for him, but she—

"This song is about the person you kiss once but can't forget," Dalton went on. "The one whose voice you'd give anything to hear. Whose scent stays on your mind for months. Even just her hair. You remember the way her hair smells. The one who gets into your head and won't get back out."

Ava froze. Her eyes met his and suddenly it was just the two of them there.

"The song is called 'Always London.' Because it's always been you."

LonDOs
Falling in love

LonDON'Ts
Giving up (ever!)

Read the entire Sophia and Ava in London series

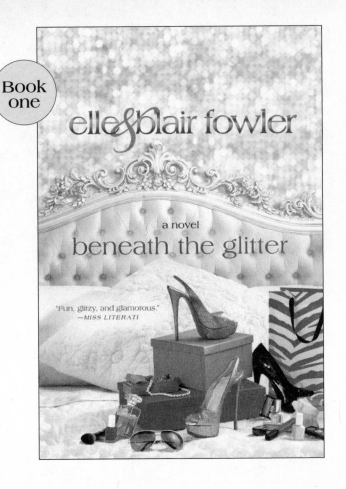

Book one

elle&blair fowler

a novel

beneath the glitter

"Fun, glitzy, and glamorous."
—MISS LITERATI

St. Martin's Griffin